MURDER ON FIRST

B A ERICKSON

Filbert
Publishing

Reclaimed Haven

Murder on First

B.A. Erickson

http://BAEricksonBooks.com

Claim an entire Starter Library, get in on contests, fun stuff, and freebies when you become a VIP reader.

http://bethannerickson.com/vip/

CONTENTS

BOOK 1

PREFACE

It was unlike any nightmare he could have imagined.

He groaned, the wadded bandanna muffling guttural sounds escaping his lips. Tears dampened the blue cloth twisting into his cheeks. His hands felt clamped behind him, duct tape digging into his wrists. He was fairly certain they'd disjointed his shoulders.

But that was the least of his worries.

With cold precision, they grasped the food processor lid, chopped at the chute, shortening it by half. They flicked the switch and it whirred to life.

His cries erupted anew as they inserted his fingers. Groans escalated to squeals as bloody flesh splashed into the container. He fainted. They smiled.

While humming a snappy melody, they grasped his other hand and inserted each digit. The food processor groaned as it sliced through living bone. Seeing the container full, they unlatched it from the base and flung the contents against the wall before reconstructing the device and resuming. They then worked on his toes, his nose, and finally his flaccid, quivering penis. They stood over the sanguineous mass that was once his body and watched for signs of life. Then, final twitches erupted through what was left of his limbs. With one clean swipe, they sliced each side of his neck. Blood oozed from the new wounds.

With their work finished, they silently exited the house. Blood dripped from their hazmat suits as they slid into the inky night of small town Minnesota. One streetlight buzzed in the quiet alley; a lame attempt to expunge darkness. One of them proceeded to the van and slid open the door. Plastic lined the interior. He stepped inside and removed the white, crinkly suit as another man exited the vehicle with two large labradors. Another man stood at the door watching the huge dogs lunge forward.

"Suppose he's dead yet?" he said as they approached.

"Dunno," the other one answered, holding the door wide. "You sure they're hungry enough?"

"These bastards will eat anything," he replied. The man unlatched the hounds and they leaped inside.

"Finish 'um off," he whispered.

Chapter One

INCISIONS, NEWSPAPERS, AND NED

She gazed at her broken body in the mirror. A large incision swept across her torso, butterfly tapes curled at the edges making a grisly sight even more gruesome.

"How did it come to this?" she mumbled.

She held a bandage against the incision and gingerly pressed tape over it. She winced. Then she placed the next piece of tape over another stretch of gauze. Then another, and another, and another. Within a few minutes, she managed to cover the entire wound. She dabbed at pink goo drying on her waist and slid her shirt over the mess.

"Nobody'll ever know... I hope."

She tossed extra bandages and tape into her purse and slid it over her shoulder, pausing to steady herself as a stab of pain pierced her abdomen. "Gotta be careful." She grabbed her leatherbound folder, recorder, reporter notepads, and proceeded to her car. Nausea washed over her. She paused.

"Perhaps I should have waited."

However, with insurance running out, medical bills raising, and finances draining she knew she had to get to work. She hated what this had done to her body. How this situation impacted her career was certainly unsettling. Plus, she disliked starting a new job when she didn't feel 100 percent.

But she was a consummate professional. She'd figure out how to do this. After all, the Crossroads Herald covered a quiet swath of Minnesota. The chances of a big story breaking, one requiring a lot of time and effort, were slim to none, especially on quiet fall mornings.

Nope, all she had to look forward to in this town was a long parade of city council stories, school board reports, and an occasional feel-good piece. Should be easy. She twisted the door knob and winced.

"It's gonna be a long day," she mumbled.

———

The award-winning weekly, Crossroads Herald, served central Minnesota's small section of land that housed more farm animals than humans. Hailing itself the "Turkey Capital of the World," it was difficult to travel from town to town without noting copious silver barns dotting the terrain. Thick, white feathers lining the highways would also tip off the smarter than average visitor... not that this section of Minnesota received many of those. With an agricultural bliss vibe permeating the area, you'd think a small town newspaper would provide a reduced stress zone compared to its big city cousins. But you'd be wrong.

Newspaper publisher Bart Lundquist struggled with every aspect of his biz. Reporters came and went like a cool summer breeze. Photographers were harder to keep than outdoor flowers in January. His only graphic artist threatened to quit to become a full time mother. That would be odd considering she didn't have any children. Finances always balanced on a knife blade.

His sales staff sucked. Finding a good sales person that didn't emit a creepy vibe was one of Bart's greatest challenges. If he found someone the locals tolerated, the person couldn't sell worth crap. If he found a salesperson who had mastered the craft, the locals viewed him with suspicion. Today's sales staff consisted of himself and Dick.

Dick was his brother-in-law and likely the most incompetent salesman he'd ever met. Doughy and chatty, Dick talked more than he sold.

"Good God," Bart would say, "the business owners know why you're there. Just cut to the chase, sell the ad, and move on."

Instead, Dick would meander through his conversations, getting off track, forgetting to sell the spot. If he did sell, he often got details wrong. Hell, he routinely messed up the offer, the text, the phone number, the price... you name it.

"Dude's a walking mistake,' Bart often said. "But he's my mistake."

Hence, more money problems.

Advertisers complained when their spots ran with incorrect information. Over half the ads running today were freebies to make up for massive cock-ups on previous runs.

To make matters worse, the city council threatened to ban his staff from meetings after a recent unflattering article on last week's cow dung incident triggered a brouhaha at the local cafe. Even the city clerk seemed to withhold her support of the local paper, emailing her most recent council minutes in a skeleton form, without comment, presumably hoping the paper would quit running them. This was a particularly large problem considering council meetings provided the bulk of story ideas for his paper. One meeting often ballooned into at least a few interviews resulting in many column inches of newsy news.

If it wasn't one person offended, it was another. Depending on the week, Bart had at least one prominent Crossroads citizen ticked at him for one reason or another.

Nevertheless, he labored forward... all with an overworked crew. Poor wages plus dismal public support equaled a less than favorable working environment. But, true publisher that he was, when things got terribly difficult, he retreated to the quiet, prosperous world of his mind... a place where readers revered his work and his employees loved their job. A place where one well crafted story would put his little newspaper on the map... a story so glorious, so huge, so noteworthy, that forevermore, Minnesota students would gasp in wonder as they read his detailed, accurate account.

But alas, the chances of that happening in this tiny community were nil.

But a man could hope.

A cold burst of air brushed against his unshaven cheek. He glanced up from his desk and watched Ned enter the building. "Damn," the younger man breathed, "chilly out today, eh?"

"You ain't seen nothing," replied Bart, "I took a gander at the long range forecast."

"Hope you're wrong."

"I'm not. If you think it's cold now, just wait," he said. He scribbled a few story ideas on the pad in front of him. He sighed. Minnesota winters are not for the faint of heart. Temps often don't creep above zero for weeks on end. "When winter hits," he said, "wear layers, don't forget your boots, and cover all exposed skin within a few minutes if you're going outside for any length of time."

Ned stamped his feet on the floor. Frost shards flaked to the floor. "You sound like a public service announcement." He tromped his feet a few more times before he added, "When's the new reporter coming?"

"Today."

"What's he like?"

"She."

"Female?"

"Seriously?" Bart shook his head. "The pronoun 'she' is generally applied to a female. Geez. Sexist much?"

"Not really. It's just that the last two have been male."

"Well, this one's female."

"Well, that's a switch," Ned said, "what's she like?"

"Good writer."

"Clips were sound?"

"Yup."

"Interview?"

"Via phone. Sounded competent."

"Good." Ned peeled his parka from his torso and hung it on the coat tree. He lumbered to his desk, heavy boots clunking all the way, and plopped into his office chair. "Very good. Hope this one stays a while."

Ned Stevens arrived in Crossroads five years ago and was the exception that proved Bart's assertion that "keeping photographers was harder than keeping flowers blooming in January." Originally, he didn't know if he'd like small town life but figured he'd give it a shot after he lost his job at a big-city, first class, glossy magazine. He missed his expense account. He also missed slick night life and refined women. But five years in Crossroads helped him appreciate down home cooking and the peanut shell littered floors of the local bar. Through the years, he learned to relax into a quiet life, snapping pics of wildlife, combines, and local festivals. The slower pace and lower cost of living didn't hurt either.

Truth was, he enjoyed his work. The quiet, lazy town of Crossroads offered a near perfect environment for a professional photographer. He had plenty of time to do his own thing while getting paid to meet interesting people. The picturesque palette of seasons were always a delight to capture on film. He felt like an important member of a team, working closely with the reporter and enjoying how his pictures enhanced each story. Bart always said, "There's nothing like seeing a picture of someone you know in the local paper... that's what sells copies."

To a large extent, that seemed true. Bart peppered his pages with Ned's photos, and papers sold. Put a kid in the paper and every family member bought a copy for posterity. It was win-win.

He leaned back in his chair and carefully polished the lens of his latest acquisition. Sure, the Herald would have supplied him with an adequate camera, but he preferred to use his own. As he wiped away dust flakes and stray fingerprints, he wondered what this new reporter would bring to the table. The last one clearly felt far too talented for the likes of Crossroads. He and Bart spent more than one evening betting how long he'd stay. His designer boots got soiled with cow dung on one assignment. On another, a horse sneezed on his $300 briefcase. "I swear to god, I didn't know horses could expel that much snot," Ned said. The reporter wasn't amused.

It wasn't a secret that The Crossroads Herald had a bit of trouble with employee retention. Ned didn't know if it was the low pay, long hours, or lack of community respect that kept the position of "full time reporter" a revolving door of applicants. With so many writers coming and going, editorial quality sometimes suffered. Typos, inaccuracies, and sloppy layout seemed to be the rule these days. The only thing keeping the paper alive was Bart's tenacious spirit followed by Ned's incredible photographs. Everyone loved Ned. While everyone else received regular complaints for one reason or another, Ned only received complements. Everyone loved their picture in the paper. Bart was smart enough to capitalize on that.

"If we could just find someone who stuck around," Ned lamented, "we could really make a difference..."

But, small town living in a remote part of Minnesota isn't for the weak willed. Winters are long. Nights drag on forever. Brutal weather apparently kept "riff raff" at bay... scorching summers, frigid winters... locals said Crossroads weather was downright perfect around four days out of the year.

Also, while the concept of Minnesota Nice is a true reality, it comes with a sharp veneer of outsider suspicion. Even after five years of faithful service to the newspaper, Ned was still viewed as an interloper.

Every election resulted in one of the long times locals easily capturing the win. Sure, newcomers were encouraged to join the election process, but their chances of victory were similar to the local department store hosting a successful Christmas bikini sale. Ned figured if he were to hang in there and manage to remain an active member of society, it could be possible that his grand children would have a chance at being accepted as a full member of the community. Until then, Ned viewed the town as a place to live, a safe place for his future family, a nice place to make a living, and plenty of local drama to document.

However, if this reporter couldn't clean up the editorial mess in the newspaper, Ned feared Bart would have to shutter the shop. Already, a few major advertisers threatened to withdraw ads if they couldn't maintain circulation. "Take more pictures," Bart ordered. Even then, Ned knew they needed quality editorial... and he wasn't about to become a writer.

He sighed. "Perhaps this one will work out."

———

Crossroads, Minnesota celebrated its centennial anniversary in 1969. It was evidently the best thing to have happened in the small town since... ever. Large photographs of the event still hung prominently in the town civic center.

Struggling for relevance in an ever changing world, the mayor, along with the tiny city council, often brainstormed ideas on how to put Crossroads on the map. They promoted the annual town festival in the county brochure. They paid for advertising in big city newspapers. They attempted to attract new business to the community to no avail. One look at the dilapidated elevator leaning precariously over the rail road tracks and most business people eschewed Crossroads for the next town over.

Crossfield was everything Crossroads was not. It had a thriving daily newspaper. Businesses prospered due to the nearby community college. The Crossfield school system had succeeded in poaching nearly all of Crossroad's high school students and was on the verge of absorbing the Crossroad Elementary school into its district. Already, Crossfield threatened to close the Crossroad post office and replace it with a bank of outdoor PO boxes.

Crossroad residents didn't take kindly to Crossfield's interference. To their benefit, the twenty miles expanse between them was the only thing keeping the marauding invaders at bay. Crossroad die hards loathed Crossfieldites. And the feeling was mutual.

So when the owner of the Crossfield Daily approached Ned in an attempt to lure him to the larger daily, Bart took it personally. While Ned turned him down, Bart harbored revenge.

"Mark my words," he said, "someday I'll scoop that asshole and twist his scrawny neck."

"But nothing ever happens here," Ned replied.

"Oh," Bart said, "you never know."

"It'll be tough. You'll have to find a big story, hope it happens right before we go to press, and pray the Gazette doesn't find out about it."

"Oh," Bart repeated, "you never know."

And so it went. Small town weekly versus larger town daily. Small, overworked staff versus larger, sharper staff. A tiny newspaper minus reporters versus a well-stocked editorial team.

This represented life in Crossroads the day before all hell broke loose.

Chapter Two

BLOODY LABS, A MURDER, MALLARD

It began as many days begin: with a whimper.

Mrs. Geena Larson was walking to the post office when she saw what she thought was a bloody golden lab. "It was wandering all over town... like it owned the place," she told the post mistress, "and it looked like it was limping, too."

Ike Moe spotted the second lab. "Bloody as hell. Musta been in one heck of a fight," he said.

With bloody dogs traipsing around town, Sheila Knight called the sheriff. He sent a cruiser to investigate the situation.

Ashley Stone noted a large number of cars rolling up and down Main Street as she turned into the Crossroads Herald offices. She didn't think much of it as she parked her vehicle and eased herself out of the car. She had other things to think about. A stab of pain pierced her abdomen.

"It's gonna be a good day. It's gotta be a good day," she repeated, mostly to quell her nerves. Her boots ca-thunked their way to the entrance and she paused. It felt like a damn cold morning and a very bad time to start something new. "What if I can't do this? What if I fail?" she wondered.

She didn't ponder long. The door swung open and a large man

grinning from ear to ear greeted her. His powder blue dress shirt peppered damp with what was apparently perspiration. A broad smile widened, stretching across his pudgy, pasty face. "I bet I know who you are," he gushed, "You're the new reporter. Welcome!" Ashley stood before him, stunned. He added, "Or maybe not..."

"Yes," she said, "I'm the new reporter. Ashley Stone." She extended her hand, "You sound like Mr. Lundquist."

"Bart," he said, "call me Bart." Ashley stepped through the door and Bart pointed to Ned. "That's Ned Stevens. He's our photographer. The graphic designer's out today. Name's Maisy. She's our receptionist, too. You'll meet her later." He pointed to a coat tree near the door, "Hang your parka there. Your desk is next to Ned's. Unload and meet me in the conference room in.. say... ten minutes. Ned will tell you where it is." Bart huffed dramatically, turned on his heel, and trotted to what was evidently his office. He slammed the door shut, leaving Ashley and Ned alone in the middle room of the building.

Ashley undid her coat. She sneaked a peek in Ned's direction as she placed it on the only bare hook on the considerably large coat tree. Dust clung to the wrinkles of a number of out-of-season jackets. She tucked her coat tight, hoping to keep her brand new winter ensemble fairly clean. She turned and stepped towards her desk, glancing at Ned in the process.

He looked reasonably nice. His longish, dark hair gave him a native American vibe. He sat at his desk, feet perched on top, newspaper resting on his lap. If she'd felt remotely well, she would have found him attractive, with his broad shoulders, deep brown eyes, sly grin. However today she felt old, hungry, and terribly sore. She realized in her haste, she forgot to eat breakfast. "Just make it through today..." she thought.

She noticed him eye her as she stepped towards her desk. He nodded toward a door to his right. "That's the conference room," he said. "Bathroom's there." He nodded towards a door directly across from his desk. "Bart's office is there," he nodded to the left, "you probably already figured that out. And you've already found the front door. That's about it."

Ashley nodded. "Not too complicated." She sat and examined what was evidently her desk. She decided to check it out.

She grasped the center drawer, giving it a light tug. Nothing. She pulled a bit harder. Nothing. It appeared completely stuck. Finally, a firm yank jerked it open. Paper clips and thumb tacks leaped onto her lap. She glanced towards Ned. His eyes danced as he suppressed a grin. She nonchalantly gathered the contents and tossed them back where they belonged. Then she struggled to close it again. She could have sworn she heard Ned snort a small chuckle as she jiggled the wide drawer. She ignored it.

Next she pillaged through the other drawers. Paper, carbons, and clippings littered each. An ancient, shrunken apple sat in one corner, its dried ooze gluing more papers together. She tossed it in the trash. The rusty, sticky residue gummed her fingers. She vowed to sort through the mess that afternoon.

Ashley loved the ambiance of a small town newspaper office. The scent of crisp, dry toner filled the air. It felt dusty, old... newsy. A sticky film clung to everything, likely residue from melted bees wax that used to hold various newspaper components... ads, stories, announcements... on mock up boards. Today, all the layout was done electronically, but visceral memories of the old days clung to the interior of the office.

She leaned back in her chair, observing the mess that was her new desk. It looked ancient, a pale green cast covered the metallic finish. It must have weighed a ton. Cool to the touch, it felt solid, predictable, grimy. She'd have to give it a good cleaning before she allowed Betsy to sit on it.

Ah, Betsy.

Ashley had a Windows laptop for as long as she could remember. However, after the "Big Event" and her subsequent rough recovery, her not-so-faithful companion had suffered a terminal Windows cascading failure. Ashley recalled how, in horror, she watched one blue screen of death after another materialize on her screen.

"What am I going to do?" Ashley cried into the phone, hardly able to bear even one more bit of bad news.

Her mother listened in silence.

After Ashley accepted a writing position in this remote area of Minnesota, her mother presented her with a beautiful, new laptop. Betsy.

Unbeknownst to her mother, but known to Ashley, it was a Mac. "The geek told me this one won't get that error," her mother said.

"Nope," Ashley replied, "It won't get any Windows errors."

"That's a good thing, right?"

"Absolutely."

Ashley hugged her mother, hopped into her tiny Smart car with every possession that meant anything, and drove away from her previous home with tears in her eyes.

Already, Betsy the little Mac, had become her faithful companion. The last few weeks, she managed to pour thousands of words into her interface... every one of them a flawless computing experience without errors, missed saves, or unexpected power-offs.

"Everything'll be fine. Everything'll be fine," she breathed.

As she sat gazing at her grimy desk, Ashley realized her incision was in full complaint mode. She needed another pain killer. She leaned back in her chair and placed her hand over the wound. Her fingers trembled at the memories her gesture triggered. Breathing deep to control them she said, "Is there a place to get a glass of water in here?"

Ned didn't say a word. Instead he nodded to his right.

"Conference room?" Ashley said.

"Yup."

She gingerly stood in as discrete a manner as she was able, unfolding her painful body, and made her way to the next room. Just then, Bart exploded into the center office. "Meeting time."

Drake Mallard's official title was Investigative Detective for the Crossfield Police Department. He'd held that position for the last ten years. It wasn't particularly demanding, considering the number of homicides in the area generally ran in the single digits... per decade.

But he kept his skills sharp by attending copious continuing education seminars and chatting with fellow officers online. A part of him envied his peers who recited harrowing stories of death and mayhem. But, he figured raising his family in a peaceful part of the world was worth the boredom, assuming he ever had a family. Police work was his passion, his focus, his life... for now.

When he wasn't busy with his particular area of expertise (which was basically never), he aided in investigating burglaries, patrolling traffic, and various other small town matters.

So, he wasn't surprised when the call came in.

"Bloody lab reported at Third and Mud... Crossroads."

"Crossroads?"

"Yup."

"Seriously? Can't they take care of stray dogs?"

"Evidently not bloody ones. Nobody wants to touch it."

"Sweet Mary, mother of God. Damn thing probably got into it with a raccoon." Silence. "What's the address?"

"Bloody lab. Last seen near Third and Mud. Crossroads."

"10-4. On my way."

The dispatcher continued, "Take necessary precautions. Blood. Could be a biohazard."

"Roger," he laughed, "I'll put on my hazmat."

He conducted a fast u-turn and headed east.

———

"First on the agenda," Bart said, "We have a new reporter."

"I'm aware of that," Ned said, "I was there when she arrived."

Bart narrowed his eyes. "Just because Maisy couldn't be here doesn't mean we can't conduct a proper meeting."

"Well," Ashley said, "it's just the three of us. We've already met."

"Doesn't matter," Bart said, "we'll conduct a proper meeting nonetheless." He tapped on a small stack of papers in front of him.

"You planning on using Robert's Rules of Order?" asked Ned.

"If I have to."

"Fine," Ned said, "then I'll happily accept my copy of today's agenda."

"You know we don't have a printed agenda," Bart said.

"Then it's not exactly an official meeting, is it?"

"Nevertheless," Ashley jumped in, "I'm sure everyone is busy. I'm sure we can move along." She squirmed, visualizing the small pill box in her purse holding her precious pain meds.

Both men turned to look at her. "I guess you have the floor," Ned said, "tell us about yourself."

"I don't want the floor," she replied, eyes widening.

"I want, and currently have the floor," said Bart, rearranging the papers in front of him.

"Then hop to it," Ned said, "we've all got work to do. What 'cha got?"

"Fine," said Bart, "First on my agenda: We have a new reporter."

"I think we've established that." Ned said.

Ashley nodded, cheeks reddening.

"Perhaps you'd like to introduce yourself," Bart said.

"I just said that," Ned interjected.

Bart threw him an angry glance. Then he turned to Ashley, pursed his lips, and nodded. "Go on," he said.

"Oh," Ashley said, "I suppose..."

Both men gazed at her, waiting for her to speak. "I... uh..." she said, "I don't know what to say."

"Introduce yourself," Bart said.

"Fine," said Ashley. "I'm Ashley Stone. I come from the Twin

Cities. I've freelanced for the last fifteen years, been a stringer for a number of publications back home." She stopped abruptly, then added, "You can call me Ash. Everyone does."

"Well, Ash," said Ned, "it's a pleasure to meet you."

"Likewise," piped in Bart. "Now, let's get on to business. First," he tossed the first sheet of paper in front of Ash and Ned, "we've got to finish the Senior Living Special Issue. Ash, for this project you have to interview six senior citizens who have done, or are doing, something spectacular."

Ned rolled his eyes. "I suppose you want me to make 'em all look tall, thin, beautiful, and young."

"No smart talk from you. Just get 'er done. And make 'em look good. This isn't a tabloid you're working for." He continued, "Second, Ned will give you the schedules for the meetings we cover. Most are in the evening. All are at least two hours long. All need coverage. Manage your office time appropriately."

Ned and Ash nodded.

"Third," Bart said, "Dick is fucking up everything he touches. It's up to you two to act as PR. Smooth over the big advertisers with a promise of a front page story spread."

"How are we supposed to do that?" Ned asked.

Ash interrupted, "Who's Dick?"

"Salesman. Bad salesman." Ned answered, "Don't ask."

"I don't know how you're going to fix the advertising situation. I don't care. Just get 'er done. Write complementary features on 'em. We need cash flow." He looked directly at Ash. "Finally, as you've probably already figured out, Ned is our photographer. He goes with you on every story. Period. Our readers aren't used to a large amount of editorial content. Pics sell papers. Don't get in his way."

Ash nodded. She was about to say something when Bart's phone rang. He raised his finger to interrupt her. He stood and exited the room.

Ned and Ash sat in silence a few moments before he said, "I think he likes you."

"Why would you say that?"

"He hasn't yelled yet."

"Really?"

"Yeah."

Silence hung heavy for a few moments before Ashley said, "What's up with that Dick guy? If he can't sell, why is he still employed?"

Ned said, "Dick is Bart's brother-in-law. If he fired the lazy lout, his sister would kill him."

"Oh my."

Silence descended on them again, then Ned said, "You haven't met Maisy. She's the receptionist, graphic designer, gofer, you name it. You'll like her. She's nice. Part time, though."

Ned sat without saying a word for a while longer. His gaze caught in her general direction. He seemed to be studying something about her. Finally he spoke. "Your hand. Looks like a pretty nasty IV scar."

Ashley glanced downward. A poke hole directly above a large vein glowed red. She brushed it lightly. "Cat. She can get rough sometimes."

"Doesn't look like something a cat would do."

"Well, I guess you're the expert," she answered.

Ned smiled as another moment of silence passed. "So, how did the cat do that?"

"Playing," Ashley said, "playing rough."

"That's one hella cat," Ned said. Then he added, "If you plan on using that lie again, you may want to remove some of the tape residue." Ashley winced.

Their conversation was mercifully cut short when Bart entered the room. He tossed a piece of paper on the table. "Bloody lab," he said. "Go cover it. Write a brilliant story. Sell newspapers."

"Bloody lab?" Ashley repeated, "as in a dog?"

"All the details I have are on the paper. Now hop to it."

Bart exited the room, leaving Ashley and Ned alone. Ned

grasped the paper and read it. "Should be interesting," he said. "Looks like a lab got into it with a 'coon."

"Coon?"

"Raccoon."

"I knew that."

"Then what was your point?" Ned's eyes sparkled.

"Dunno."

"Let's get moving." He passed the paper to Ash. She read the information and began to mentally write her lead. She followed Ned out of the conference area and paused by her desk. She grabbed her notepad, flip camera, leather portfolio, and Betsy. They headed out the door.

———

Officer Drake Mallard pulled into the Crossroads Area Post Office parking lot. Groups of residents stood in small knots outside the door. Mallard counted four, approximately three to five people per. He strode to the closest one.

"Anyone here call in an emergency?"

A few group members mumbled in response. Mallard moved on. "Anyone here call in an emergency?"

A pudgy women to his right said,"That was me. I saw a stray lab near here. Golden lab. It was bloody."

"How did you know it was blood?"

"It was red."

"Could the red substance have been something else?"

"Maybe."

"Where was the animal last located?"

"Right over there." She pointed to an empty space of gravel around ten yards from the tip of her finger.

"Well, it's gone now."

"Yup. Labs have a way of doing that."

Mallard scowled. "What way did it go?"

The woman pointed to her right.

Mallard walked back to his car and slipped inside. "God, I hate this town," he mumbled. He fired the ignition and threw the car in gear.

———

In the parking lot of the Crossroad's Herald, Ned stopped short as Ashley proceeded towards her tomato red Smart. "I'm not getting into that thing."

"Why not," Ash asked.

"Seriously? I have a reputation to maintain. Anyone sees me in this thing and I may as well volunteer my nuts for their rear view mirror."

Ash stopped short. "Seriously? Your masculinity is dependent upon the vehicle you're in?"

Ned said, "No. But it sure affects other's perception thereof."

Ash laughed. "You said 'thereof. Kudos!" Then she added, "I love my Smart. Great gas mileage. Perfect size for one. Plus, I can park anywhere."

"Parking may be an issue in the big city, but really... I doubt you'll have trouble finding a spot here." His arm swept the vast expanse of the main street. Empty parking spots outnumbered cars by ten to one. "Hell, you don't even have to know how to parallel park in these parts. Just drive on in and you're good to go." He paused, then added, "We're taking my truck."

"Fine," said Ashley, "but next time, I drive. You need to experience the glories of my car. Plus, I wouldn't mind seeing your... er... nuts hanging from someone's rear view."

"Yeah," said Ned, "Sure. Hold your breath waiting."

He strode towards a half ton pickup and clicked the fob. The vehicle chirped to life. He opened the door and hopped inside. Ashley pulled the gargantuan door open and stood a moment. It would take quite a heave-ho to get inside that thing.

"What 'cha waiting for?" Ned chirped, "You're about to find out what it's like to ride in a real vehicle." He patted the seat beside him. "This baby'll take you anywhere you want to go. In style. In comfort."

"And my car can't do all that?" Ashley said. Then she added, "Got a hoist?" She paused gazing at the mile-high seat in front of her. "I'll probably need one to get in this thing. Either that or a step stool."

Ned revved the engine. "What did you say?"

"Nothing."

Ashley strategically placed her right foot on the running board and grasped the door frame with her left hand. She gingerly pulled herself towards the seat, but a stab of pain pierced her incision. She grimaced.

"You need help getting in?" Ned glanced in her direction.

"Nope. Doing fine."

She gave the maneuver another go, and this time hooked her left hand through the hand-grasp above her head and used it to pull herself upward. Meanwhile her right hand pushed against the door. Her abdomen screamed as she heaved forward, but she managed to wrench a portion of one buttock on the seat. She paused, breathing deep. Then she gingerly wiggled the rest of her bottom into the truck. Her hands shook and a tiny river of perspiration trailed down her temple.

"Jeeze," Ned said, glancing in her direction, "You OK?"

"Yeah," she answered nonchalantly, "I'm just sore. Tried working out last night. Just about did me in. I'm super stiff today."

"Sure," Ned answered.

Ashley gazed at the note Bart gave her. "Ned," she said, "what kind of story do you suppose Bart's looking for? I've run a dozen leads through my mind and I just can't get a handle on how to start this thing."

"Don't work too hard," he answered, "He's just testing your chops. If you can make this story work into something newsworthy, he'll figure you can write anything." He engaged the pickup and exited the parking lot. He continued, "Just write the story.

Nothing fancy. It's not exactly hard news, but it could still hit the front page depending on what else comes in this week."

They drove in silence until they approached the post office. Cars lined the streets and the crowd had expanded. Officer Mallard's police cruiser had returned and was parked directly across from the flag pole. Ashley gave Ned her best side eye. "Hmmm… no open parking spaces. I told you we should have driven my car."

"Nah," Ned said, "we'll just go over there. You mentioned you like to exercise. Guess you'll get some." Then he broke into one of his gorgeous smiles. "I don't like to park in the thick of things anyway."

"I suppose I could use a work out," Ashley said, "but I'd rather it be voluntary rather than forced."

Ned laughed as they rolled to the end of the street. He swung a left and kept going until he reached the end of the parking snag. He pulled the vehicle in place and threw the shift in "park."

"I suppose we'll both get a nice walk this morning," Ashley said.

"This hardly constitutes a nice walk," said Ned. "I like to count my walks in miles, not half blocks."

"No comment," Ashley said.

———

Officer Mallard watched the crowd grow. "Damn people. Small town folks'll get excited over nothing," he grumbled. He sat back in his cruiser. "I'll never find that mongrel."

He flipped on his radio and spoke into the mic. "Mallard to dispatch," he said, "No sign of said canine in Crossroads."

The radio hissed a few moments before it sprang to life. "Dispatch to Mallard. Monitor the situation."

"10-4."

He dropped his head against the seat. Damn. He threw the car in gear and maneuvered away from the scene.

He passed Ned Stevens as he exited the area. He walked next to a woman who carried what appeared to be reporter equipment. "Damn. The Herald's here. Just what I need, bad reporting on a non-story," he groaned.

He nodded to Ned and kept moving. He proceeded to patrol each street, noiselessly gliding down each, slowly scanning the terrain for the so-called bloody lab.

"It's gonna be a long day."

————

"Ned, my man!" Ashley watched a lanky fellow ambled towards Ned, his hand outstretched. "It's been too long!"

Ned laughed and clasped his friend's hand. "I know. How long has it been... a week? Two?"

"Ha," replied Lanky, "you know it, Superstar. We gotta get together at beer-o-clock sharp! We've got catching up to do."

The men nearly doubled over as their peals of laughter melted into the surrounding din of conversation. Ashley stood silent, patiently waiting for sanity to prevail and the men to act with even a small semblance of professionalism.

Finally, Ned turned to Ashley. "Ash," he said, "This is Ike. Ike... Ash."

"Nice to meet you." Lanky (a.k.a. Ike) reached a long bony hand towards her. Ashley obliged, grasping his knuckles.

Ned said, "Ash is our new reporter."

This small sentence elicited peals of laughter from Ike. "Seriously? How long do you suppose this one'll last?"

Ned shrugged. "Who knows?" Ashley threw Ned her icy stare. He continued, "Ash comes to us via the big city. Drives a Smart Car. Probably drinks froufrou coffee."

Ashley interrupted. "Hello Ike. It's nice to meet you." She turned to Ned. "Any chance we can get to work?"

"Have at it," he replied, nodding towards the crowd.

Ashley stepped away, leaving the men to chat amongst themselves. She spotted a small knot of women and decided to start there. "Hello," she said, "I'm Ashley Stone, the new reporter at the Crossroads Herald. Any of you know anything about the lab?"

The women fell silent and gazed at her. "Dunno," said one, "I'm just here to watch." Another said, "Everyone's here so... well... so am I."

Ashley politely thanked them and moved on to the next knot of gawkers. "Hi," she said, "I'm Ashley Stone, Crossroads Herald's reporter. Anyone here know anything about the lab?"

One of the men looked at her suspiciously. "Got a press pass?"

"What?"

"Press pass."

Ashley said, "I don't believe I need one."

"Just messing with you," the man laughed. "Nah. Just here waiting for some action."

"You could talk to Officer Mallard," said another.

"Officer Mallard," Ashley repeated.

"Yup. Mallard. Drrrrake Mallard." He spoke in low, dramatic tones.

"Yeah. And I believe you," Ashley quipped.

"Seriously," a younger man said, "That's his name."

Ashley thanked the men and proceeded to the next group.

Nothing. She paused and breathed deep, pondering her next move. Then she noticed Ned making his way towards her. "Hey," he said, "Ike saw the dog. If all else fails, interview him."

Ashley said, "Good idea. Thanks."

"Not really," he replied, "I already snapped my shots. I just need you to get the story." He grinned.

"Has anyone ever told you that you're annoying?"

"All the time."

Then it happened. In a flash.

Ashley was interviewing Ike for his take on the big bloody lab story. Ned was floating in among the crowd taking candid shots, hoping to find something usable for another photo essay. His flash sparked like a small bolt of lightning every time he snapped a pic.

The crowd members murmured between themselves, some exiting due to boredom. Then it happened.

It began with a shrieking howl, then crescendoed from there. Every pod of gawkers instantly fell silent and all heads turned towards the animalistic sounds.

Within moments of the eruption, Geena Larson gasped, "What's Justin T. doing?"

Ashley followed Larson's gaze and her eyes fell on a scrawny middle schooler carrying what looked like a large knapsack. He stumbled, screaming. As he neared, Ashley noticed tears running down his cheeks. A trail of mucus dangled from his nose. His denim covered knees appeared discolored. The palms of his hands glowed bright red.

"Sweet Mary, mother of God," Larson whispered.

Ashley's jaw dropped. At that moment, she felt a warm hand rest on her shoulder. She turned. Ned stood next to her, eyes wide, horrified look on his face.

"Holy hell," he whispered.

Chapter Three

CROSSROADS SUPERSTAR

The folks of Crossroads, Minnesota, population 513, hadn't seen anything like it before. They'd survived tornadoes, budget cuts, power outages, sewer breaks, acts of God, and what was considered (by some) satanic attacks. But the moment Justin T. staggered towards the post office forevermore replaced them all, including the 1969 town centennial, as the most exciting community event. Ever. His shrieks would live in infamy, verbal descriptions of his demeanor, his clothing, his facial expressions would be mimicked (in various, ever escalating forms) for decades.

Justin T. delivered the Crossfield Gazette to residents of Crossroads every morning (minus Sundays and certain holidays). It irked Bart to no end that a fellow Crossroads citizen would patronize that odious, competing publication. Just because they were a daily, could pay their staff better wages, had a better (unearned, in his opinion) reputation, and bulldozed through every story, scooping him on a regular basis didn't mean they were better.

Either way, he liked Justin's family. He graduated with his father back in '79 and befriended his mother years ago. Last year was rough on Justin's family. His mother was diagnosed with Lyme disease and suffered intense fatigue since then. His father lost his job at the county jail due to budget cuts. His sister had gone rogue, hooked up with Ike Moe, and suspected she was now pregnant, although her parents were yet to receive these little bits of information. As of yesterday, it appeared as though hard-working Justin T. would be the only person in that family who would "turn out." Now this.

Given their precarious financial situation, Bart couldn't hold it against them that they'd allow their son to don the Crossfield Gazette knapsack and deliver his direct competition. After all, poor Justin was basically on his own, using his earnings to purchase crazy things like clothes, food, a few used console games, and general school supplies. So far, Justin had done a fine job, raising himself. But it was painfully clear he'd need some serious help after seeing whatever it was he saw.

What happened to Justin T. on that fateful autumn day forever cemented Bart's decision to keep his complaints about Justin delivering the Crossfield Gazette to himself.

———

It began as any other day. Cold, crispy snow, frigid wind made his skin erupt in a million goose pimples. Silence stung his ears, even birds weren't awake at this hour. He enjoyed this moment... the brief window just before the sun rose and the town rested in serene slumber. Even wild animals crept quiet, always keeping a safe distance.

He tramped through back yards, up alleys, always carefully placing the newspaper between the screen door and main. That's where people liked it. That's where the biggest year end tips lied.

In the big city, paper carriers rode bicycles and tossed their wares onto lawns, driveways, roofs. Not here. Small town folk got special treatment. Right inside the door... that's where the paper belonged.

He recalled Saturday morning's route, nothing unusual, just serene silence punctuated by frigid wind nips. He really liked non-eventful days. The mornings he didn't encounter dogs, cats, raccoons, or cranky residents made for a perfect route. He had Sundays off, no paper. He had Monday off. Holiday. Although it would certainly bite into his weekly income, Justin appreciated a little leisure. On those days he could sleep in... all the way to 6 AM.

Today he ran behind schedule. It was tough not to oversleep after a couple days broke his rhythm. Sure, he'd miss a couple hours of school today, but he needed the income. He decided to explain it to his parents later... if they ever found out. They were busy with their own trouble and rarely kept track of him.

He proceeded through his route, steps accelerating as he neared the end. He checked his watch, gratified to note he wouldn't miss much school. On the last block he threw it in high gear and raced to finish. He zipped through the yards, whipping open screen doors, throwing in the paper, and slamming them shut... all with the efficiency of a pro.

He was just performing his maneuver at the Alexander Kaufman residence when he unexpectedly slipped on the cement stoop, landing with a dull thud on his right side. Dazed, he paused a moment before he noticed the stench, the utterly horrific, nasal piercing, stomach churning, horrible odor of insanity, rot, violence. Terror flooded his being as he raised his hand and it arrived in his field of vision dripping with coagulated goo. In spite of every macho lesson his father ever taught, he involuntarily shrieked in a most undignified manner. When he realized he was surrounded with the goo, another garbled bellow rose in his throat.

Before he could ascertain what was going on, he found himself wallowing in the mess, attempting to rise, but slipping back to his knees, onto his shoulder. He fought the mess, wrestling it like an invisible invader. He rolled about, unable to rise, the frigid goo permeating his clothing, coloring his skin.

He was covered in the stinky mess. It hung in long strings

making him appear like a marionette whose cut lines dangled from his fingers. He cried for help, but no one arrived.

Despite pain shooting from his various scrapes, he managed to maneuver himself to his feet and stagger forward appearing like an amateur propelling himself forward on an ice rink. He vaguely pondered the escalating shrieks filling the void of silence, then realized the sound originated from his own throat. Panic welled in his belly as putrid slime clung to his clothing, smeared to his body, splattered his face. The the odor choked his nostrils so bad, he could actually taste the scent.

He staggered away from the house, limping, gasping, groping... hoping to somehow escape whatever it was that choked him, hoping to erase the images now seemingly tattooed in his memory.

He managed to stagger to the post office as adults surrounded him.

"What happened," gasped one.

Another steadied his shoulders, but quickly retracted when their hands smeared into the gelatinous slime.

Flashes popped on smart phones.

Justin collapsed in a heap. "Help me," he murmured.

———

Ashley heard the screams. She watched the crowd turn and gasp. She saw Justin stumble towards the post office.

She smelled coagulated blood. Its pungent odor pierced her nostrils causing her to gag.

Already exhausted, sore, and hungry, she slapped her hand over her mouth, the other arm pressing against her horizontal incision as if to keep her innards intact. Her world spun as nausea choked her throat. Then she felt a firm hand on her shoulder.

"You OK?"

She steadied herself and breathed deep. The nausea somewhat dissolved. "I'm fine," she gasped. "I think I forgot to eat."

"How do you forget to eat," Ned asked.

"Dunno," she choked, "I just didn't think about it." Then she added, "What's that stench?"

Ned nodded towards Justin. "Looks like it could be him." A clot of people surrounded Justin. "I should probably get some pics," said Ned. "You gonna be OK?"

"I'm fine," Ashley said, "you move along. I'll try to get some quotes."

Ned floated amongst the crowd, discretely snapping shots of the event. Ashley pulled out her recorder and spoke to a few gawkers for reaction quotes. When Drake Mallard hit the scene, both Ashley and Ned darted straight to him.

"Officer Mallard," she said, "what is your comment on this situation."

Mallard paused and squinted at Ashley. "How am I supposed to know? I haven't even made it to the scene. Get out of my way." He marched forward and shooed the crowd aside. "Ambulance is in route,' he announced, "now quit crowding him." He headed to Justin, occasionally demanding, "Step back. Step back. Give us room."

"That wasn't the most stellar example of journalistic acumen," said Ned, commenting on Ash's conversation with Mallard.

"I kinda hoped no one noticed," replied Ashley.

Just then, Lanky strolled by. "Hey Superstar. Pretty exciting, eh?"

Ned nodded. "Not bad."

"Superstar?" Ashley asked.

"Long story," said Ned. Then he added, "Better call Bart. He'll want something ASAP. We can't publish until Monday, but we can get what we have on the website." He paused, eyes narrowing. "Damn. Looks like the Crossfield Gazette will scoop us on this one, too."

Ashley glanced over her shoulder. A scruffy man carrying a notepad and recorder made his way through the crowd. A tall cameraman followed. The reporter's hunched back and ragamuffin hair swooped like oily curtains around his craggy face. His wadded shirt peeked out from under a wrinkled jacket. He apparently didn't own an iron.

"That's Hugh Harrington," said Ned, "Your competition."

Ashley's eyebrows rose. "I didn't realize this was a competition."

"Never think otherwise." He nodded towards the photographer. "Hey Snap." The man bobbed his head in return.

"I assume that fine fellow is named 'Snap?' Seriously? A photographer named 'Snap?'"

Ned laughed. "Yup."

"Is he friendlier than his buddy?"

"Nope."

———

"Stage one complete. It took less than 80 hours from completion to discovery."

"Seems rather long."

"Not really. Small town. Not much action."

"I would have thought discovery would have taken place earlier in a small community."

"Not necessarily. Long weekend. Columbus Day."

"That's still a holiday?"

"Yes."

"How politically incorrect." Pause. "Are you monitoring the situation?"

"I am. Very closely."

"You'll send regular reports?"

"Yes."

"Wonderful. Carry on."

———

With the crowd dispersed, with the first draft of her article written, Ashley leaned back on her couch in supreme comfort. She ate a bowl of cheesy rice with vegetables and had (most importantly) consumed two Tylenol. Not the regular kind, the good stuff. The kind with a hit of Codeine. Her oncologist told her she wouldn't need it long, in fact she'd stretched out her prescription far longer than she expected, saving the "good stuff" for very important events, like starting a new job, discovering her new home town was the site of Minnesota's latest murder, needing to work late, and meeting (likely) the most gorgeous man she'd ever laid eyes on.

But they were co-workers. Nothing could come of it. But she could dream.

She sat back and allowed the numb happiness of prescription laced joy wash over her. She rested her hand on the enormous incision.

Its pain seemed to have settled down for now, almost becoming an invisible companion. "Today you misbehaved, my love. How dare you throb like that. It was hard to work."

She chuckled at her absurd situation and took another long swig of hard lemonade. She knew she probably shouldn't mix narcotics with alcohol but today had been a particularly challenging day.

She closed her eyes, trying to erase the memory of the awkward moment. It happened after they returned to the office.

At that point in the day, Ashley felt exhausted, grimy, and exceedingly hungry. She'd marched to her desk and lowered herself to her seat. Her incision screamed as she dug through her purse searching for a "good" Tylenol.

Ned approached her desk with an SD card in his hand. "Want me to dig through these shots and give you what I think will work? Or, do you want to review all of them?"

Ash cringed as she paused, gazing at the card. "I trust you. Give me your best."

"Sounds great," he answered. Then he said, "Have you eaten today?"

"Nah. No time."

"Me either. Wanna get something?"

She paused as a lump formed in her throat. "After what I've seen today, I don't think I'll ever eat again. I can't get that stink out of my nose."

Ned chuckled. "I know what you mean. I've never seen so much blood." Much to Ashley's chagrin, Ned pulled a chair next to her desk and sat. She'd have to find her pill later. He continued, "I don't believe I've ever seen so much blood before... and I've taken pictures inside a slaughter house."

Ash groaned. "When did you do that?"

"I'm a man of many mysteries," he said, leaning back in his chair. He flashed a perfect smile.

"Definitely," Ash mumbled. Another stab of pain made her throw caution to the wind. She grabbed her purse and started digging. She pulled out the bottle and shook two pills into her palm. She popped them in her mouth and swallowed.

"Don't you need water for that?"

"Obviously not."

Ned studied her face for a moment before he said, "What were those?"

"Tylenol."

"In that bottle?"

"Headache," she answered.

"They're prescription," he said, "they must be pretty bad ass."

"Really bad headache."

Ned placed the SD card on the desk, seemingly satisfied with her explanation. He shook his head as he said, "I still can't believe what I saw today."

"I know," Ash whispered.

"As god is my witness, I never believed a human body could... could... do that."

"I know," Ash repeated.

"I mean really? A shovel? They used a snow shovel to scoop him up."

"How do they know what — or who — that was?"

"Well, Kaufman lived there. He hasn't been seen since last week. It really isn't a stretch."

"Yeah. But how will they identify him?"

"DNA, I suppose. There wasn't much of him left. Those dogs must have been really hungry."

Ashley's stomach performed a flip. "I suppose."

Ned closed his eyes. "I'm still amazed."

"Me, too."

Just then Bart entered the room. "I hear we've got a gory one."

"That's an understatement," Ned said.

Bart held a piece of paper out to Ashley. She stood, extended her right hand and grasped it. As she did so, her jacket shifted, giving Ned a view of the entire right side of her shirt. She sat and gazed at the paper.

Bart said, "It's the press release from the Crossfield PD. You can use some of the information for your story." His face glowed crimson with excitement. He rolled up his sleeves and continued, "We can't go to press with this until Monday, but we can get it on the website. Write fast, before the Gazette scoops us." Then he added, "I need spectacular pics for this, Ned. Watermark them all so that fucking Gazette can't swipe 'em." He took a moment to catch his breath. "The Gazette will get the story out first. We can't help that. But where they'll go wide, we'll go deep. Ashley, I need spectacular reporting on this. We'll beat 'em with quality, not quantity." Then he added, "That goes for both of you. Show me some excellence." Ned nodded as he watched Bart saunter away, enter his office, and slam the door. He turned to Ashley.

"No pressure, though," he said laughing.

"None whatsoever."

"Welcome to the Crossroads Herald." They paused a moment, smiling at the absurdity of the situation. Finally Ned spoke. "I can't help but notice you're still stiff. That must have been one heck of an exercise session last night."

"Yup," Ash answered.

"Also, your pain pills. Seemed a bit much to take a prescription for a headache."

"Not really," she answered. "I reuse bottles."

"Sounds reasonable," he said, leaning closer. "But I have one more question."

"What would that be?"

"What's that big spot on your shirt?"

Ash gently grasped her torso as an embarrassed flush flooded her cheeks. "I don't know what you're talking about."

"Yeah. I think you do." He rested his head on his hand. "Something's going on. We've got a big story to cover. I'm just wondering what I'm dealing with."

She gingerly opened her jacket and peered downward. "Well I'll be darned," she said, "I guess I spilled."

"Yeah," Ned said, "IV punctures, pain pills, obvious bandaging, now drainage. It's clearly nothing."

Ashley didn't reply.

"I don't know what the big secret is, but it doesn't seem to inhibit your ability to do your job... so far. We've got big stuff going on. You're taking pain pills. I hope you're not in over your head."

"I'm fine," she said.

"Probably true," he answered. But sometimes things like this are easier to handle if you've got a friend."

"And are you applying for that position?"

Ned paused. "Dunno," he said, "I seem to have peeved you." He added, "We're going to work together. We're about to spend a lot of time together. I just want to make sure you're OK so we can get everything done on time."

Ash breathed deep, then said, "I'm not peeved. I'm just hungry, stinky, exhausted, and have a lot to write before I get to go home. I'm not sure I can swallow anything after everything I've seen. It's my first day here and it's turning into a really bad day."

Ned said, "It'll get better. Promise. Bart's a blow hard." He paused, looking pensive. Then he extended his hand. "I've got an idea. Come here."

Ash stared at it a moment. "You want to hold my hand?"

He laughed. "No. I want you to follow me."

"But you're sitting."

He stood. "Follow me." He marched to Bart's door and opened it a sliver. "We'll be back in a flash."

"Where you going?" Bart's voice bellowed.

"Doesn't matter. We'll be right back." Ned nodded to Ashley. "C'mon. Bring your stuff." He exited the building and strode directly to his pickup.

"Where we going?" Ashley asked, scrambling behind him. The medicine had evidently worked its magic on her throbbing incision. The pain felt quite tolerable at this moment.

"You'll see," he said.

Ashley climbed into the behemoth and sat back, enjoying the sensation of Codeine flowing through her veins. Ned joined her, fired the engine, and threw the truck into gear. Neither said a word as he sped down the road.

———

Ashley swallowed another large swig of the ice cold hard lemonade. It felt wonderful to be home, bathed, fed, and relaxed. She lifted the bottle to her lips again.

She recalled watching Ned drive as they proceeded towards their mystery destination. He rolled past the Kaufman house and she watched the yellow hazard tape flutter in the breeze.

"Weird day," Ashley whispered.

"Yup," Ned answered.

They drove in silence as they left town and headed towards Crossfield.

"Did you bring your laptop," Ned asked.

"Always," she answered.

"Good," he said, "Pop it open."

She leaned forward, grasped her laptop bag, opened it, and pulled out Betsy.

"I'm taking you to Crossfield," he said. "We need to eat." He added, "On our way, we've got twenty minutes to kill. Let's pound out that story."

"In the truck?"

"Yup. It's a great place to write. No interruptions. No phones. No Bart." Then he said, "Bet you can't do anything like this in your little rattle trap."

Ash actually laughed. "Yeah, I admit it. My Smart's cab isn't the size of a small office. I'm not sure Betsy would comfortably sit on my lap in there."

"We can try it sometime," Ned conceded, "you'll never know until you try."

They cruised down the highway, bouncing ideas off each other, comparing notes, discussing accompanying photographs. By the time they got to Crossfield, Ned and Ash had already hammered out the majority of her story. "I'm always amazed at how much I can get done when I'm out of that crappy office," Ned said as they rolled into the parking lot of a small cafe. "It's almost magical." He paused, a satisfied smile on his face, then added, "We can grab a bite, then polish what we've got on our way home. It'll be done before we hit the office. Works every time."

Ash breathed deep. "Thanks," she said, "I really owe you one."

"No problem," Ned answered, "glad to help.

And that's how Ashley's illustrious career at the Crossroads Herald began. Her first official assignment was a story that would impact her life far longer than she expected. It would have a profound affect on not only her health, but the trajectory of her career, and would take her places she never imagined. This story would offer a chance at happiness... if she could extend herself enough to accept it. She'd face her own mortality and most feared adversary.

She'd lose friends, search for love, and risk her life on more than one occasion.

But at this exact moment, as she sat sipping her hard lemonade, enjoying her codeine haze, she felt happiness, pure unadulterated contentment, and had no idea the terrifying depths of the story she was about to research.

And the door to utter madness was triggered by a simple golden Labrador.

Chapter Four

AN ANNOYING INFECTION

Ashley awoke the next morning laying in a puddle of moist, warm liquid. The pink pallor shining on her new white sheets told her she'd sprung another leak. She leaped to her feet, cringed, then grasped her incision. She momentarily forgot the pain until it pierced her belly. She paused a moment, waiting for the stabbing sensation to subside.

As she hobbled to the bathroom, she stripped off her shirt and pulled at her soaked bandages. She paused to gaze into the mirror.

At each end of the incision, the wound opened like a tiny, gaping mouth, each side drooling pink liquid. A new "mouth" opened in the exact center of the wound. It drooled as well.

She sighed. Fuck.

She grasped some gauze and gingerly dabbed at the drippy mess but some of it already formed a delightful crust that stuck tight to her skin.

"Better take a shower, gorgeous," she mumbled.

She stripped off her remaining bed clothes, hopped in the shower, and allowed the water to sweep her body clean. Afterwards, she rebandaged her wound, dressed, and pulled off her bed sheets. After she threw them in the washer, she grabbed her telephone and dialed the number.

"Dr. Pence's office."

"Yes. Ashley Stone here. May I speak with her nurse?"

"She's with a patient. May I take a message and have her call you back?"

"Yes. You have my number. Tell her my infection hasn't gotten any better. It appears I've started leaking from a new hole last night."

The other voice on the line said, "Would you like to make an appointment?"

"Not if I don't need to," Ashley said, "I just started a new job and really can't take any time off."

"I'll speak with the nurse."

"Thanks."

Ash hung up the phone and pondered her situation. "I never should have taken a new job before I was completely well," she mumbled. But when would that be? At best her situation was precarious. At worse... well, she preferred not to think about worst case scenarios.

She breathed deep and poured a bowl of toasted oats. "At least I can try to eat healthy... in case I don't die in the foreseeable future." She smiled at her morbid sense of humor.

There she was. A walking time bomb. An expensive woman with more medical bills than common sense. Who starts a new job when they're in her situation?

Lots of people, she supposed. After all, how do you pay medical bills without an income? Yet, she couldn't help but think it was a mistake to move, start writing for a small town paper, and transfer all her medical records... all before she felt completely well.

But when would that be?

She shook her head, trying to remove the copious "what ifs" from her mind.

She scooped more cereal into her mouth and savored the faint crunch of a vaguely soggy nugget.

"I'll be OK," she thought. "I'm not dead yet. Heck, things could even turn out. Miracles happen."

Her phone rang.

———

Ashley sped to work, hoping an early arrival would earn her a longer lunch break. Sadly, Dr. Pence wouldn't prescribe any new antibiotics without examining her wound. That was the bad news. The good news was that she could squeeze her into her schedule at 11:30. Ash hoped she could slip away, get to Crossfield, arrive at her appointment (it would be a miracle if the doc wasn't running behind schedule), and back to the Crossroads Herald office within an hour and a half... assuming the doc didn't insist on culturing the drainage.

If everything went slick, it would be difficult, but definitely doable, in her opinion.

She arrived at the office to find Bart and Ned already there, discussing the story.

"This is good," said Bart, "but I need more."

"Well, you've got what you've got until the authorities release more information."

"Yeah, but you should be able to do better than them. That Drake Mallard is one dim bulb. Interview the people he won't think to interview. Scoop the cop if you can."

Ned turned and flashed a brilliant smile at Ashley. "You came back. Awesome."

"Why wouldn't I," said Ash.

"You'd be surprised at how many one-timers we get here," said Bart, "And after yesterday, I wasn't sure I'd see you again."

"I knew she'd come back," said Ned. His eyes gazed at her in a most uncomfortable fashion, "She's a trouper."

"Uhhh... I'll just disregard that entire exchange," said Ashley, "how did the story look?"

Bart bellowed a loud barking laugh. "I like this one. Sticks to the topic at hand." He continued, "Good introduction. But as I was saying to Ned, we've gotta step up our game. The Gazette is gonna kill us unless we get something better than them. I want to scoop them in every aspect of this. I want you and Ned to take every spare minute you've got to examine this story from every angle. And by that, I mean every... damn... perspective." His eyes narrowed. "By that I mean... get dirty if you have to."

Ashley's eyebrows knit together. "Are you talking publishing speculative tabloid journalism?"

"I don't care for labels," said Bart. "I do care about sales."

Ash's eyes darted to Ned. "And what do you have to say about this?"

He shook his head. "I'm not willing to go tabloid on this. I like to err on the side of journalistic integrity. I think we owe that to our readers... and to the poor dude who died. Sales are one thing. Turning this into a community brouhaha is another."

"Well," said Bart, "I own the paper. I'm the boss. I call the shots around here."

"Well," said Ned, "I own my camera. I'm its boss. It'll take pictures of what I want it to."

They both turned to Ashley. She pondered a moment then said, "I need quality clips. If I start writing tabloid, I could hurt my long term career. I've never aspired to write trash, but..." She never finished her sentence. If she had she would have said, "I've got bills to pay. However, I may not need to worry about my long term reputation anyway. If I were to die in the near future, it wouldn't matter how I covered this story, unless I want to consider my legacy..."

She turned to Ned. He seemed nice. He sure was gorgeous. She turned to Bart. He signed her paychecks. She stood silent for a moment before she said, "I wouldn't feel comfortable profiting from another person's misfortune." She sighed. "I'm with Ned on this."

Bart snorted. "Fine. Do it your way. But if papers don't fly off the shelves, you're both fired."

Ned laughed. "Yeah. Sounds fine to me."

———

Ashley struggled through her morning, setting up interviews, trying to squeeze information out of the Crossfield PD dispatcher, and continually grasping her wound, trying to ascertain how spongy the gauze was. The last thing she wanted was another leakage situation, especially in front of Ned.

Speaking of Ned, he was particularly attentive. He offered her coffee. He said he'd proofread her work. He offered to collaborate on the next installment. He asked her opinion on various photos.

Ashley remained professionally aloof, focusing on her work, declining each offer, so she could sneak out for her appointment.

Finally, at 10:30, Ned said, "Do you think we should head out of the office and find the local scuttlebutt on this situation?"

Ashley glanced at her watch. "Sure. We should take both vehicles. I have to head out for an early dinner."

Ned's eyes narrowed. "What time do you need to buzz out?"

"Elevenish."

"Why the early dinner?"

"Personal."

Ned nodded. "Fine. Grab your gear. I'll start the truck."

Ash paused, pondering the equipment she'd need on this particular run. She grabbed her notepad, recorder, and Betsy. She followed Ned out the door. Outside, she repeated, "I'll follow in my car."

"Nah," said Ned, "This won't take long. Besides, we need to come up with our plan of action. We'll discuss is in route."

Ash paused again, resting her hand on top of her incision. She realized she probably should have swapped out the bandage before she left the office. She sighed. "I need to leave in half an hour. I'll take my car."

Ned stopped and turned to her. "What's up? We both know lunch hour begins at noon."

"Noonish, I was told."

"Eleven isn't noon or noonish. What's 'cha up to?"

"Nothing that concerns you," she said, "I just have to take care of something... something related to the move. Besides. I came to work early for the express purpose of taking a little extra time on lunch hour."

Ned glanced at her abdomen. "My guess," he said, "is it has something to do with that."

Ashley instinctively tightened her arm around her wound. "I have no idea what you're talking about."

"Just get in the truck," he said.

"I really need to make this appointment," she said.

"You will."

Ashley and Ned spent the next half hour cruising near the crime scene. Yellow tape cordoned off the area and all entrances to the house were sealed with a similarly colored yellow adhesive. Ned pointed out the houses near the scene.

"That house belongs to Sheila Knight," he said. "She called the cops. We need to talk to her to find out what made her do that. Maybe she'll spill some new information. We need to find out if she heard anything, saw anything, smelled anything... we've got to jog her memory." Ashley nodded. He continued. "Ike Moe is a buddy of mine. He apparently saw a bloody lab and called it in. You need to talk to him."

"Name sounds familiar. Did I meet him," Ashley asked.

"Yup."

"Is he the guy who called you 'superstar'?"

"Yup."

"What's the story with that," she asked.

"Nothing important today," he answered.

"Well, you're pretty interested in my personal life, just thought I'd return the favor," she said.

"Yeah," he said, "But I doubt my story is anywhere near as interesting as yours."

Ashley's eyes narrowed. "Quid pro quo."

Ned tossed back his head and laughed. "This isn't Silence of the Lambs and I'm not Hannibal Lecter." Then he added, "You're as pretty as a starling, though."

Ashley felt her cheeks warm. She disregarded his comment and ran her fingers along the spiral edge of her notebook. "I'll ponder some questions to present to Ms Knight."

Ned turned to her, his dark eyes meeting hers. Much to Ashley's chagrin, a number of butterflies erupted in her stomach. "Almost eleven. I suppose I should get you to your car." Then he added, "I won't mention the early lunch to Bart. Just get back ASAP. We have a lot to do."

———

Ashley sat in the waiting room, nausea sweeping through her throat. Medical settings generally transformed her nervous energy into an unpleasant physical sensation. She tapped her toes, glanced at her watch every couple minutes, and occasionally touched her bandages, calculating the potential moisture they could absorb. Finally the nurse entered the waiting area and called her name.

"Step on the scale," she said just after they left the waiting area.

"I hate this part," answered Ashely.

"Gotta do it. Federal guidelines."

"Yeah, but it's stupid. I just need the doc to give me antibiotics."

"Dr. Pence can't calculate dosage without your weight."

"Bet she can. Plus, I still hate it."

The nurse shrugged as she recorded the number. She led Ashley into the exam room. She gestured towards the table and said, "Have a seat." She took her vitals and asked the standard questions. With the brief medical history complete, Ash waited alone, thoughts tumbling through her mind.

Mortality statistics buzzed her brain; she determined hers weren't all that bad. The upwardly creeping scale number triggered her thoughts on dietary restrictions; cancer really was a bitch in that regard. CT scans tumbled through her memory; not real fun, unless you enjoy holding your breath and the sensation of wetting yourself. She dreaded the needles... so many needles; definitely bad.

But the loss of freedom felt like the worst side effect of everything she went through so far; she'd be chained to these people forever... assuming she maintained her current clinical status.

The scent of medical offices made her throat tighten. She noted the pungent scents of rubbing alcohol, cleaning solution, desperation, death, sickness... She wanted out. Now. She pondered skipping the appointment, running outside where the scents of fresh air, trees, grass, and faint auto fumes intermingled. But she was stuck. She needed these people. She needed to stop dripping. The door finally opened.

"How are we today," said the person who entered. She stuck out her slim hand and added, "I'm Dr. Pence. What can I do for you?"

"I assume you read my records?" said Ashley.

"I've read most of them," she answered, "You have a large file. I hear you have a nasty infection."

"Ecoli."

"From your surgery?"

"Yes."

"Let me see," said the doctor.

Ashley lifted her shirt, exposing her battered abdomen. The doctor didn't react to what Ashely figured had to be one of the most horrific things she'd ever seen. But then again, doctors clearly witnessed more gore than Ashley would likely witness in her lifetime.

"You've got a pretty strong reaction to the adhesives on the tape," she said. She ran her finger along the multiple tape-shaped welts along the nearly soaked bandage.

"Yup."

Dr. Pence pulled at Ashley's bandages with chilly, smooth fingers. She grabbed a cotton swab with a long wooden stem and swept away some of the dripping pus. She placed it in a tube. "We'll culture this to see if we're still dealing with the same strain of bacteria." She added, "I'll also get you some adhesive tape designed for sensitive skin. That should help." She pulled out her prescription pad. "I'll prescribe a broad spectrum antibiotic. Take it twice a day for two weeks. Come back if things don't clear up... or at least slow down... in the next few days." Then she added, "If the culture indicates you need a different antibiotic, I'll contact you. She paused, then said, "I'd like to see you in two weeks. That's a large incision. I read your chart and you've got some big stuff going on. I want to make sure you get through it OK." She said, "When do you see the oncologist again?"

"One month."

"Your move went OK?"

"To my knowledge."

"That's good," Dr. Pence said, paging through Ashley's medical record. "How are you feeling?"

"Like crap."

Dr. Pence smiled. "I don't blame you. It says here you just started a new job. How's that going?"

"Fine. I'm on day two and am already here."

"Does your employer know about your medical situation?"

"Nope."

"Do you plan on telling him?"

"Not really."

Dr. Pence lowered her prescription pad. "Support system?"

"I'll figure it out."

The doctor nodded. "I can give you information on a potential support group."

"You can do that," Ashley said, "but I doubt I'll go."

Pence sighed. "I'll send home a brochure." She studied Ashley's face a moment. "How is your digestive system holding up?"

"It's a challenge."

"Do you need to see a dietician?"

"Nah. I'm figuring it out."

She paged through the file. "I see you've gained a few pounds. I'll send you a brochure on a low residue diet." The doctor wrote a few words in Ashley's file. "You might pick up a few tips." Ashley nodded. Pence continued, "Tell me about your new job. It seems a little early to get back to work full time."

"Well," Ashley said, "I have these medical bills..."

Pence laughed. "I understand. But most people in your situation need more time to recover."

"Wish I had that luxury. I know it's early. I hurt. All the time. But I need the job. Didn't think it would be real demanding, but then we had that murder in town."

"I heard about that," said Pence, "You're covering it?"

"Yup."

"For which paper?"

"Crossroads Herald."

"At least it's not the Gazette. Dailies have to be harder than weeklies."

"Yes. But the Internet evens the playing field. We have to get fresh content up daily."

"I hadn't thought of that. Will you be able to handle the stress of work, deadlines, and your illness?"

"Guess we'll find out."

Pence nodded and jotted a few notes in the file. "How's the pain?"

"It's bad sometimes."

"What do you do?"

"I pop a pill."

"You can't use narcotics and drive."

"I know."

"You don't do that, do you?"

"Nope."

"Your file says you've received Tylenol with Codeine, Vicodin... anything else?"

"Nope."

"How are your prescriptions holding up?"

"Fine. I try to take over the counter unless it really hurts. However, I wouldn't mind a few more of the good Tylenol."

"That's probably fine at this point in your recovery." She jotted notes in the file again. "I'll write a scrip for more Tylenol." She stood. "Do you have any other questions or concerns?"

"Nope."

"Very good. I'll see you in two weeks. I hope you're feeling better then. If your pain doesn't ease in a reasonable amount of time, don't hesitate to call. In the mean time, please try to limit your activity and give your body time to heal. Also, look for a support system. You shouldn't do this alone."

———

Ashley left the office with a prescription in her hand, fresh gauze on her incision, and a small packet of brochures. She chucked the literature in the trash immediately upon exiting. She took two steps, then paused. She turned and fished the brochures out of the receptacle and gazed at them before tucking them in her purse. She walked to her Smart.

She pondered pain meds, murders, and support systems as she proceeded. She was just clicking the "unlock" button on her fob when she saw him.

Chapter Five

SUPREME SURPRISES

The phone vibrated in his pocket. He paused a moment, scanning the room. He discretely stepped towards a quiet corner, grasped the phone, and lifted it to his ear. He whispered, "I'm here."

"Everything is going according to plan," intoned the voice on the line, "Target number one is exterminated. Number two will be dispatched soon."

"Do we have a tentative location for number two?"

"Yes. However, identity isn't confirmed yet. We have our suspicions. We will proceed when we have a solid ID and elimination plan."

"How long before you figure that'll happen?"

"We'll let the heat die down, confirm identity, formulate the hit, then you'll receive your orders. Until then, maintain a holding pattern."

"Any complications from the recent project?"

"Nothing huge. New reporter. She seems rather nosy. We've got a guy watching her in case she digs too deep. He'll do what he can to keep her off the correct trail. Plus, with our insider at the police department, we don't anticipate many complications. The locals in this area are pretty dim when it comes to issues like this."

"That sounds fine. Thank you for the update."

"We'll be in touch."

"Thank-you."

————

Ashley paused and gazed at the large pickup parked next to her tiny Smart. Ned leaned against the hood looking like a million dollars. A sly smile played on his lips. His eyes studied her in a way that made her tingle. "Well I'll be darned," he said, "fancy meeting you here."

"Fancy that."

"Medical center. That's a funny place for an early dinner."

"Agreed."

His brown eyes sparkled as he said, "I hear the cafeteria's excellent. Did you have the pot roast or meat loaf?"

Ash laughed and said, "What are you doing here?"

"I had an errand to run. Saw your car. It's rather unmistakable." His eyes scanned her body. She wasn't sure if he was checking her out or making sure she wasn't leaking.

"Indeed," she said.

"Well, I figured I'd swing by to make sure you're OK. Medical centers have a way of attracting sick people."

"I'm fine," she said, then added, "I'm not sick."

"You look better than fine," he agreed, eyes smiling, gently scanning her face. "Mighty fine," he said. They stood a moment in awkward silence. He added, "I hope you're OK." His tone sounded genuine.

"I'm fine," she mumbled.

"Glad to hear it." He paused, sweet eyes capturing her gaze, caressing her vision, making tingles erupt up and down her spine. The moment she wasn't sure she could stand his soulful eyes one more second he said, "Despite your early lunch hour, have you eaten yet?"

"Nope."

"Wanna?"

"Yup."

He flashed his perfect smile. "Meet you at Mel's."

————

The thing about small town living is that while surface temps are generally toasty warm, dig just a little deeper and you can hit some supreme surprises. It's especially easy to underestimate small town business owners. They may look like a local yokel, they may act simple, but the facade presented rarely reflects the person behind the mask.

Case in point: Maisy Mills.

Maisy worked off and on for Bart Lundquist for over a decade. She began as a part time teenage receptionist. She moved onto graphic design and the layout department (translation: she received a larger desk) shortly after nearly graduating high school. These days she pulled back her hours under the guise of needing "me" time. The truth was far more interesting.

It was just a few years back that Maisy discovered she couldn't live the lifestyle she desired on an entry level news desk wage. Most newspaper workers slave at their positions for the love of the job, the adrenaline rush of a tight deadline, the camaraderie of fellow writers, the ego stroking sensation of becoming published, and the right to condescendingly pontificate about scooping a competitor. Suffering for her craft, even if her craft consisted of photoshopping a stove onto a new ad, didn't appeal to Maisy. She wanted money. She wanted a living wage. She wanted freedom. She had important activities to finance.

So she tried Avon... but discovered she didn't like selling makeup. Then came Amway. Again... Maisy didn't care much for selling something as boring as soap. It was during one of her sales presentations, as she patently drew circles onto the white board illustrating the immense financial opportunity that could afford every single Amway distributor, that she noticed it: men staring. And not just staring, they gawked.

As she struggled through the presentation, she couldn't help but note the unbridled lust pouring out of the eyes of at least three of the men in attendance. She didn't ponder it too long, instead vowing to gather her things and exit the room pronto.

But she couldn't.

Before she left, she was surrounded by eager customers not only buying her wares, but a number of fairly wealthy business men discreetly slipped their business card into the palm of her hand. "Call me. Any time," they purred.

Maisy pondered this newfound development as she drove home in her rattle trap Pinto.

After receiving a few uncomfortable telephone calls from these men, many of which desired pictures of her in various stage of dress, Maisy began to recognize a business opportunity.

Within a week, she decided to send her new "fans" a a couple sensual pics. They demanded more. When one of them asked where her blog was, an idea sparked. At first, she posted fairly tame photos. Then they got a bit more graphic. Then she created a members only section where she portrayed an idealized version of small town life, conveniently "forgetting" to dress for most of her photo shoots. Once she had mastered the fine art of the selfie stick, she scheduled interactive, nude podcasts and bouncy videos. Before she knew it, she had a thriving Internet porn enterprise under the name of Maisy Muffbottom. Today she had more investments than she could spend.

Of course she couldn't share any of this information with the folks in town. In fact, she was surprised she hadn't already been busted in her sure-to-be labeled "ungodly" activities... but she liked money. After all, she had the body and business acumen. Her only regret was not creating an online name a little more dissimilar to her own.

So, she continued her business, tucking away her earnings into various enterprises, while quietly trudging to work part time at the newspaper to make it seem as though she was completely innocent of any and all illicit Internet activity.

When she found herself navigating a large crowd outside the post office on the fateful day of Crossroad's first (alleged) murder in recent memory, Maisy figured it might be prudent to high tail it to the newspaper office to see if they needed help covering this developing event. When she arrived, Bart sat alone at his desk.

"Hey Bart," she said.

He lifted his head and smiled. "Maisy. Glad you're here."

"Yeah," she answered, "I figured something was going on. What happened?"

"Looks like someone was killed."

"In Crossroads?"

"Yup."

"Yeow." Daisy leaned against the door jam and pursed her lips. "Who was it?"

"Police aren't talking yet. Word on the street is that it happened at the Alexander Kaufman house. Lots of blood. Cops used shovels to pick up chunks. Sounds like dogs got in there. If they catch 'em, they'll have to pump the stomach. Ingested evidence, I suppose."

"Jeez," said Maisy, "That's... weird." She added, "And gross."

"No kidding."

Maisy furrowed her brows and pondered a moment. "Who's covering this?"

"I've got Ned on it. The new girl is writing the story."

"She actually arrived? She any good?"

"Hope so."

"Can I run second squad if she can't handle it?"

"As always," Bart said, smiling. "I count on you to have my back."

"Always," she said.

———

Ashley and Ned sat the cafe booth. Silence enveloped them as they quietly waited for the waitress to appear. Ashley pondered her doctor visit, hoping the new meds would curb the leaking incision. She glanced at Ned, wondering how to approach this little lunchtime meeting. She didn't have to ponder long because Ned broke the ice.

"I'm feeling like eggs. A second breakfast. What are you going to have?"

Ashley studied the menu. "I feel like pancakes."

"Sounds good." Ned dropped the menu to the table with a flourish. "I'm ready to order." He grinned and gazed at Ashley. She dropped her eyes to the menu. "And juice. I definitely want juice."

"Coffee for me, I need the caffeine boost," Ned said. Then he added, "So... what's up?"

Ashley lifted her gaze. "We're ordering breakfast. That's what's up."

"Nah," Ned said, "I'm not talking about that. I'm wondering how your doctor visit went."

"It went fine," Ashley replied.

"That's good. They gonna take care of that oozing wound?"

Ashley eyed his face. She pondered lying, but thought better of it. "Yup."

"What's up with that," Ned asked.

"Nothing, really. Besides, I'd rather not talk about it."

"Sure," he said, "but you should know... it would probably be better if I were in on the secret." Ashley furrowed her brows. He continued, "We're going to work close together. Heck, I'm like your partner." He paused, then continued, "I could help you get to appointments and stuff. Without a brouhaha. Without Bart knowing anything..."

Ashley pursed her lips. "I won't need any assistance. Nothing's wrong with me."

"Fine," said Ned, "It's just that sometimes it's nice to have an ally. And I like having you around." He added, "Besides, infections that drip enough to soak through bandages will probably need follow up. My sister's a nurse. I know medical shit."

Ashley nodded. "Thanks." She pondered a few moments, weighing the pros and cons of saying anything to a near stranger. It didn't feel right. So far, every person who knew the truth about her condition either treated her with kid gloves or slowly disassociated themselves from her.

Not this time. She was starting fresh.

However, a tiny twinge of fear rose in her belly. This task could be monumentally easier with an ally... assuming Ned would fill such a role. He seemed genuinely nice. He seemed like he could be a valuable person to have in her corner. She decided to test the waters. "OK. Fine. I had a minor surgery before I came here. Couldn't put it off so I went ahead and did it."

"What kind of surgery?"

She paused, forming words in her mind before speaking them aloud. Every scenario ended badly so she decided to lie. "Nothing serious. I just need a bit of follow up, then I'll be done with the whole sh'bang."

"But what did they do?"

"I'd rather not get into it," she said.

"Fair enough. I'm here if you need anything."

She smiled. "Thanks."

Their meal progressed without event and Ashley found herself back at the newspaper office with a pile of papers on her desk. "Write the obits," Bart ordered. Ashley fingered through the pile, briefly reading each, then started typing.

————

Officer Drake Mallard stared at the ream of paperwork resting on his desk.

"Just a bunch 'a nothing," he mumbled. He pulled out photos of the crime scene. A slurried mass of tortured red flesh glared up at him. "Bunch 'a nothing," he repeated, tossing the photos onto the pile. Every photo filled with bright red flesh, drying blood, and paw prints. He cringed. What bothered him more was that every pic wasn't as sharp as he had hoped. He grumbled, "Damn photographer didn't use a high enough resolution."

He pondered his options and lifted a list of names. He read each aloud:

"Geena Larson... Ike Moe... Troy Tonn... Sheila Knight... Justin T..."

He created a file for each person. "I'll start interviews tomorrow... after I reexamine the crime scene and take decent pics." His phone rang.

Meanwhile Ashley had finished the obits, vaguely realizing that the murder victim wasn't included on the list. "They still don't have an identification," she whispered.

She constructed her own list of interviewees which included some of the same ones in Mallard's files. Her's also included a few brilliant suggestions from Ned... people Mallard likely wouldn't include unless he actually lived in Crossroads. Ned had named descendants of town fathers whose families had lived in Crossroads longer than anyone, the folks who knew the goings on of pretty much every family in town. These people included members of the Shaw family, the Temple family, and the matriarch of all matriarchs, Old Lady Crossroad.

Ashley wondered what she was getting herself into, interviewing big wigs on her first real story. She glanced over at the next desk and peeked at Ned, who seemed engrossed in digitally manipulating a few of his photos. She pondered his dark hair, deep brown eyes, and strong arms. She closed her eyes and imagined the sensation of his hand resting on her shoulder. Despite her desire to be independent, it felt terribly comforting feeling his warm touch. She breathed deep.

She ceased her imaginings and opened her eyes. Just then she watched his lips form into a smile. She refocused her energy on the task at hand.

"How's it going over there," he asked.

"Just fine," she chirped.

"Soon done with the obits?"

"Got 'em done already."

"Well," he stood up, "Shall we start our interviews?"

"Absolutely," she said a little too confidently. She gathered her gear and slipped Betsy into the carrying case. They'd just stepped outside when her eye caught a flash of gold. She didn't have a chance to process this event before a large yellow lab leaped in front of her. It not only leaped in front of her, it turned its head, ears cocked, and lunged towards her. It not only lunged towards her, it tackled her.

They tumbled to the ground with a dramatic thud. As Ashley's head struck the pavement with a thud, she heard strange yells... perhaps they were screams... erupting from somewhere.

Chapter Six

MALLARD'S SHAME

Officer Drake Mallard, in his decades on the force, had never encountered anything like this. Dried blood flaked from every surface in every corner of every room of the tiny house. Drake noted what appeared to be intermittent clear areas where the labradors had "cleaned up," so to speak. Streaky tongue prints spread across to various areas on the blood soaked surfaces and paw prints peppered the entire house, even smearing windows, cupboards, and kitchen appliances.

"God damn," he mumbled.

He cordoned off the area immediately after the discovery of the murder(s). This morning he personally gathered more evidence, some that had been left behind, some he figured he'd missed the first time around, and he thoroughly photographed every inch of the scene using the highest resolution setting on his camera. Now, according to his most recent phone call, the crack CSI teams directly from the State of Minnesota would arrive and process the place. He hoped to impress them. They would arrive shortly, but knowing state officials, he figured they were likely running late.

Given the grisly nature of this crime, he wondered if Big

Brother thought he was incapable of a good process on the scene. He'd show them. So while he waited for the big wigs to arrive, he bagged some obvious evidence, some not-as-obvious evidence, carefully noting its original location as well the photo number in which the object would appear. He squatted, examining the underside of tables, silently congratulating himself on the thoroughness of his observations. He found a few drying chunks of flesh and studiously bagged them, feeling pretty good that he didn't gag as he did so. He spoke quietly into a recording device, memorializing his thoughts, acts, reactions, and brilliant observations.

After around 45 minutes, Mallard heard a vehicle's wheels crunch to a stop. He peeked out the front window. It was the state van. He continued his work. He listened to mumbling voices outside amplify as the CSI agents approached. A rock formed in his stomach when he heard the tone change from casual to angry.

"What the hell is a local doing in the house," he heard.

"How do you know he's in there?"

"Where else would he be?"

"If anyone's in there, heads are gonna roll," said another.

Mallard acted casual as the outside door swung open.

"Is someone in here," called a voice.

"Officer Drake Mallard," he replied, "I'm gathering evidence, helping you get a jump start."

"Idiot," said the voice, "Get out of there... try not to destroy anything."

Mallard stepped towards the door. "I'm perfectly capable of gathering samples for forensics."

"Out of the house. Now."

Drake stepped outside and two scientists glared at him. "You realize you have likely tainted the evidence, right?"

"I've done no such thing," he replied. "I'm trained to do this."

"No. No you're not." The person paused, then said, "I need your name and badge number. Now."

Mallard obliged, then handed over the evidence he gathered.

"We'll need the camera," they said.

"It's mine. Doesn't belong to the force." Mallard slipped out the SD card and held it towards them.

The scientist held out his hand. "Camera. Card. Now."

"It's mine. Not department. This one's way better than theirs."

The scientist's eyebrows rose and eyes intensified. "Hand everything over."

Mallard cringed as he obliged. "I want it back." The techs obviously didn't appreciate his efforts. "Heads'll roll if I don't get it back. In mint condition."

Then they told him to stand perfectly still while they called his superiors. After a short conversation, they demanded he remove his shoes, pants, and shirt, and turn them over as part of the evidence package.

"No fucking way."

The CSI person handed over their phone and Mallard heard his superior yelling. Mallard didn't say a word, immediately deciding to quit arguing. He reluctantly opened his coat and unbuttoned his shirt.

"I'm only doing this for the sake of the investigation," he mumbled. The scientists didn't say a word.

He disrobed, right there on the sidewalk, handing over each piece of clothing until he stood wearing his tightie whities. "I can keep these, right?" The man bagging his clothes said, "As far as I'm concerned you deserve to stand there stark naked."

"Oh, you'd love to see that," said Mallard, "but you'd probably get intimidated."

The other man rolled his eyes.

He stood, shivering as the frigid wind bit his nethers, when another agent tossed a Tyvek suit his way. "If you're done being a dick, put this on. When you've done that, sit on the lawn and await further orders. Good luck keeping warm."

"I'm a professional," he said, "and that is demeaning."

"Sit."

"Fuck you." He dressed, then gingerly sat on the cold ground.

As he sat shivering, despite his best efforts, even though he had cooperated in every way he was able, Drake felt a reprimand on the horizon.

———

It happened too fast. One minute Ashley was walking out the office door. The next she laid flat on her back, a huge golden Labrador on top of her. She was too stunned to make a sound as the animal's tongue slathered her face. Then pain ripped through her abdomen as the animal's thick claws scratched at her belly, soiling her jacket. She tried to push it away, but its wiggling, heavy body heaved towards her. Unable to slow the onslaught, she contorted into a ball, eyes clenched shut, arms shielding her face.

The next thing she recalled, the dog ripped away from her and Ned's voice pierced the air. Then it was joined by Bart's. Then a few more unidentified individuals joined in.

"Holy shit!"

"God damn."

She heard Ned's voice say, "Ashley! Holy shit!"

Someone yanked the dog away for a moment before the animal leaped on her again and restarted the whole process. It clearly didn't attack her as much as it engaged in overzealous affection. She felt someone heave the large animal off her again and Ned dropped to his haunches beside her. "Ashley. You OK?"

She groaned as she attempted to straighten her body, but recoiled. Her eyes clenched shut as unadulterated pain consumed her body. "Dunno," she groaned.

She felt hands pull at her arm. She opened her eyes. "Did it bite you," Ned asked, pulling at her jacket. "You picked a hell of a day to not zip up."

"I don't think I got bit." He helped her to a sitting position. It took a few moments. She continued, "It kept licking my face."

Ned paused, smiling. "I can see that."

Ashley placed her hand on her cheek. It felt slick with slime. "Oh god," she moaned.

"Rather smelly, too."

"Fuck."

Ned laughed. "Glad to see you're OK."

Ashley made one attempt to stand, but fire ripped through her body. She grasped her abdomen and grunted. Ned sobered. "Sure you're OK?"

"No," she whispered, "I'm not sure."

"Need an ambulance?"

"No." Her ears turned red at the thought. She added, "Not in a million years."

Ned lowered his lips to her ear and whispered, "What can I do to help?"

Ashley pondered a moment, then said, "Get me to your truck?"

He nodded. "Sure. Can you make it?"

"Hope so."

"Well," he said, "I'll help you." He gently grasped her elbow and eased her to her feet. He felt a tremor vibrate down her arm half way through the process. Then a tiny, nearly silent, squeal escaped her lips as her body unfolded. After that, her entire body quivered.

"You OK," said Bart's voice.

Ashley turned towards him. "I'll be fine," she called, "I think I'll run home and clean up." A fake twittering laugh exited her lips. "Weird morning, eh?" They stood in silence a moment as Bart eyed her.

He ignored her tag line. "Going home to clean up might be a good idea. You don't look so good."

Ash's eyes were drawn to a large man hugging the offending Labrador around its chest. The animal tried to leap towards Ashley again, tail wagging wildly. The man struggled as he held the dog in place. Bart said, "Animal control's on the way."

She nodded, seemingly balancing on her own. That's when she realized Ned's arm was around her shoulder, steadying her.

"Can you walk?" said Ned.

"Absolutely," Ash mumbled.

"You might want to have a doc take a look at 'cha before you call it a day," said Bart.

"Think so?" said Ashley

"Well, you're bleeding," said Bart.

"What do you mean," said Ashley as she scanned her hands, arms, fingers.

"Your shirt. It's all red," he said.

Ashley's face darted downward towards her abdomen. A bright red stain bloomed on the front. "Oh shit," she mumbled.

She felt Ned turn her around and lead her away from the scene. "I'll take her to the ER," he called over his shoulder.

"I want an update," said Bart.

"Sure thing."

Once they were alone, Ned said, "You sure you're OK?"

"Not really," she whispered.

He led her to his truck and guided her to the passenger door. "Let me see what we're dealing with."

"Probably popped my incision," she answered.

"Fine," he said, "but let's see it."

Ashley paused.

"Look, you've got to trust somebody. May as well be me." His dark eyes searched hers.

Months of solitude pressed on her soul. She knew she could likely handle this crisis alone, but the thought of a friend to lean on seemed terribly enticing. With his rock star looks, with those perfectly fitted jeans, with those sincere eyes, with the incredible pain in her belly, she couldn't help but think Ned would be a nice person to have on her team. She nodded. "I'll let you take me to the ER," she said.

"Mighty big of you," he said, "You gonna show me what we're dealing with?"

"I'd rather not."

Ned gazed at her. "I know I can help if I know what's going on."

"Seriously," she said, "I'd rather keep that part of my life private."

"It's not exactly private when you're bleeding all over a parking lot... and eventually my truck."

"I'm sorry. I'll be careful. If I mess it up, I'll pay to have it detailed."

"That's not my point."

"I know," she sighed. "It's just that..."

"Come on," he said. "It can't be that bad."

"Oh, it's not good." She added, "We should probably get going. I kinda feel dizzy."

"That's fine," he said opening the door to his vehicle. "Whenever you're ready, I'm good to go."

"Thanks," she said. He helped ease her into the passenger seat. "Jeeze," she said, "I wish you'd get a lower vehicle."

Ned chuckled. "I'll have to do that someday."

He drove her to the emergency room, careful to avoid potholes. Ashley appreciated that. She closed her eyes and held a wad of tissues against the red bloom on her shirt.

"You OK," Ned occasionally asked.

"Fine," she breathed. But her quiet tone alarmed him. He drove faster.

When the bloody jumble of tissues tumbled to the floor of the truck, his eyes darted towards her. She had either fallen asleep or had passed out. Alarm gushed into his belly.

"Ash," he said, "you sleeping?"

She didn't respond.

"Ash," he repeated, "what 'cha doing?"

She didn't respond.

He accelerated the vehicle and within minutes had bounced into the unloading bay at the local emergency room. Staff trotted out to meet them.

They loaded Ashley onto a gurney and rolled her into the building. Ned tried to follow but was stopped. "You need to move your vehicle," said an attractive nurse.

"Will I be able to see her?"

"Who are you?"

Ned paused a moment, then said, "Her brother."

"Come back. Then we'll talk."

Ned hopped into the truck and sped to a parking spot. Then he trotted into the hospital. He was relieved to hear Ashley's voice coming from one of the tiny rooms.

He felt a nurse touch his elbow. "Your sister is over there." She pointed to a dark door. Doctor is examining her. You may want to wait."

Ned nodded and stepped towards the room. He cracked the door and almost stepped inside. He couldn't decipher the conversation taking place, but he could see the object of the conversation.

The doctor lifted her bloody shirt, exposing her abdomen. Despite his sister's graphic stories, despite volunteering to be her frequent guinea pig pin cushion, Ned gasped at what he saw.

Laparscopic scars were the first item on the list followed by an 18 inch incision held together with battered, curling steri strips. On each side of the incision, stained gauze apparently caught continual dripping ooze. The skin around the wound was filled with angry red welts in the perfect shape of adhesive tape. The doctor seemed nonplused at the sight and instead was droning questions that Ashley answered in a guarded whisper. As he spoke, he peeled away bandages and the entire gruesome mess glowed in the harsh ER lights.

Ned breathed deep and slipped the door shut. He strode to the waiting area and sat. He closed his eyes to quell emotions rising in his throat.

––––––

Ashley didn't like this doctor. He seemed cold. However, many docs acted that way these days.

She relaxed into the stiff bed and closed her eyes as the physician examined her wound.

"You appear to have an infection."

"I'm aware of that," she mumbled.

He pulled at the butterfly strips a bit and occasionally dabbed the liquid oozing from various points in the incision.

"When was your surgery again?"

"It'll soon be a month."

"Where was the surgery?"

"Twin Cities."

"And you're up here... why?"

"New job."

"Do you have a regular physician?"

"Yes."

"Have you seen him concerning this?"

"Yes. I saw her this morning." Ashley listed the meds she was taking, including the antibiotics. She also recited her complete medical history, prognosis, and current developments.

The doc paused and breathed deep. His eyes met hers. "You realize you shouldn't be working yet."

"I need the money," she replied, "and the insurance."

"Yes, but you're in a fragile state. You certainly shouldn't be in a position where you'll get attacked by stray dogs."

"I didn't anticipate that."

"Most people don't anticipate things like that." He continued, "You must slow down. Your incision is a mess. I can cobble it back together, but you have to realize you have a myriad of splices inside your body. Any one of them could have split when all this happened."

"I need an income," she replied. "I have to work. I'm a writer. It's a desk job. Who would think this could happen in a situation like that?"

"That's beside the point. You should be at home convalescing."

"That's not going to happen. I wish I could do that, but I can't."

He paused, apparently pondering his options. "I'd like to admit you overnight. Make sure you don't have any internal bleeding."

"Do I really need to do that?"

"I'd recommend it. When you came in, you were unconscious."

"I just fell asleep."

He shook his head. "It's not safe to send you home. I want to admit you." He added, "Just for 24 hours."

She paused a moment before she said, "I don't know..."

"What's your life worth?"

"I have a deadline. I just started this job. It provides medical insurance..."

Just then a nurse entered. "Ms Stone, your brother is here."

Ashley's eyebrows crinkled. "Brother?"

"Yes. Your brother. Ned. He's here and would like to see you."

Ashley broke into a light panic. "That may not be a great idea..."

Ned poked his head into the room. "Hey Ash," he said, "How 'ya doing?"

Ashley's face blanched when she realized her entire secret... her belly... lay exposed in all its gory glory. She clawed at the sheets hoping to cover the worst of it. Then she saw Ned's eyes slide directly towards the mess.

Her incision. The bane of her existence. It mocked her like a gruesome grin. Even catching a glimpse of it herself took her breath away.

Terror flooded her thoughts. She couldn't stop the inevitable. He'd see it. He'd see everything. She watched for his reaction, but there was none. Instead, he strode into the room and said, "What's up, Doc?"

Chapter Seven

BLOSSOMS

Dr. Troy Tonn studied the golden Labrador standing in front of him. Its tail wagged wildly every time he caught its eye. He leaned over and glanced at its underside. "A girl," he mumbled. He touched its back and the animal erupted in wiggles. "Simmer down," he whispered. The dog leaped upwards and planted a slimy kiss on his cheek. He laughed. "Seriously," he intoned, "simmer down."

He stroked his hands down the dog's sides, checking its form. The animal went wild at the sensation. Dr. Tonn flipped on a digital recorder and said, "Golden lab. Around a year old. Very friendly." He placed the recorder on the table and squeezed the animals belly with his fingers. He retrieved the recorder and continued, "No apparent abnormalities." He lifted her canine lips. "Teeth look good. Some blood staining around the muzzle. Doesn't appear to originate from the animal's circulatory system. As he examined the teeth, he pulled out a piece of what looked like raw meat from between two molars. He placed it in a petri dish.

"The CSI team," he continued, "asked that I perform a gastric lavage."

He turned off the recording device and set it on the exam table. He stroked the animal's head.

"Poor girl," he said. "What did they do to you?"

Her tail thumped on the hard surface.

He gently injected a sedative into her front leg. Her eyes glazed over and she slid to her belly. Then her head sank downward.

Dr. Tonn worked diligently and gently. He inserted a lubricated plastic tube down her esophagus, then began the suctioning process. After the majority of the stomach contents drained into a dish, he injected saline solution into the tube, then repeated the procedure. After three times, Tonn was satisfied that he'd removed anything of note. He poured the retrieved stomach contents into an evidence jar and placed it in the specimen refrigerator. He'd contact the CSI people later.

He gazed at the unconscious dog and pondered. He recalled his conversation with the head of the CSI team when they delivered the bouncing mass of yellow fur to his office.

"Perform the gastric lavage. If there's evidence of human flesh, put it down. Immediately. Then we'll need the corpse."

Tonn wondered how a nice critter could get tangled in such a mess. Everything about this case seemed off. Dangerous animals don't melt into a puddle of affection when touched. Vicious predators don't flirt. Unacceptable animals never tried so hard to play.

"I don't think I can put you down, little girl," he said.

He stroked her head, considering his options.

———

"So... you going to tell me what's going on?" Ned sat next to her bed. His elbows rested on his knees while leaning towards her. He spoke in a quiet voice.

"I'd rather not."

The physician entered the room. "I still think she should stay the night. I've booked a room."

"I really can't," replied Ashley, "Unbook it. Besides, my brother's here," she glanced towards Ned, "he says he'll keep an eye on me."

The doctor turned towards Ned. "You realize there's a very real possibility that she could experience some internal bleeding. You realize she has some major digestive reconstruction... stitches you can't see? This situation is dangerous enough that she could bleed out if one of those stitches tore. You realize she should be under medical supervision... especially after what she's been through."

Ned's eyes narrowed. Ashley could tell he was trying to form a sentence that would garner him more information about her health situation. She intervened. "He's fully aware of everything. I'll be fine. I know it. The fall wasn't that bad."

"It was pretty bad," Ned said, eyes narrowing.

"I'm not staying here," said Ashley.

"Well," the doctor said, "I'll give you my card. If you have any issues whatsoever, you make sure you call me. I'll give you a list of possible complications and if you see any of them coming on, you must get her to the ER as soon as possible. Understand?"

"I do," said Ned, glancing towards Ashley.

"Her surgery was pretty intense," said the physician, "she needs to see her regular physician tomorrow." He added, "Also, I think she should see her oncologist before her regular appointment. I know she was supposedly knocked over by a dog, but if she fell for any other reason... such as a met in her brain, she'll need an immediate CEA to check her tumor markers, possibly a CT scan."

Ned eyes widened. "I'll make sure she does that." He turned to Ashley, "She can certainly be a bit stubborn at times."

The doctor continued, "Understand you're leaving against my medical advice."

"I'm fully aware of that."

"You can really hurt yourself."

"Again... fully aware."

"But if you experience any of the symptoms I've laid out on your discharge papers, you need to come here immediately."

"Yes. I know."

"Fine," he said, turning to Ned, "I hope you know what you're getting yourself into."

———

They were half way home when Ashley broke the silence. "You can just drop me off at my house."

Ned threw her the side eye and said, "Over my dead body."

Ashley stiffened. "What's that supposed to mean?"

Ned kept his eyes on the road. "It means I made a promise to the ER doc and I intend to keep it."

"What promise?"

"Seriously?" he said. His fingers tapped the steering wheel. "You even supported it."

"Supported what?"

"The fact that your 'brother' would keep an eye on you tonight."

Ashley paused. "That's not how I see it. I supported the notion that you'd take me home. I figured you'd ask how I'm doing tomorrow when I get to work."

Ned chuckled. "That's not what I signed up for."

They rode a few more miles before Ashley spoke. "Then... exactly what did you sign up for?"

Ned glanced at her. "You're coming to my house. I'm watching you tonight."

Ashley broke out in a chortle of a laugh, but stopped short when she grasped her abdomen. "Seriously?" she croaked, "I can't do that."

"Why not?"

"Well, for starters, I don't have any fresh clothes."

"We can stop by your house to get some."

"I don't have any of my morning stuff."

"Again... why can't we just pick some up at your house."

"What about my cat?"

"You don't have a cat."

Ash slumped in her seat, then cringed as she straightened back up again. A few miles passed before she said, "I can't stay at your house."

"Why not?"

"It's unseemly."

Ned laughed aloud. "Unseemly? Who talks like that?"

"I do. And don't make this about my language. I don't think I should stay at your house."

"Too bad. If the roles were reversed and you heard that list of possible outcomes from the ER, you'd do the same thing."

Ashley sat quiet for a while. She closed her eyes and mentally examined the sensations ricocheting through her body. Despite the meds administered in the ER, her body ached. A thick gauze bulge rose from her belly and dull discomfort throbbed throughout her abdomen.

She whispered, "How 'bout a compromise?"

Ned glanced at her. "What would that be?"

"What if you stayed at my house? I have all my clothes, gear, and meds there."

He smiled. "Brilliant. How 'bout we make a fast detour to my place so I can pick up some stuff?"

"Sounds great."

———

One year ago, the terrorist organization Republic National Forces, (a.k.a. the RNF) exploded in a dizzying hemorrhage of top secret information; every member compromised, remaining operatives scattering like cockroaches. With even their deep cover, retired, and benign operatives exposed, RNF organizers struggled to cobble their once flawless network back together. But reunification was next to impossible.

Then the madness escalated.

As months wore on, it became clear that remaining members were getting picked off, one at a time. Given their numbers, if someone's goal was to eliminate everyone, they'd have to work long and hard to accomplish the task in one lifetime. But these surgical strikes on former members disconcerted the masses.

Every former member cringed at the thought of exposure. They changed their names. Some had covert plastic surgery. Many settled as best they could in America's heartland and adopted covers complete with wives and children. Others opted for the hermit life... but nothing worked. With the slow spread and tenacity of the assassinations, each knew they would eventually be discovered.

Now the murders occurred more often and it became quite clear that a shadow organization was in the midst of forming, strengthening, and had stepped up their goal of eliminating the RNF in its entirety. One could only assume its goal was to fill the vacuum created when the RNF blew and take its place as the most powerful and influential shadow terrorist organization on the planet.

David McNally, long time RNF member and former #3 in the organization, couldn't have that. His cover, wife, and partner was completely aware of his past, present, and future plans. Yet she loved him. And he loved her. To watch his long time friends, comrades, and coworkers fall, one by one, was too much. Despite his wife's pleas, he had to jump into the fray one last time to hopefully stop the madness.

He and his trusted ally, Jim, a.k.a "Mr. Big Hands," accompanied him.

Their final RNF sanctioned assignment to recover the list of operatives before it became exposed failed miserably. But, the exposure wasn't due to their incompetence. Instead, turncoats within their own organization plotted its demise.

McNally suspected it was these same individuals behind the current slaughter. With a mountain of dead bodies in their wake, most notably those in a TGV, high speed train, the double-cross exposed by that final RNF assignment would forever make

McNally and Jim leery of any organization whose stated purpose was to promote any particular agenda.

McNally and Jim studied this latest wave of assassinations with a keen eye. By their calculation, so far all the murders occurred along America's coastlines and deep within European nations. Each could be easily explained as a gangland event or tragic accident. But the recent murder in Crossroads possessed all the earmarks of an RNF assassination and hit far too close to home. Clearly, if this was a bonified hit, the tentacles of this new organization were becoming a concern.

Back when they settled in Minnesota, both Jim and McNally agreed that living in Ely would be a perfect place to maintain invisibility to any international terrorist organizations. But, they were evidently wrong. Due to the suspicious nature of this hit, they decided to make the trek to Crossroads, check things out, and decide how proceed from there. However, they had to be careful. If McNally's hunch was correct, he and Jim were in for a world of hurt if they were spotted.

So, today they made their way towards Crossroads in a very plain sedan, wearing utterly average business clothes, regular hair cuts, muted colors, employing blend-in mannerisms. McNally hoped for an average mission of above average surveillance and reconnaissance.

But, the best laid plans...

Ned and Ash stepped into her tiny house, Ned carrying a small satchel of what he called his "gear." Ashley hobbled to the couch and gingerly slid to a sitting position.

"You sore?" asked Ned.

"Yup."

"Want a pain killer?"

"Nope."

"Why not?"

"I want to be coherent."

"How 'bout something non-prescription?"

"I might go for a couple of those. I don't want any narcotics. Don't want to get hooked. Plus, I like driving."

Ned laughed. "The chances of you getting 'hooked' are pretty small. Also, chances of you driving tonight are even slimmer."

"I know," she said, "but I don't want to chance anything."

"Fine," said Ned, "But don't let the pain get ahead of you." He added, "Your belly looks sore."

Ashley didn't answer. Instead she sank deeper into the couch and closed her eyes. She listened to Ned rummage in the kitchen. She heard the cupboard open. He filled a glass. Then he called, "Where's the Tylenol?"

"Bathroom," she answered, cringing because even speaking loud caused her abdomen to flame with anger.

She listened to him him head towards the medicine cabinet before she sank towards unconsciousness. For a brief moment, she felt cared for, warm, and very safe. She enjoyed the sensation. When she felt the seat cushion sink beside her, she opened her eyes. Ned sat next to her, studying her face. A strange sensation twittered in her stomach. She focused on it. It wasn't pain. It wasn't her incision tearing open. She smiled when she realized it was a lone, but very active butterfly.

"Got your pills."

"Thanks."

She grasped the glass and accepted two shiny caplets from him. She downed them in a single gulp.

"You're pretty good at that stuff."

"Acquired skill," she said.

They sat a moment before he said, "So... are you going to tell me about it?"

"About what?"

"We're doing that again?"

She didn't speak for a while. Then she said, "I'd rather not talk about it."

He looked pensive. "I won't pressure you. But it looks like you could use a friend." She didn't answer. Then he said, "Do you have Netflix?"

For a moment, she didn't speak. Then she said, "I had surgery."

He leaned back into the couch cushion and said, "I figured that."

"I know." Then she added, "It wasn't very good."

"I kinda noticed that myself."

She sighed, seemingly carefully forming the sentence before she could speak it aloud. She finally said, "It's just that when people know, they look at me different."

Ned glanced towards her. "How so?"

"Pity... in a 'you're screwed' kinda way." She added, "Many people launch into long, gory, fatalistic stories of people similar to me. None of them have happy endings."

A sarcastic smile spread across Ned's face. "Well," he said, "that's not very nice."

"No kidding." Her words hung in the air for a while. Then she said, "I know you heard the ER doc say 'oncologist.'" Her chin quivered a bit.

"I did," he said matter-of-factly.

"So, I suppose you figured it out, then."

"Well, it didn't take many smarts to do so." He paused, then added, "I haven't figured everything out, and I don't know if what I've presumed is correct, but it doesn't really matter." He turned to her and their eyes locked. "I know you. I've seen how strong you are." He added, "I like what I see and I know what I need to know."

Tears formed in the bottom of her eyes. "Thanks."

"No thanks needed," he said, resting his head deep in the cushion. He stared at the ceiling as he said, "I don't have any intentions of leaving. And when I look at you, I'm not going to try to one-up your story." He turned towards her and added, "When I see you, I intend to look at you in a 'I'd really like to love you' kind of way.'"

Her eyebrows rose. She didn't reply. Instead, she turned away, eyes wide, tension spreading across her face. Then he said, "Well, isn't this awkward." He added, "I sometimes talk too much."

She chuckled, face melting a bit. "Not awkward," she said, "Just surprising." She added, "I've never gotten that response before."

His eyes veered back to her, "Why surprising? You're a knockout."

Now she laughed harder, grasping her abdomen in the process. "Yeah," she said, "I'm a real looker with all this blood, pus, bandages, welts, steri strips..."

His eyes narrowed. "Don't sell yourself short. You're a great writer. You're a kind person. You're exceedingly strong. You've got a will of iron. Plus, look in the mirror. Holy shit, nothing this gorgeous has crossed the city limits since Maisy Mills sashayed into town. And from what I can tell, she doesn't have one tenth the brain power you have in your little finger." He laughed and added, "Those are awesome traits. I wish you could look in the mirror and see what I see."

She stared at him, dumbstruck. "Since when is cancer, or anything associated with it, attractive?" Then it hit her: it had been a long time since she said the "C" word aloud. Saying it that way made it real. The sound of that word exiting her lips cut her psyche. More tears formed.

Ned said, "Only a shallow fool would discount someone because of that. Remember, my sister's a nurse. I know that modern medicine has come a long way when it comes to treatments, survival rates, and quality of life issues."

"I guess the world is filled with shallow fools then. Besides, talking with someone about survival rates, quality of life, and treatment is hardly dating material."

Ned hoisted his body forward. "I'm done. Get over here. I'm hugging you whether you like it or not." She laughed and he gingerly pulled her head into the nook of his arm. "Just stick with me. We'll get through this one way or another."

Full fledged tears escaped her eyes, but she didn't allow crying sounds to exit her lips. Instead, she spoke with a hard lump in her throat. "I hardly doubt that." She swallowed the lump and added, "Be careful. I'm a time bomb."

"Blah, blah, blah," he said.

She felt his warmth permeate her skin, filling her strength reserves and granting her an optimism she hadn't felt in a long time. She melted into his embrace, allowing herself to float along with the scent of his maleness. Her hand slid to his chest and rested over his sternum. The regular lub dub of his heart vibrated her fingertips and comforted her as she closed her eyes. Sleep crept towards her, erasing the exhausting events of the day.

————

Another nondescript sedan rolled into Crossroads precisely at sundown. That was by design. A grey car entering town at its greyest point was as anonymous as it gets. It cruised down the near empty streets, rolling to a stop one block from the tiny house surrounded by yellow police tape. Two men exited. Each had a subtle bulge on the right side of their rib cage... a holster.

"You ready," said one.

"Oh, yeah," said the other.

Little did the residents of Crossroads realize life was about to get quite messy from this point forward. Lives would end, some would be forever changed, and for others... they had no idea that an adventure of a lifetime was about to begin.

"Let the mayhem start."

BOOK 2

Chapter Eight

OOH LA LA!

Spotlights sliced through the darkness and the squealing drone of female fans cut the silence.

"Three minutes!"

Ace Chase fluffed his hair, glancing at his band mates as they prepared to hit the stage. He sighed, unsure if he could do this again.

But the tour was a rousing success with close to 10,000 attendees at this arena alone. The group was flirting with sales of $250,000 so far. Single numbers were through the roof. Yet his smiling mug had barely graduated from teeny bopper magazines to a couple more mainstream tabloids. Tabloids. Filled with conspiracy theories. He sighed.

Despite his agent's best efforts, he couldn't make it into any higher level mags like GQ or even People.

The entire enterprise struggled for relevance beyond the hard core teeny bopper demographic. It all felt hollow and Ace could sniff the stagnant scent of oblivion in the near future.

Already band members were bickering about their sophomore effort. None of their follow up singles could match the success of "Ooh, La La." In fact, their subsequent releases all failed to make the top 100. To make matters worse, every member of the band abhorred that vacuous, repetitive ditty.

And the hair. He hated the hair. The oily, piled high mess was all the rage, and scores of prepubescent males mimicked the messy mop atop his head.

He disliked every bit of it, but vowed to act professional to the end... unlike one of his bandmates who snuck curse words into the lyrics at each event.

"Don't do that," said their manager, "we've got kids in the audience."

"Shut the fuck up," the band member replied.

Ace stayed out of the dispute.

He often pondered his situation. Somehow the music he longed to create had been viciously replaced by inane, teeny bop, faux angst, and his onstage enthusiastic antics didn't reflect his personality in any way shape or form.

He had many more concerts on this leg of the tour... and the thought of continuing towards each event nearly broke his heart.

"Two minutes."

He glanced at his band mates.

"Ace! Ready to go?" said his band mate. He hopped up and down, attempting to sharpen his performance attitude.

"Yup."

"Hair looks good. New gel?"

"Thanks. No."

"Ready for another round of Ooh La La?"

"Not really."

His band mate sobered. Then he whispered, "Me either."

They paused listening to the screaming fans.

"Look," said Ace, "I know this is temporary, but jeez."

"I know." His bandmate grimaced. "At least I have enough money to be set for life."

"Pretty much," Ace agreed, "assuming we don't do anything stupid."

Both sets of eyes flew directly to a third band mate... the rebel... who treated cash like an inexhaustible commodity."

"One minute!"

Ace smiled. "Guess we better get going."

The bandmate touched his arm. "We can do this. Just focus on your bank account."

"It's getting harder. Did you notice none of our followups were able to climb the chart?"

"Yeah."

"Do you realize it's very likely that we'll be in the exclusive club of one-hit-wonders?"

"The thought had crossed my mind... but there are worse things than that, right?"

Ace smiled. "I suppose."

"I say we enjoy it while we can and get out when the getting's good."

"You'll do that with me?"

"Absolutely. I can't wait to live a hair-gel free life."

They laughed.

"Well, my dancing shoes are good to go," said the band member, "Let's do this, Ned... I mean Ace."

————

The warmth permeated her, creating sweet sleep, calming dreams. In this placid world, pain was nonexistent and worries were replaced by storybook endings. She never wanted to leave.

But as consciousness crept towards her, she became vaguely aware of reality, of dull pain in her belly, of Ned's heart beating under the palm of her hand. If she could have slipped away, she would have. Except somehow, during her little nap, she made the fatal mistake of slumping. During that process, her innards had evidently glued together in a twisted, sticky mass and trying to straighten her spine caused intense discomfort.

"Ned," she whispered. He didn't respond. "Ned," she repeated.

No answer. She tried to pull away, but was certain someone had inserted multiple knives into her belly. "Ned," she increased her volume as she tapped his sternum.

He groaned. She squealed as her body, pressed against his, stretched in synch with his. Her pain spiked to a new, unpleasant level.

"Ned," she said again, "I need a pill... something... anything."

He jerked awake and she squeaked in protest. "You OK," he asked.

"Not really. I think I need narcotics."

"Oh dear god," he gasped, stiffening, "what can I do?"

"Narcotics. Two of 'em. Next to Tylenol."

He gingerly pulled away while she scrunched her face to try to quell the squeals rising in her throat. After he left, she sat, knees next to her chin, eyes clenched, sweat dripping from her temple.

When he came back he said, "Need to go back to the ER?"

"No," she said, "I'm not going back there. I slumped. Now I can't straighten out. I'll be fine. Just hand me pills."

He dropped two in her palm and handed her water. "Here ya go."

"Thanks," she whispered. She closed her eyes and rested her forehead on her knees. "Just give me some time. I'll be fine. This has happened before. It's temporary"

He sat next to her. "You sure?"

"I sat too long," she answered. "Give me a minute."

"Hey nudie boy. What' 'cha got cookin' under the tyvek suit?"

Officer Drake Mallard sat sullenly outside his superior's office, grimacing each time another verbal barb hurled his way.

"CSI team is p-i-s-s-e-d..."

Mallard pretended not to hear.

"I smell a demotion..."

Mallard attempted to maintain his dignity despite his ridiculous getup. The white tyvek suit crinkled each time he moved. The blaze white booties were stained with dried blood, dirt, and assorted office dusts. Mallard disliked the hoodie portion of the suit, feeling as though it mocked his aura of professionalism. He wondered if and when he'd get his clothes back.

"Those uniforms are expensive,' he mumbled.

"What 'cha talking about over there," called a voice. "Got an imaginary friend?"

"Fuck you."

Laughter filled the room. Finally the office door opened. "You may enter."

Drake stood and turned, but not before throwing his coworkers a vicious side eye. He relaxed his face and entered his superior's office. He stood, waiting for an invitation to be seated. It didn't arrive. "What the fuck were you thinking?"

"I'm fully trained in forensics."

"Not for this kind of scene. I specifically told you to wait for the team."

"I thought I'd show initiative."

"Initiative?"

"Indeed."

"Well, it didn't work."

"My apologies. But the evidence I gathered was clean."

"Hardly," barked his superior, "most of it is unusable."

"Not by any standards of evidence," replied Mallard. "It was a clean scene with a clean gathering of evidence. My photos were thorough. High resolution, too. The evidence was processed by the book."

His superior leaned back in his chair. "No. No, it wasn't. Not by any stretch of the imagination." Then he added, "Forensic methods have changed since you graduated from the academy. What hasn't changed is the chain of command." He leaned forward, "I told you not to enter the house. You entered. You screwed up the crime scene." Mallard didn't react. "I'm not sure what the penalty will be, but you will be punished for this." Mallard didn't flinch. "You understand?"

"Understood."

"Any questions?"

"I only want to know when I'll get my uniform and gear back." His superior broke into a hearty laugh. "Seriously?"

———

Ashley slept like the dead. Ned poked her, only to verify that she hadn't expired. She hadn't.

She laid stretched on the couch appearing to have passed out. He barely slept all night. Instead he watched her sleep, pondered Crossroad's recent murder, and constructed possible backstories explaining Ashley's incision.

She appeared zonked out. "Perhaps I should have only given her one pill..."

But, she asked for two.

He sat across from her, pondering their next move. Do they go to work? Call in sick? He couldn't imagine how anybody could function after a night of pure unconsciousness.

He didn't have to ponder the situation very long because just then, Ashley moved. She groaned. Then, her eyes opened. It took a moment for them to focus. She finally spoke.

"Oh dear god," she gasped, "what have I done?" She groaned. "I took narcotics last night, didn't I?"

Ned laughed. "Yeah. You were really out of it. But, you seem fine now." She turned and tried to pull herself to a sitting position. She didn't succeed. "Need help?" he asked.

"Nah," she said, "I can do this." She added, "I feel pretty damn good, though."

He watched her struggle a few moments, then he stood. He stretched his hand towards her. "Just take it before you pop another hole in your belly."

She extended her arm and grasped his hand. She felt his

warmth enter her skin. It felt really good. She tried to ignore the sensation by saying, "I've been laying down too long. I do best if I'm up and down. Movement helps the most. Give me a minute and I'll be right as rain." Ned gently pulled her to a seated position. She didn't squeal.

"Right as rain," Ned said, "that would be a miracle."

"Seriously," she said, "It's not as bad as it looks. Right now, I feel better than... well, since the surgery."

Ned examined her. Pale and frail, it was clear she hadn't been eating enough. Her short hair made the bed head appear quite insane. Her abdomen was now a rainbow of colors ranging from yellow to red... and each moist hue had evidently dripped down to the couch. Ned counted three small puddles on the once pristine cushion. She sat for a moment, breathing deep, and then said, "If you'll help me stand, I can get ready for work."

"You're working today?"

"Got a big story."

Ned scrutinized her for a moment. "I really think you should take the day off."

"I'll be a different person once I get moving around," she countered. "Just wait and see. You'll be surprised." Then she added, "I know it's bad, but I always look like this when I get up."

Ned's eyebrows raised. She didn't particularly appreciate the incredulous look on his face. He pondered a moment. "Fine," he said, "but you have to eat some breakfast, you have to keep it down, and I insist you take it easy... all day."

She eyed him, "Seriously? You're creating conditions for my employment? You think I'm not capable of taking care of myself?"

"Nah," he laughed, "Nothing of the sort."

"Well, it sounds that way to me."

Ned pondered a moment, then said, "So far, it appears your skills have been lacking when it comes to post surgical care. Remember, my sister's a nurse. I picked up a lot from her. Trust me, take my advice and you'll recover much faster." He erupted into his dazzling smile. Ashley's butterfly flitted in her belly. "So," he said, "ready to stand?"

She nodded. He pulled her upright and she wobbled. Ned wrapped his arm around her waist and steadied her. She closed her eyes. "Just the narcotic," she breathed. Ned didn't argue. She pulled her attention away from the butterfly and said, "I'll run to the wash room and get gorgeous." He laughed. "Be out in a sec," she said.

"Hey," he added as she stepped away, "Got any upholstery cleaner?"

"Why?" He pointed to the moist spots on the couch cushion. "Damn it," she mumbled. "You don't have to clean that."

"Nothing else to do."

"Kitchen," she said. "Cupboard by the door. I'm really sorry."

"Don't worry about it."

———

McNally and Jim rolled into Crossroads. "Not much to do here."

"Perfect place for a cover. Bad site for surveillance. We can't hang around in one spot too long. People will notice anything unusual pretty fast."

Last night, they decided to set up headquarters in a small, nondescript Crossfield motel. Its dingy interior and ramshackle exterior reminded McNally of the Bate's Hotel. But the tiny room was easy to sterilize with no electronic bugs, recording equipment, or anything out of the ordinary.

They rode in silence after reaching Crossroads to survey the crime scene, each man mentally preparing himself for what was sure to be a disconcerting day. Then they spotted the small cafe. From that vantage point, they could see Main Street as well as the tiny house surrounded by yellow tape. Jim drove into the parking lot. "Let's see what we're up against," he said.

———

The cold air bit Ashley's nose as she and Ned walked the perimeter of the crime scene. The pungent scent of dried blood, rotting flesh, and chemicals pierced her nostrils.

"Think they'll ever figure out what happened here?"

"Hope so," said Ned. He snapped copious photos as he spoke.

Ashley felt a bit woozy after last night's narcotics. She knew she probably shouldn't get behind the wheel until her body had completely processed them, so she didn't argue when Ned offered to drive. Besides, her little Smart still sat at the newspaper office.

She glanced around, then lifted the yellow tape and tiptoed closer to the house. She proceeded directly to a window and peeked inside.

"What 'cha doing," Ned called.

"Nothing," she answered.

He joined her. "We shouldn't be here," he whispered.

"Tell me something I don't know."

She proceeded to the next window and peeked inside.

"See anything?"

"Not much," she said, "someone closed the shade. But I can kinda, sorta, see around it."

Ned joined her. Gazing at the blood streaked walls he said, "Damn. Messy."

"Understatement of the day," she answered. "Get pics."

"Already on it."

Ned snapped photos furiously as Ashley spoke low into her recording device. She stepped away from the window and continued to recite her thoughts. She heard Ned say, "Damn."

"What is it," she said, turning towards him.

"Paw prints. I was wondering what these smears are, but they're paw prints."

"Damn," she said. She gingerly exited the perimeter and paused, noticing a flash of silver in front of her, around ten feet beyond the edge of the crime scene. She approached it, gingerly poked it with her boot, and examined it.

"Hey Ned," she said, "can you come here?"

She heard his camera snap a couple more times, then he joined her. "What 'cha got?"

"What's that," she pointed to the shiny object resting in the snow in front of her.

Ned bent to examine it. "Dunno," he said. He squatted, staring at it.

A small silver object glistened in the snow. It looked like some sort of key, circular head with a sleek shaft. Completely smooth in every way, it looked futuristic, dangerous, mysterious. Ned picked it up. "Well... what are you?" Then he added, "Think it's connected to the murder?"

"Dunno," said Ashley. "We should probably turn it in to the police."

Ned laughed. "Yeah, that would be the smart thing to do. I probably shouldn't have picked it up, eh?"

Ashley said, "Dunno. It's the most awesome looking key I've ever seen."

"Yeah," said Ned, "No markings whatsoever." He turned it over in his hand, examining it from every angle.

"Weird."

They paused a moment. Then a sound pierced the silence. "What the fuck are you two doing here?"

Chapter Nine

MAISY

Boom waka waka, Boom waka waka, Boom waka waka. The music droned across the basement, red lights glowed dim. "What do you want, big boy," she purred, "I'll give it to ya."

Maisy Mills, a.k.a. Maisy Muffbotom, gyrated in front of the web cam, her feather boa resting soft between two ample breasts. "You know you want it," she murmured. She grasped a riding crop with bejeweled fingers and occasionally whacked it against her bare thigh.

She wore a leather corset strung tight, pushing her breasts skyward. She jiggled them seductively. Her fish net stockings, and eight inch heels made her already long legs appear to go on forever. Nothing else covered her body except a tiny hat. She bent over in front of the camera. "Whoops," she chirped, "I dropped my crop. Where could it have gone?" She shimmied towards the floor, turning various directions, giving the web cam a 360 degree view of her body. She heard a disembodied voice groan. Mission accomplished.

"Closer," said the voice. "Move closer," it gasped. A few moments passed in silence. Then it added, "Can you tweak your nipples again." Somehow, it wasn't a question, it was a command. The mood darkened a few hues.

"No problem, honey," she answered, careful to keep the atmosphere light. "You've got three more minutes." She swayed her hips, lifting her arms over her head. She stroked the skin of her arms as she glanced a light trail towards the swell of her breasts. She closed her eyes and traced circles around her areolas. Although she appeared relaxed, enjoying the sensation, her ears strained to detect any dissatisfaction from her customer.

"Better not be shorting me again."

"I'd never do that," she purred, "You're one of my favorites." She picked up the crop and massaged each nipple with it. She slowly rotated her hips, spreading her legs as she sank to a squatting position. She glanced at her monitor to make sure she gave her customer just enough of a view to get off, not enough to be completely satisfied.

"Jeeze, woman," said the voice, "you're killing me."

A sly smile spread across her lips. "Just tell me what you want. I'm all yours... for another minute."

"Look here," said the voice, "I paid for you. I own you. Now jiggle those tits and stick your finger up your ass. Now." He added, "That's what I want."

"No need to get rude," she chided, "just let me grab the lube." She gyrated a few more times and pulled her nipples. She heard the voice groan. She smiled. He was definitely aroused. She turned around, bent over, then tapped a button installed on the desk, hidden from the viewer. The screen went blank. Time over.

"Asshole," she mumbled, "I'll have to make sure to block you."

———

Ashley watched Ned stroke the key with his thumb before slipping it in his pocket. Officer Drake Mallard stepped out of his cruiser and marched towards them. "I said," he bellowed, "what the fuck are you doing here?"

Ned smiled stiffly. "How ya doin', Mallard. Great to see ya. Chilly today, eh?"

"You didn't answer my question," said Mallard, "what the fuck are you doing here?"

Ned shook his head. "You can probably guess. I mean, really..."

"Don't get punchy with me, Superstar."

Ashley broke in. "I'm just working on a story for the newspaper."

"Which rag?"

Ned rolled his eyes. "I'm sure you could guess..."

"We're not really a rag," she intoned, "but it's for the Herald."

"Piece of shit rag, if you ask me," said Mallard. He added, "You don't have permission to be here. Get the fuck off the property. This is a crime scene."

"You know," said Ned, "we're outside the crime scene tape. Technically we're not in the crime scene area. We're just checking things out."

"Without permission," said Mallard.

"How do you know we don't have permission?"

Mallard stepped forward and was now inches from Ned. "I know this because the person who could grant you permission to poke around his property is now a bloody puddle. A very large puddle of disembodied fragments."

Ned's eyebrows rose. "Well, that's a violent way to go, eh?"

"Don't get smart with me, Ace." The final word in his sentence dripped with sarcasm.

Ned said, "No problem. We can go." He nodded towards Ashley. "Let's get back to the rag."

Ashley nodded. Mallard scowled. As they walked away, Ned mumbled, "I get extra points for not mentioning the word Tyvek."

Ashley's brows knitted together. "I don't know what you mean."

"I'll explain later. Back at the office."

After she entered the pickup, Ashley grabbed her notebook

and started writing, forming sentences, fleshing out her story. "Get any good pics," she asked.

"Yup. You know it."

"Good."

She scribbled until they made it to the office. "I'll get the pics transferred to my computer right away," said Ned. "Want me to separate my favorites?"

"Absolutely," said Ash, "I love your eye."

He paused. "Only my eye?"

"Yup." She grinned. Then she added, "Good one."

Ned threw back his head and laughed. God, he looked gorgeous in the morning sun.

———

Alexander Kaufman lived an unheralded life. Plain in every way possible, he thought he hit the jackpot when he married Ingrid. Everything would have gone according to plan if it hadn't been for his pesky sister in law.

You see, Alexander had much to atone for.

Born in a rural village in Germany, Kaufman was a sickly child. Tall, exceedingly thin, lanky to his core, he couldn't seem to attract a buddy, let alone a girl friend. He soldiered through his teen years alone, dejected, angry. It wasn't until he turned 17 that he discovered his first true friend... at least he believed this person his friend. Too bad he was incorrect. The exact moment they met seemed tattooed on his brain.

He was at the local grocery store, fingering a HotWheels Corvette. Its baby blue hue glistening as he turned it over in his hand. It was cheap, but he didn't have cash on him. In fact, he didn't have any money whatsoever. Two inches from homeless, even if he had funds on hand to purchase the tiny vehicle, he probably wouldn't use it on such extravagances.

He figured he didn't need toys anyway. Yet, the thought of that little gem in his pocket gave him pleasure beyond words. He missed the little things in life, the tiny comforts most people take for granted. Things like heat, bathrooms, couches, televisions... food. He was just resigning himself to the fact that he was an impoverished good for nothing waif when he heard the voice.

"Just take it. I'll cover for you." Alexander turned. A grinning man stood beside him. "It's a beaut," he said, "I don't know why you shouldn't have it." Something about the man made his stomach knot. He wasn't sure he wanted anything to do with him. However, he didn't appear to be someone he should ignore. He answered.

"Uhh, because I can't afford it?"

"I'm not so sure," said the man. Dressed in utterly average clothing, his eyes shined bright as he spoke. "I think you should take it. You deserve nice things as much as that self entitled brat." He motioned to his left where a child silently examined a package of tiny green army men. He said, "I'll cover for you."

Alex pondered a moment. He wondered if this person was legit. He glanced at him out of the corner of his eye. What if he were an undercover cop? What if he were a member of store security?

He wondered what the consequences of theft would be. He pondered what his mom would think. Realizing if he got caught, he'd wind up in jail... a place where he'd receive three square meals a day, a warm bed, free television privileges... he figured he didn't have much to lose. He slipped the toy into his pocket and stared at the man.

"Very good," he said, smiling.

"Fuck you," said Alex.

"Even better."

They walked out of the store together with nary a clerk noting his deed.

Thus began the unholy friendship between Kaufman and Mr. M., recruitment official, agent groomer, and rising star of the RNF.

Kaufman desired love, acceptance, true friendship... and the RNF needed men. It was a match made in heaven.

He trained vigilantly, honing his craft long after other agents ended their day. Alexander could sink so deep into a new character, a new persona, that he could literally lose himself inside his newly constructed world. Watching Alex, Mr. M. often had the disturbing notion that Alex actually believed his cover stories. As an agent, this was a particularly useful trait. As a human being, this could present problems when dealing with reality. But no matter. M. knew Alex was replaceable... he certainly wasn't promotion material. He figured they'd get as much as they could out of him, then toss him aside once he was spent.

But Alex defied all expectations. He didn't have to work at achieving "average" status and could get by with nearly any crime because no matter what happened, Alex never stood out. Alex reveled as he rose through the RNF ranks, surprising Mr. M. beyond all imagination, receiving more complicated assignments as time wore on.

Then one day it ended. He supposedly made one small mistake that potentially exposed some of the inner workings of the RNF. His bosses rambled on about a silver key... something exceedingly important. Someone saw Alex touch it and now it was gone. Alex had no knowledge of a key, but he could smell the stink of excommunication nearby.

He jumped into action, conducted his own investigation and... found said key tucked away in one of his secret stashes. He didn't remember taking it. He didn't remember stashing anything. He presented the object to Mr. M. hoping for exoneration. He received nothing. In fact, he felt like he was framed by an invisible entity he couldn't confront.

Without a trial of any kind, he was convicted and sentenced to death. But they trained him well. Before they carried out the sentence, he slipped away... vanished... before anybody in the organization noticed. Before he left, he pocketed the one item he knew could give him the best assurance of survival: the large silver key.

He had no idea what it unlocked. The first time he saw it, like the tiny blue car, he knew it would be his someday, and his someday had evidently arrived.

Key in pocket, he fled to the USA to the one place he figured he'd never be discovered.

Boy, was he wrong.

———

Ashley's ears still burned. She didn't expect the greeting she received when she arrived at the office.

"Ashley's back!" Bart yelled.

A woman, presumably Maisy Mills sat at the reception desk smiling. She stood and clapped when Ashley entered.

"You look like crap," said an (evidently) moody Dick.

"Thanks," Ashley said, "I'm fine. Just a few bruises." Trying to change the subject, she said, "Gonna finish my story."

"Where you at on that?" said Bart.

Ned broke in. "She's got some good stuff going. We talked to Mallard this morning. I got some great pics, too."

Ashley continued, "I got official police documents faxed here." She added, "Did they arrive?"

"They did," said Maisy, "On your desk."

"Well, get on it," said Bart, "Glad you're OK. Get to work."

Ashley nodded. "Sure thing."

She sat, then winced. Ned sauntered to her desk and sat on the corner, his back to the rest of the crew. "You OK?" he mumbled.

"Yeah," she murmured, "Still little sore."

"Not surprised," he said, concern spreading across his face. "Need a pill?"

"Nah. Not yet. Definitely later, though."

She typed, dug through papers, and scrutinized details. She disliked the newspaper computers so she used Betsy, her faithful Mac, and synched everything with a cloud service. She studied Ned's photos and selected the ones she felt best illustrated her story. When she finished, she emailed everything to Ned for proof-reading. If he thought it looked good, she'd send it to Bart for his approval.

After she heard the ping of Ned's email program, she turned in her chair and said, "I appreciate your proofing"

"Already done? I'm impressed." He clicked his mouse a few times, examining the screen. "Yup," he said, "everything opened." Then he added, "No problem on the proof reading. I do it all the time. I'm just glad I didn't have to write the thing."

She laughed. "I'm glad I don't have to take the pictures."

"Guess we're a good team," he said.

She paused a moment, last evening's events rolling through her mind. She realized she liked Ned. Probably too much. After her diagnosis, she decided she wasn't going to like anyone. But there he was. He knew she was sick. He knew it was the big C. Yet he didn't shy away. This man puzzled her. She pondered rethinking her "don't get close to anyone" policy. She decided to think about that later.

"I think I'll run to the rest room and check the bandages," she whispered, leaning towards Ned, "keep reading."

"No problem." He looked deep in thought as he narrowed his eyes and focused on the text.

She was just stepping towards the door when Maisy touched her arm. "I couldn't help but overhear. Small office," her eyes darted towards Ned's desk, "but what kind of bandages are you checking. Dog bites? Did you hurt yourself? You OK? Is there anything I can do to help?"

Ashley's cheeks reddened as she said, "Nah, it's nothing. I'll be fine. Just a couple souvenirs from yesterday. Seriously, it's nothing."

Maisy studied her face. "Listen," she whispered, "I've heard about you. You're good. We can't lose another reporter. Bart will drive me mad if you go. Seriously... I want you here. Let me know what I can do to help."

Ashley laughed. "You're funny. I'm fine. Seriously." She added, "I better get moving."

She entered the rest room and latched the door. She gingerly lifted her shirt. The bandages didn't look as damp as she expected. She smiled. She carefully undid the tape and peeled them away from her skin. She dabbed away moisture before opening a new package of gauze, pressing it against her abdomen, and taping it in place. She was careful to apply the tape to the least damaged skin. She tossed her used bandages into a zippered plastic bag. "No evidence," she whispered, "Must leave no evidence."

————

Alex Kaufman's luck wore out after coming to the US. He married Ingrid, a perfect cover story, in a small ceremony with the promise her family wouldn't meddle in their lives. Then, her sister-in-law's husband unexpectedly died. Ingrid insisted they take her in.

He tried every argument against the arrangement, citing ridiculous religious beliefs in the hopes he'd get his wife to submit to his authority. It didn't work.

He tried to get rid of the relative... from anonymous threatening mailings to hair raising exorcisms, to no avail. The woman wouldn't leave. Pure frustration poured through his veins and the protection of his cover story turned into something far more sinister.

After much soul searching he would be the first to admit that she became a bit of an obsession... and "bit" would be defined as a complete obsession. After embarking a psychological tangent worthy of a most seasoned psychopath, the line between reality and cover story became terribly blurred. Due to his actions, he was soon arrested and ordered mandatory psychiatric evaluation.

Then luck shone on him again.

The psychiatrist turned out to be an old friend... a fellow deep cover RNF member who was miraculously unaware of his expulsion. Said member arranged to have his records expunged from the system, create a new cover that disallowed any visits from former family members, and grant Kaufman his freedom.

He jumped at the chance.

With the silver key as his only possession, as a wanted man in every sense of the word, Kaufman made his way to Crossroads and lived an anonymous life in an average town.

Then all hell broke loose.

Chapter Ten

SUPERSTAR REVELATION

Ashley sat at her desk feeling supreme. She'd done it... her first week of work was complete and rousing success. She glanced at Ned. She was taken aback at how the crinkles around his eyes stirred the butterfly that seemed to have taken up residence in her belly. She breathed deep to capture her breath.

"I don't believe I've seen you smile before," he said.

She summoned the cognitive ability to construct a coherent sentence. "I don't believe I've felt like smiling since I met you."

"Well..." he said, "I think that could be an insult."

She laughed. "No. Just a hard week."

"Well, it's not every day that you get to start a new job, get attacked by a crazy canine, and get to see the doc."

Ashley laughed. "Agreed."

He leaned back. "I think we should celebrate."

"Agreed again,' she said. The words exited her mouth before she had time to ponder the consequences. She hadn't expected a "we" in her celebration plans. But given the fact that she didn't need any narcotics since last night, two Tylenol had made the afternoon bearable, she figured a small celebration was in order.

"Well," said Ned, "I think I have something in mind."

"Like what?"

"Surprise."

She paused, studying his face. "I'm not sure I like surprises."

"You'll like this one," he said.

"You think so?"

"I know so."

Ashley laughed. It felt comfortable engaging in a verbal tennis match. She hadn't done that in a long time. Cancer tends to wipe out word play... at least for her. Unless, of course, she was high on narcotics. Then all bets are off. One shot of Dilaudid, a powerful narcotic injection, and she turned into a complete comedienne... a very bad one, but quite the semi-funny lady nonetheless. She had all her nurses in stitches (ha) and the food service people delighted in entering her room. Everything was hilarious. Every word out of her mouth, a joke... a really bad joke.

But today was a narcotic-free day. And she enjoyed the lively verbal spar. That had to be a good sign.

Ashley shrugged. "I guess I'm in your hands."

"Don't I wish," he replied.

"In your dreams," she shot back.

Both laughed.

"Hey you two." Both broke each other's gaze, their eyes focused on Maisy, "I'm right here," she said. Ned spouted into another a round of laughter. "Seriously," she spoke again, "I know it's Friday. I know the recent excitement has simmered down. I know you've got some time to kill before you can go home, but... if you two are going to blatantly flirt right in front of me, I'm going to have to do something about it."

"Like what," said Ned.

"Like... I don't know. But cut it out. I'm getting jealous." She laughed and drew a can of diet cola to her lips.

"You shouldn't drink artificial sugar. That stuff'll kill you," said Ned.

"Nah," replied Maisy, "it'll just give me cancer."

Alarm shot through Ned's face. He glanced at Ashley. Happiness drained from her eye and her laugher was replaced by a faux smile.

"Did I say something wrong," said Maisy, "I just felt the tension meter jump two degrees."

Silence hung thick for a few moments before Ashley spoke. "Nah. You're fine. You didn't say anything wrong." She added, "Absolutely nothing. I always drink diet cola. Who needs all those sugar calories?" Her voice trailed off, betraying the unsure nature of the sentiment.

"No kidding!" said Maisy, "I'd blow up like a balloon if I didn't watch my caloric intake."

"That makes two of us. I recently put on some weight and it's a bugger to get off."

"I know," cried Maisy, 'I tried that whole eat meat all the time... got so stopped up I never figured I'd get anything out again!"

The blatant nature of Maisy's statement melted Ashley's sadness. She laughed. "Yeah, I tried that one. My breath turned toxic."

"How bout the vegan one?"

"Plenty of fiber," said Ashley, "Lots of hungry."

"Oh... I once ate only raw food. That one was crazy."

"The all rice diet got boring."

"You two sound nuts," said Ned.

"When I was vegan," said Maisy, "I ate lot of nuts. Blew up like a balloon, too."

"Seriously," said Ned, "we should move on."

"I liked the all liquid diet. Lasted a whole morning on that thing," Ashley said.

"Oh, that one was bad. I've never craved solid food more. Chocolate milk doesn't do it for me."

"Either way," said Ned, "let's move on. We've got to wrap up the day. I've got big things to do."

"We?" said Maisy, eyes sparkling.

"Yup." A smile spread across Ned's face. "I'm going to show Ashley the town."

Maisy broke into laughter. "That'll take ten minutes. What do you have planned for the rest of the evening?"

Ned turned towards Ash, "I guess she'll have to find out. I'm not spilling."

"Well," said Maisy, "aren't you two cute. However, if you're going to go all sweetie pie, you better take it down a notch when you're in the office. All this flirting is going to give me diabetes."

"Sorry," Ash said, "I'd hate to be responsible for your diagnosis." Her eyes twinkled. "I don't know what got into me. Guess I'm enjoying finishing my first full week here."

"Kudos on that," Maisy said. Then a spark of mischief ignited. "Also, I know what'll get into you if you two keep carrying on like this." Her eyes sparkled. Ashley's ears reddened. Ned didn't react.

"Oh Maisy," he said turning to her, "You know you'll always be my first love."

"Don't 'cha know it, Superstar." Their eyes locked for a moment as a slow grin spread across Maisy's face. Clearly enjoying an inside joke, Ashley couldn't remain quiet.

Her eyebrows furrowed. "Hey," she said, "I've been wondering... what's up with all this Superstar stuff?"

Ned's ears reddened. He stammered two times, attempting to start a sentence. Maisy spoke. "He hasn't told you?"

"Told me what?"

Ned said, "It's really nothing. We should move on and get back to work."

"Seriously," Ashley said, "'It's nothing?'" She leaned back in her chair and bit her lip. She pondered a moment and said, "You'd say 'it's nothing' after our conversation yesterday? The one about secrets? And now you're keeping what is evidently quite a large secret from me?"

"Ooh," Maisy said, "You two have secrets? I love secrets." Everyone ignored her.

Ned breathed deep. "It's not a secret," he said, "more of a... not an embarrassment... more of an unfortunate period of my life."

"Oh," Ashley said leaning forward, "now I have to know. I

insist." Her eyes caught Ned's line of sight. His face looked slightly pained. She turned to Maisy, "What could be so horrible?"

She grinned and replied, "Ooh La La."

Ned groaned. "Seriously, Maisy. I'd rather not discuss this. Not before my big night."

"Oh," Maisy said, "I think she should know." She quickly added, "As your work partner and friend, she definitely deserves to know."

"Know what?" said Ashley.

Maisy didn't say a word. Instead she opened her desk and pulled out a colorful CD.

"Maisy..." said Ned, "You don't need to do this right now..."

She said, "One moment please." Her head disappeared under her desk. Ashley heard her fumble around for a bit, then the distinctive wrrrr of the CD drive opening caught her attention. She listened as Maisy placed the CD in the drive and tapped the button. It wrrred and clicked in place. Her head popped back into its previous position. She grasped her mouse and murmured something incoherent while she did some clicking. Ashley glanced over at Ned.

He looked a bit embarrassed, but a playful smile danced on his lips. "I can't believe you have that," he said, "I'm impressed."

"Oh," Maisy said, "I don't throw anything... especially a gem like this." She added, "This one's bound to be a classic."

She clicked a few times and said, "One more second. Gotta turn up the volume."

"Get 'er nice and loud," said Ned, who now had a full smile on his lips. "I don't want Ashley to miss one moment of true glory."

"You got it," said Maisy. A few seconds later, music filled the room.

"Hey," Ashley said as recognition filled her face, "I've heard this song."

"Who hasn't," yelled Maisy, "Damn thing clogged every radio station for an entire summer."

Ashley glanced at Ned who was now standing, twirling, and

exhibiting some mad dance moves. He held a pencil like a micro-phone and sang with the lyrics.

"Ohhhh la la baby... ooh ooh ooh la la"

"Hey," Ashley said, "You sound good." She shimmied in her chair, enjoying the beat. Her memories filled with pleasant thoughts of warm summers, friendships, and lazy days lounging at the lake.

Ned danced towards her and held out his hand. She laughed and placed her fingers on his palm. He pulled her upright and danced around her. By now, Ashley laughed out loud.

"Oohhhh la la... baby you're mine... mine all mine..."

When the vocal solo hit, Ashley's jaw dropped when she real-ized Ned had a striking similar voice to the one on the CD. When he hit the high note just right, her jaw dropped.

"Oohhhh la la. Baby, baby you're mine."

The song wound down and faded into silence. Ashley stood transfixed, puzzled at this display of... of... she wasn't sure what she was watching.

Maisy broke the silence. "Ashley Stone," she stepped out from behind her desk and said, "I'd like you to meet," she gestured towards Ned, "the unforgettable..." Ned's eyes sparkled, "Ace Chase."

Ashley's eyebrows collided. "Ace Chase?"

"At your service," Ned said, grasping her hand and bowing slightly. "Please excuse the hair. Crossroads doesn't have enough gel in stock to keep up that appearance."

Ashley's jaw dropped. "That was you?"

Ned nodded. "Yup." He added, "In the flesh."

"That's why people call him 'superstar,'" said Maisy. "He really is a bonified superstar." She grinned at him.

"Was," corrected Ned, "I was a superstar." He pondered a moment then added, "Actually I think the term 'one hit wonder' is more appropriate."

"Nah," said Maisy, "I've seen the concert footage. You were and are a superstar in my book. You're the only person I know who can sing like that, out dance everyone on the floor, all while keeping your hair taller than anyone I've ever seen."

"Well, aren't you sweet," said Ned, "Oh, and I really appreciate your bringing this up... right before my first big date in years. Class act." He glanced towards Ashley.

"You know," said Ashley, "this only enhances your appeal. Quite mysterious, if you ask me." She added, "Plus, it's not a date. We're just hanging out." She looked pensive. "Superstar. That's the the most exciting thing I've heard in a while."

Ned laughed. "I aim to please." He paused. "Date or not, I think tonight will be exciting."

"Agreed,' said Ashley.

"That whole superstar thing explains his Hollywood looks trapped in a map dot of a town in the middle of Minnesota, don't you think?" said Maisy.

"I imagine," replied Ash.

"You two," said Ned, "you gotta stop. I'll get a big head."

"Never gonna happen," said Maisy, "you already cut off all that hair."

Just then Bart entered the room. "What the hell's going on here? Sounds like a god damned concert complete with gushing fans."

"Just reliving the good old days," said Ned.

"Fuck that. You've got a story to cover. Pity you peaked in your teens."

"I haven't peaked yet," said Ned with mock despair spreading across his face.

"Well, then give me some great pics and maybe you'll peak as a photographer," countered Bart.

"Oh, you know it," said Ned, "You'll love what I got this week."

"You always say that."

Ashley interrupted the banter. "We've got the next installment ready to go."

Bart said, "It's not on my desk. It's not remotely finished until I see it."

"I'll email it right now," said Ned, "it's written, proofed, and I attached the magnificent photos." He added, "Ash did some great work on this one."

"Get cracking with the email," said Bart, "and grow up. No more dancing in my office. No annoying music either. We're professionals."

"Got it," said Maisy. She winked at Ned.

———

The day was forever etched in Ashley's memory. After some minor abdominal pressure, she went in for her annual physical. When she mentioned her complaint, her family doc said, "Well, it's probably nothing, but I suggest we do a colonoscopy. I can feel a little thickening... it's likely just some matter, but it may be helpful to see what's going on in there."

Ashley wasn't sure she liked that idea. Her older relatives occasionally shared horror stories of "the prep." Fasting... emptying bowels... sports drinks... none of it sounded pleasant. After she surfed online to consult Dr. Google, she was hesitant to submit to her doc's advice, especially after reading about the "industrial medical complex" in the USA and how they (along with evil pharmaceutical companies) milk everyone out of their hard-earned cash.

Was her family doctor a disease mongering quack? She couldn't be sure. One thing she did know. Something nagged at her, begging her to check it out.

Against her better judgement, she decided to follow her physician's advice. She sucked on lemon flavored popsicles, ate lime gelatin, and chug a lugged green sports drinks the entire 24 hours before the big day. It was pretty unpleasant. Around 2 am the next morning, the worse was over and she caught a few hours of sleep. At 6 am she, along with her escort, entered the surgery center.

Nurses inserted IVs. She answered a million questions. Then they wheeled her into the procedure room. She answered more questions, then everything went dark. "You'll get orange juice when you wake up," they said, "and you won't remember a thing."

She awoke to a stone quiet recovery room. She wasn't conscious more than a few minutes before someone led her to the changing room. "How did it go," she asked.

"The surgeon will speak to you shortly."

"I'm famished. I can't wait to guzzle some of that orange juice they promised me."

No answer.

She dressed and a nurse led her to a vinyl recliner. "I'd love an orange juice," she said, "My belly's screaming... so hungry."

The nurse smiled sweetly and said, "The surgeon will be here shortly." She left Ashley alone in the little cubicle. Still woozy from the procedure, she closed her eyes and felt sweet sleep descend on her. When someone tapped her shoulder, her eyes flew open.

It was the surgeon. He didn't look happy.

Chapter Eleven

FARMHOUSE LOVE

Ashley sat in the warm comfort of Ned's truck. With her little Smart tucked in its garage for the night, with Betsy resting on her desk at home, Ashley looked forward to a quiet evening celebrating completing her first week at the Herald. However, she couldn't help but feel just a bit naked without her gear. She clutched her purse.

She turned and watched Ned navigate the pickup towards destinations unknown. Usually she'd balk at not knowing the complete itinerary, but for some reason, tonight she didn't care. She breathed deep and relaxed, knowing she was in safe hands.

However, when he turned down a bumpy, gravel road, she paused her relaxation to say, "Now I'm really curious.. Where are we going?"

"You'll see," he said.

Silence. She broke it again. "Superstar, eh? What was that like?"

"Surreal. Exciting. Frustrating. Interesting."

"That's quite a string of words."

"It was like a dizzy dream. One minute you're hot and everyone in the biz is panting at your door. The next it just kinda sorta fades and nobody will take your calls... even if you're only contacting them to say 'goodbye and thanks,'" he said.

"That's weird."

"Nah. They think they're important and they probably are."

"Yes, but if you had a relationship... even if it's a business one... you'd think you could at least have a final contact before you go."

"Nope."

She pondered a moment then said, "Despite the crappy business people..."

He interrupted. "They were great business people. If it weren't for them, I'd never be able to afford this job."

"That's beside the point. Making money is one thing. Treating people badly is another. In my opinion, you can't be a good business person and treat your clients bad. But that's just me, I suppose."

Ned laughed. "It is just you. There was a long line of one hit wannabes breaking down the door. They make their money and move on."

"Pretty sad, if you ask me."

"It's reality."

"Well screw reality."

"Sure. Why not," Ned laughed, "I'll bet it's easy to bend reality to your own wishes... especially if you're a cancer patient. It's not like you have to deal with trivialities like reality..."

Ash shot him her best chiding look. "That was a low blow. Give me my fantasy or leave me alone."

"Oh," Ned laughed, "I can give you fantasy."

She smiled and turned away. Silence descended for a few miles. Then she spoke. "I'll bet it was magic when you were on stage, though."

"It was," Ned agreed, "When those spot lights hit, it was heaven. Singing to crowds that size... the utter energy of their cheers vibrated my bones. The scent was intoxicating. If I could go on that stage again... I probably wouldn't do it. It's more addictive than heroin."

"I can imagine." Then she asked, "How do you replace something like that?"

"You don't," he said. It's an experience completely its own. It's kinda how I'd imagine love could be. The first time you fall in love, it's magic. It's irreplaceable. Every time after that is excellent as well... just in a different way." He turned to glance at her. "Am I making sense?"

"I suppose," she answered. She allowed a few more miles to pass before she said, "Do you think there's any way to recapture the sensation of that first love?"

"Nope. And I don't think I want to try." His eyes furrowed as he continued, "My first love was magical. But it was immature. If I were to fall in love today, I think the experience would be far more satisfying because I've grown up. I know what I want. Love today would be so much better than before."

"And if you got the chance to take the big stage again? Do you think it would be better the second time around?

Ned threw back his head and laughed. "Not in a million years." He chuckled a moment. "I don't go backwards. I've lived that life. I'm living this one now. Love is one thing. Fame is another. I have no intention reliving the pressure of filling stadiums. The insurance was mad expensive. The group always bickered. Nah... I love the quiet life."

"So no reunion tours for you?"

"Nope. I'm happy." A grin spread across his face. "They tried to get the group back together a couple times. I refused. They replaced me and the come-back bombed."

"Oh," she said, "the fans missed you?"

"Nope," he said, "the group didn't have a catalog deep enough to support the tour. Fans were done with us. It had nothing to do with me." He paused, then continued, "I'm just glad I wasn't there to watch it crash and burn. That must have hurt."

Ashley nodded. "Yeah, that would sting."

"Indeed."

They sat in silence a few moments, then Ned said, "Ah... we're here." He turned and flashed her one this best, most dazzling smiles. "Wait 'till you see what I've got on tap."

———

He knew he shouldn't have done it. He was breaking every code in the veterinary medicine conduct book. But, she was just too cute, too friendly, too... perfect.

Dr. Troy Tonn stared at the wiggling mass of yellow fur in front of him. "Sadie,' he said, "you've made me do a bad thing." The lab rolled on her back and writhed on the floor. He leaned over and scratched her belly. "You've made me a bad person," he said, "but how am I supposed to put you down?"

He stared at the dog's innocent eyes and sighed.

He latched a leash on her crisp collar and led her to his pickup. Together, they drove to the the animal crematorium. Once there, they got out, entered the building and latched the door. Troy methodically cleaned the oven, scraping excess ashes into a small box. It wasn't difficult, it had been years since anyone cleaned anything in that building. Once the box was filled, he flipped on his phone and dialed a number.

"Hey Ike," he said, "I need you to do me a huge favor."

Later that day, the CSI team arrived at Tonn's office. "We're here to collect the remains of the stray animal you boarded here.... Golden Lab, female, the one implicated in the murder on first."

The receptionist stared at them blankly, then buzzed Dr. Tonn. He came out to greet them carrying the jar holding Sadie's stomach contents."

"Here you go," he said. Then he offered the ash-filled box. "Unfortunately, the tech didn't realize we shouldn't cremate the dog. This is all that's left of it."

The head of the CSI team turned red. After around 15 minutes of name calling, chiding, and shame, they left in a huff.

"Good job you incompetent boob," said the receptionist with a grin spreading across her face, "I know what you did."

"Thanks for not spilling the beans," he said.

"I couldn't have killed that sweet dog either," she answered, "your secret's safe with me."

Tonn smiled. "I know a good dog when I see it. That Sadie is a gem."

"Already named it?"

"Yup."

The receptionist pondered a moment. "Think they'll be back?"

"Doubt it."

———

McNally and Jim sat in their hotel room. "This week was a nixie," said Jim, "Nothing. Nada. Nil."

"I know."

"You sure this is organized?"

"Yup."

"No new activity since the elimination. Why do you suppose they're not moving?"

"They're waiting," said McNally.

"For what?"

"The right time."

"That could take a while."

"I know."

Silence clung in the air. Then Jim said the one sentence neither of them, up to this point, dared mention. "How do you suppose Janet and Jennifer are faring?"

"They're nervous. Scared. But they're fine."

"You sure?" said Jim.

"Talked to Jennifer last night. Nothing unusual's going on."

"Ha," said Jim, "you and I both know that 'nothing unusual' means big trouble."

"Yup."

Another long stretch of silence ensued. Jim spoke again. "What's your prediction of what will happen next?"

McNally appeared thoughtful. Then he said, "They'll have to move soon. I saw the CSI team in place. They looked legit. I saw the Tyvek wearing cop getting his due. There's some crazy shit going down... lots of distractions." He paused, eyebrows scrunched. "It appears the local newspaper is conducting their own investigation, I imagine they could stumble on something sooner or later. Hope it's not something that will endanger them." He continued, "Crossroads appears to be a hub of some sort. I've seen more than a few out of place faces. If the organization's still looking for something, there's likely something to be found." He drummed his fingers on the table between them. "I'm not sure who's behind this, but they'll reveal themselves when they need to. We'll be waiting."

"Organizations with this kind of reach rarely make mistakes."

"If this is a new organization or if the RNF's rising again, either way, it'll be a new incarnation, new name, new leaders, new everything. I figure that's why they're assassinating everyone with ties to the former group."

"You'd think they'd try to recruit 'em first. Some of the dead include some pretty savvy operatives."

"Too savvy, from what I can figure. If they get ahold of you or me, you can be pretty sure it won't be for recruitment purposes," said McNally

"Touche."

"Hence, Janet and Jennifer's fear. We need to stop this before they find our families."

"If they touch them, there will be hell to pay," said Jim, stroking his chin with his massive hand.

———

The pickup turned onto a twisted, narrow driveway. Snow humps hugged both sides of the truck as they advanced forward. After enduring a minor case of claustrophobia, they finally entered a large clearing and rolled to a stop.

"Well... here we be," said Ned.

Ashley's eyes scanned the area. A rickety barn rested to her left, its red paint peeling, its walls definitely not at a 90 degree angle. A white shack, perhaps a chicken coop, lay directly in front of them. To her right was a small farm house. Plain, simple, homey; the sawhorses outside the front porch betrayed the fact that it was undergoing some sort of remodeling.

Ned opened his door and stepped outside. Ashley did the same.

"So," said Ned, "what 'cha think?"

"Depends," she replied, "What am I looking at?"

Ned laughed. "It's my house."

"I thought you lived in town."

"I do," he said, "but this is where I'm going to live once I get it... habitable."

"Oh," said Ashley. She scanned the yard. The grove surrounding them contained some of the largest oak, elm, and cottonwood trees she'd ever seen. The snow under her feet was neatly piled, making a clean path to the house.

Ned turned toward her, eyes appearing strangely hopeful. "Want the grand tour?"

"Of course," she answered, trying to decipher why she suddenly felt a pang of unease.

Ned grasped her hand and led her towards the barn. "This is the barn," he announced.

"Yup," she answered, "I've seen one of these before. I kinda figured this would be it."

Ned laughed nervously. "The thing that's fascinating is that old wooden barns are becoming rare. Many are allowed to fall into ruin. Some are torn down. Many have been replaced by the steel variety. But this little guy... he's all mine and he's all original."

"He's kinda leaning, too."

"Ah," said Ned, eyes bright, "but I have plans to fix that. I recently got this place. So far I'm working on the house, barn's up next... got lots to restore." He added, "I even found a guy who specializes in straightening these things. Kinda exciting, eh?"

"Well, that's very cool," said Ashley.

Ned continued, "If you step inside..."

Ashley interrupted. "Is it safe?"

"Perfectly," he said, "If you step inside you can see all the stall markers are there."

"Awesome," she said."

"Cows would come in from the back pasture through that door, and enter their own stall for milking."

Ashley pondered, "How did they know where to go?"

"Dunno," said Ned, "They just did it."

"Huh."

"And up here," he continued, pointed towards a hole in the ceiling next to the right side of the building," is the hay loft." He added, "We can climb up there, if you're interested."

Ashley examined the worn ladder leading to said hole. "Perhaps next time," she said, "when I don't have any open sores."

"Oh," he looked alarmed. "Sorry. I forgot."

"No problem."

They stepped outside and he pointed to the white building. "Chicken coop. Awesome building. Probably shouldn't go in there either, avian flu and all."

"No problem."

He sauntered to the farmhouse, chattering about acreage, orchards, gardens, and other rural topics. He was about to open the screen door with flourish, but it broke off its hinges. He fumbled with it a moment, ears reddening, before he set it on the porch. "Not exactly the entrance I was hoping for," he mumbled.

Ashley laughed. "No worries. As long as the floor holds me, I'll be happy."

"Oh," he said, "this baby is solid."

"I'm sure it is."

The anonymous staff rolled Ashley to the operating room. She silently counted white tiles pass across her field of vision as they chattered inane conversation. Once inside the cold facility, they asked her to shimmy from her gurney to the table. "Can't I just get on the floor and walk to it," she asked.

"Nope." She wiggled to the other table and laid still. "Make sure you aren't laying on your hospital gown," said a woman, "We'll need to take that off once you're asleep."

Ashley grimaced and did as she was told. She despised the notion of laying, totally exposed, while someone sliced into her. She still didn't believe she had cancer. She fully expected to hear the words, "There was a mistake. You're completely healthy." But, it didn't happen. At least not yet.

Instead she joined an elite group of humans called Cancer People. In this world, everything is overshadowed by the most insidious of specters: Cancer (with a capital C). From the moment of diagnosis until death, Cancer and Ashley would be forever linked. No matter what, Cancer would be her constant companion, ghostly shadow, puppeteer, and darkest nightmare. From this day forward, she'd have to learn how make peace with Cancer, or die trying. Either way, Cancer was here to stay. For the rest of her life.

The nurse pointed out various members of her surgical team. Ashley didn't see her surgeon. She shivered. "Don't worry," said a voice, "you won't notice the cold once you're out." She glanced at the clock. Five minutes to go. A fire alarm went off. In a panic, her eyes shot towards the woman. "Don't worry," she said, "just a fire drill."

Then a voice said, "Ready?"

Of course she wasn't ready. Who could be ready for what they were about to do? Yesterday, she felt perfectly fine. Today she was getting ready to enter a new, and unknown, chapter of her life. She didn't know what lay ahead, but she had a hunch it wasn't going to be great. Was she ready? Did she have a choice? "I suppose I'm ready," she mumbled.

The room darkened, then faded to a solid black.

Chapter Twelve

MYSTERY OF THE KEY

Ashley sat at the tiny kitchen table, hand resting on the shiny linoleum, thigh resting against the chrome leg. The thickly painted white cupboards shined in the blazing light cascading from the fixture above her head. The kitchen smelled like Grandma's house.

"So," she said, "How long have you lived here?"

"I don't live here," he said, "it's not quite habitable yet."

"Probably," she said, "but I see some definite promise."

"So do I," he said, mood ratcheting up another notch. He hunched over the stove, appearing to cook some sort of egg concoction. Cheese spread over the counter, ham appeared to be one of the ingredients, and the toaster emitted a plume of smoke.

"Sure you don't want any help?"

"Nope," he said, "I got this."

"Well... I hate to say anything," she said, "but I think the toast may be on fire."

He lunged to his left and yanked the toaster plug out of the socket. He fished the flaming bread out of the device and tossed it in the sink. She said, "You sure you don't want just a little help?"

"Do I look like I'm in over my head?"

"Yeah."

He laughed. "In that case, sure. Help away. But be aware I'm perfectly capable of doing this myself."

"I didn't have any doubts."

She chopped vegetables, he sautéed them. Eventually, they achieved two fine omelets. She made the toast.

"I thought you'd like a fresh meal that you didn't have to prepare. Sorry 'bout the mess."

"No problem. I love cooking."

"I guess that's a good thing. You pretty much saved the meal."

She laughed. "Nah, you would have gotten the hang of it."

They ate in silence. Then she said, "What are your plans for this place?"

"I hope to restore it."

"Restore? Define."

"I'm not sure what you mean. I mean 'restore.'" He added, "I've seen some people restore a site, but it doesn't look like then original. That's not restoration. That's remodeling. What I aim to do is make the house look as close to the original as I can." He glanced around. "I love this era of construction. The painted wood ceilings are perfect. I love the hardwood floors. The rooms are small, but they're cozy. The porch may be sagging, but I'll get it right as rain. I'll probably update the heating system, though."

"And insulation?"

"Yeah. That's why I don't live here. Place is freezing in the winter. Summers are nice, though. I can even hit a few good days in autumn. But she needs a lot of TLC."

Ashley smiled. Silence descended as they each savored their food. "This omelet is perfect," she said.

"No doubt."

A few moments passed. He placed his elbow on the table and leaned towards her. "I've gotta ask you something."

"What would that be?" she answered.

"This murder. I just don't get it."

"That makes two of us."

He fished in his pocket and withdrew the key. "I've been

thinking about this thing all day. I couldn't figure out what it could be. So, I did a Google Image search on my phone and I found one picture that kinda sorta matches."

"Oh yeah?"

"Yeah. But here's where it gets weird."

"How so?" She slipped a fork full of eggs on her tongue.

"It looks like it could be a key. A super modern safe key... maybe even a safe deposit one."

"Weird. Most of the ones I've seen are ancient. Go to the local bank to get a safe deposit box and the key look like it came straight out of the wild west."

"Yeah, they do. But this key? It looks like one from a fancy dancy bank in Europe. They also make portable lock boxes that can use something like this."

"Europe?"

"Yeah."

"That's weird."

"Gets weirder."

"How so?"

"There's a notch here." He pointed towards the top. "It's different than the key in the picture. I haven't figured out what it does. But it looks a little worn."

Ashley examined it. "You're right." She added. "Weird."

"Weird is right," said Ned. He leaned back in his chair and sighed.

"How would a key like that wind up in Crossroads?"

"Good question," said Ned, "especially near Alex Kaufman's house."

Ashley pondered a moment, then said, "What do you know about him?"

"Kaufman?"

"Yeah."

Ned scratched his head. "Kaufman was religious. Real religious. He pretty much kept to himself, though. Everybody knew he was an ex-con with a hella bad gambling habit. He tried to hide it, but it was pretty obvious. His past was mysterious, he never talked about any of that."

"Weird."

"Yeah," said Ned, "he was a recent transplant. Never really joined in anything."

"Nobody thought that was... odd? I mean, I can't see how you could live in such a tiny community and not join in."

"Yeah. I just figured he was a kinda shy, keep to himself type guy, but since I found this key... in his yard... outside his grisly murder scene... dude's just jumped up from ordinary shy guy to interesting."

Ashley looked thoughtful. Then she said, "Do you think we should take this key to Officer Mallard?"

"That Tyvek-wearing asshole? Not on your life. He'd muck it up somehow."

Ashley laughed. "You don't like him, do you?"

"Not really."

"You don't hide it well." She paused, then said, "Never underestimate the power of cooperating with local authorities."

"Never underestimate the arrogance of a small town cop."

Ashley laughed. "Then I vote we keep it... for now."

Ned smiled. "Agreed." He picked up the heavy key and slipped it into his shirt pocket. Then he stood and held out his hand. "Enough work. Let me show you the rest of my mansion."

Ashley grasped his fingers and stood. She winced and Ned stepped towards her. "You need another pain killer?"

"Nah," she answered, "I just sat too long. Once I stretch, I'll be fine."

He led her to the living area. A dusty couch rested sullenly on the back wall. A wooden rocker, covered in filth sat next to the window. Ashley said, "That couch looks old. Kitchen set is ancient. Did the previous owners leave their furniture?"

"Yup," said Ned, "every piece."

"That's crazy," she said, "and sad."

He led her up the narrow staircase and pointed ahead. Bathroom's to the right, the bedroom is left. Check out that closet space."

"Awesome."

"It is," he said, stepping towards an entire wall of cupboards. "These farmhouses aren't known for storage areas. This one is unique in that regard. And check out the size of this bedroom."

Ashley stepped forward and peeked inside, half wondering if he was luring her towards a bed. He wasn't. The bed lay in large pieces across the floor.

"I should probably tidy up," he said.

Ashley said, "Nah. Looks lived in."

He laughed and wrapped his arm around her shoulder. His touch generated ripples in her belly. The warmth of his arm penetrated her skin... it felt nice, normal, excellent. She closed her eyes and savored the sensation. They stood in silence before he said, "Boy... I sure wish I had the nerve to kiss you."

The butterfly in Ashley's belly flitted frantically. She didn't say a word. It was one thing to allow him to touch her. It was quite another to embrace. And to kiss? Her mind couldn't comprehend how she'd handle that sensation. She didn't know how to respond to his statement.

He turned to look at her. She didn't return the gesture. She felt him gently tug her towards him. She offered some minor resistance. He paused, then continued until she was in a full fledged, yet gentle hug. Against any good sense within her, she rested her head on his shoulder.

She knew she should step away. She knew it was only honest to leave the room. She knew all this, yet, for some reason, she ignored the impulse. Any cancer person knows better than to start a new relationship on the heels of a diagnosis. Every cancer person except her, evidently. She missed human touch. Their conversations thrilled her. She longed to feel the body of another press against her. Ned made her feel alive. He gave her hope. She knew she could face anything with him by her side.

But what about him? Was it fair to drag him into her drama?

Her future was far from certain. She battled the big C once, she didn't know if/when it would rear its ugly head again.

She didn't know what to do. She didn't know what was appropriate. She realized Miss Manners probably didn't have a chapter in her etiquette book covering this scenario.

Interestingly, while her mind pondered options, her hands made the decision. On their own volition, they slid to the small of his back while her cheek rested on his sturdy shoulder. He felt warm. He smelled fabulous. She savored the descent into the depths of his aura. She could only imagine how wonderful he'd taste.

They stood in their soft embrace too long. Yet her body lingered, enjoying everything that comprised Ned Stevens. Her mind screamed for her to leave... exit... escape.

For his part, Ned could have maintained that position forever.

She took half a step away when she felt his embrace tighten. Alarmed at the change, she glanced at his face and immediately deciphered his intent. Warm, hungry eyes met hers. As he neared, she realized her life was about to capsize. She wasn't sure how she felt about this new development, but instinctual terror flooded her veins while primal urgings anchored her in place. Her butterfly was about to puncture her innards. Her knees felt weak. She knew she should refuse his advance, but she seemed unable to move. Before she could ponder the situation, his lips touched her's.

Every reservation melted into a puddle of warmth. He tasted better than she could have imagined. His embrace made her feel safe, happy, invincible. Wrapped in the toasty cocoon of his arms, she felt every worry melt, every concern vanish; tumor markers ceased to exist, cancer was a distant, fading memory.

She felt his hands slide to the small of her back. Her hands had somehow climbed to the smooth area just between his shoulder blades. If she couldn't control herself, she'd soon find her fingers tangled in his hair.

Their kiss escalated in urgency. She broke the moment, abruptly lowering her face. She breathed deep.

"Jeeze, Ashley," he gasped, "You're killing me."

She didn't reply. Instead, she threw caution to the wind and pulled his face towards her. As the current of the moment carried her forward, she realized she didn't want to end this first fabulous intimate moment in recent memory.

Passion rose. Their limbs entangled. Before she knew what was happening, she realized she was launching towards the ancient dance, evolution's folly, her first sensual encounter since the big C entered her life.

But Cancer is cruel in every way imaginable. Like an invisible, dark passenger, its sole goal is to interrupt life, poke its ugly face into every happy situation, always remind its victim that it is truly in control. Always. Forevermore.

Any new hope is quickly dashed by reality. Every happy encounter is shaded with the reminder that nothing lasts forever. If a spot of happiness appears, Cancer must rear its face in the sharpest way possible. Cancer wins. Its partners must never forget it.

Ashley's reminder came the moment Ned pressed her against the wall. With her shirt unbuttoned, the two potential lovers continued their awkward scrambling, attempting to remove clothing. That's when Ned temporarily forgot the big C. As he groped for her pant's waist band, his fingernail caught on her bandage tape. It pulled away from her welted skin. She yelped. The moment broke.

"I am so sorry," he breathed, "I didn't remember."

Tears sprang to Ashley's eyes. She slid to the floor, only realizing once she sat, she likely wouldn't be able to get up again. Then she sobbed.

"I'm so sorry," he repeated, lowering himself to his haunches. "I'm so sorry." He sat in front of her.

Silence enveloped them. Finally she said, "I can't do this."

He touched her hand. She pulled away, patting her bandages, then buttoning her shirt. He touched her face. She pressed her cheek against his hand. "I'm so sorry," he said, "I just forgot myself."

"That's fine," she said.

They sat in defeated silence, awkwardness suffocating them. She released his hand.

Finally Ashley spoke. "You didn't do anything wrong. No need to apologize." A tiny sob hiccuped through her lips. He watched her pull her emotions in check. "You didn't do anything wrong," she repeated. "That was awesome." She smiled bitterly. "I just forgot that I shouldn't engage in that kind of activity."

Ned's eyebrows knit together. "I'm not sure what you mean."

"It's just the... cancer," she said. "I'm not sure where I'm at with it. I'm pretty sure it's not fair that I get together with anyone at this point." She paused, a small tear making its way down her cheek. "I'm not sure what you have in mind, but my dating anyone is probably a bad idea." Ned relaxed a bit. He didn't say anything. She continued, "It's not like I figured we'd be serious or anything... I'm not being presumptuous. It's just that I'm not a one night stand kind of girl. And even though I really like how you taste, I think we should just be friends." She added, "And that's even a little too dangerous for my comfort level."

Ned didn't respond. Instead, he studied her face. The way his eyes penetrated her soul made her avert her eyes. His gaze promised nights of pleasure. Stability. Love. She couldn't allow that. At least not yet. She had to stop him before he made a massive miscalculation. She had to break the moment.

"You gonna say anything," she asked, her voice sounding harder than she intended.

He shook his head. "Nope."

She dropped her eyes. She knew she blew it. She probably just ruined the only potential friendship she'd allowed since... well since Cancer. She cursed her luck. She cursed genetics. She cursed whatever she could possibly curse for putting her in this situation.

Then she felt his hand on her cheek. Her eyes darted to his face. To her horror, it was nearing. She felt is lips touch her temple. Then he kissed her forehead. Then he traced a trail to her ear where he whispered, "I don't know about you, but I don't base my current actions on future outcomes that may or may not happen." Ashley's butterfly awoke. "I make my determinations based on the present moment. And right now, I really want to love you. I've wanted to do this since the first day we met." His fingertips trailed her cheek. His lips brushed her hairline. His hand cupped her shoulder in a most pleasant way.

He continued, "I get it. You're dealing with cancer. That's tough shit, to be sure. But cancer doesn't scare me. You being alone, however, does." He pulled her face towards his. "Just let me love you."

He unbuttoned her shirt, slowly, button by button. Her butterfly danced in her belly as cool air kissed the hot skin of her stomach. His eyes focused on the tangle of bandages.

She gasped in horror, realizing someone outside the medical community could see her shame, the ultimate ugliness, her scar.

He leaned back and carefully stroked each bandage. He raised his eyes and caught her gaze. "I think you're beautiful... in every way. I'm glad they caught the cancer and got it out of you. I'm glad you're well enough to be with me here, right now." He leaned towards her and their lips touched. "Please let me love you."

Chapter Thirteen

POOR TONN

Ike Moe sat next to the golden lab, scratching its ear.

"Poor girl," he said, "I wonder what they did to you." He paused to rub his chin. "Come to think of it," he said, "if I were smart like you, I'd get the fuck out of here." He studied the dog a moment, then whispered, "I should talk to Troy when he gets here... both you and I know what's going to happen. You lived with those monsters. Hell... I know what they're capable of." He breathed deep. "The tide's shifting and it may be a prudent time to pull stakes and run." He sighed. "But I'm too tired to start over... again. Fuck."

He glanced at his watch. 9:20. Ten more minutes. He stroked the dog. A rock formed in his stomach. He knew he shouldn't have accepted the cash. But he did. Now he was in over his head.

"If I could, I'd return it," he mumbled. The dog whined and rolled onto her back. He scratched her belly. "I hate this," he said, "I hate feeling like this. I hate doing this. I hate knowing this." He paused. "I wish things could go back to the way they were before this shit storm."

Ike sighed, weighing the consequences of ditching town. He

realized it would be a futile act. "They'll find me. They always do. I just hope my situation turns out better than Alex's."

He took a long swig of his beer. He gulped it down. He raised the bottle. "To Alex. To Dr. Troy Tonn. To the whole fucking world!" He sat in silence.

———

Their limbs entangled. Various pieces of clothing lay spread across the floor; the only sound, their synchronized breaths.

He entered careful, slow. The sensation flinging her to new heights of ecstasy.

Ned was certainly a man of many surprises. First, she didn't expect him to want her, especially in her broken condition. Second, she didn't expect he'd accept her after realizing her whole cancer ordeal was far from over. Third, she never expected him to be such an incredible, gentle lover. Dear God, Ned Stevens appeared to be far more intoxicating than any narcotic.

Never, in a million years, did she think she'd completely disrobe for a man again. With all her incisions, needle pokes, and scans... who would want to love something so scarred... so used up.

She shook her head. There it was. Cancer invading her pleasure yet again.

She tried to pull away from those thoughts, but each time his belly pressed on hers, she felt her scar strain. She tried to ignore the sensation... the pain invading her pleasure... but Cancer will not be ignored. Its quiet insistence endures.

"I shouldn't have allowed this before I could properly school a man on what hurts and what doesn't," she thought. But how would anyone broach that topic?

Scenarios flitted through her mind: "Excuse me sir, but when you mount me, be sure to do so in this manner so as to not disturb my incision." Perhaps something like this would work: "When engaging in sexual copulations with a cancer patient be sure to avoid bandaged areas, do not engage in twisting actions unless previous consent has been granted, and above all, do not remove any clothing unless a verbal contract has been drafted concerning said item." She would have laughed at such ridiculous thoughts except at that moment, another wave of ecstasy neared. "Mustn't think of cancer... mustn't think of cancer... Can't let Cancer do this to me."

Her arms wrapped around his shoulders. He felt sturdy. She loved that.

"Hey," he whispered, "You doing OK?"

"God, yes," she gasped.

He grinned. "Let's try this." He looped his legs around hers, pulled her close, and rolled to his side. She squealed, the movement creating a stab of pain. Alarm spread across his face. "You OK?"

"Just felt odd," she whispered.

"Sure you're fine?"

She kissed him.

Then, he slowly rolled to his back, pulling her along with him. Straddling his groin, she pulled herself upright. It felt good. Really good. Her body reacted to the sensation.

"Dear god," he moaned, "you've got to slow down." He groaned. "Holy shit..." She gyrated her hips. "Seriously," he gasped, "slow down. I can't let this end."

She would have lowered herself to kiss him, but truth was, it felt great to extend her torso and if she were to go down there, she wasn't sure she'd be able to get back up again. So she remained, enjoying watching him writhe with pleasure. She realized one of her bandages had loosened and was now flapping. She tore it off with a wince and tossed it aside.

Without warning, he snapped to a sitting position. He wrapped his arms around her bare shoulders and said, "So help me God, now that I've got you here, I'm not about to come yet." He kissed her. Hard.

His strong arms pulled her tight. His lips possessed her. And she allowed it.

"I'll think about cancer tomorrow," she thought.

"You'll think about cancer now." Cancer won't be ignored.

But, for the first time, passion temporarily overrode the gruesome conversation. Thoroughly engrossed in the moment, she allowed herself to explore new levels of pleasure, vistas of intimacy, trust unlike anything she'd known.

After what felt like forever, he finally shuddered and allowed himself to collapse onto the dusty carpet. She gingerly joined him, pulling off his body and resting beside him, her head perched in the nook between his arm and shoulder.

"I never thought making love could be like this," he said. She didn't reply. She watched a smile spread across his face. "Not gonna say anything?"

"Nope."

He laughed.

He turned to his side and wrapped his other arm around her. He kissed her cheek, then made a trail towards her lips. There, he savored her taste as he held her tight.

"You'll never be alone as long as I'm alive," he whispered.

She didn't reply.

———

After the surgery, Ashley remembered little of the actual procedure. She recalled a garbled conversation in the recovery room, but most of her memories began after she awoke in her hospital room. She recalled searing pain, exceeding fatigue, and cold like she never knew existed.

She shivered her way through the first day.

"What did they find?" she kept asking.

No answers.

"What all did they do?"

"You'll have to talk to the surgeon."

"I'm hungry. Can I eat something?"

"You can't eat or drink until your colon wakes up."

"When will that be?"

"Few days... give or take."

Without answers, without food, she closed her eyes and slept. She hobbled through the hospital halls, happy in the assurance that doing so would wake up her digestive system faster. At least that's what the nurses said. It didn't seem to work. Hunger gnawed at her innards. She hobbled and wobbled wherever she went. If it hadn't been for the powerful narcotics controlling her pain, she would have been miserable.

Instead, life was a hoot. Everything humored her. Her pain, while quite vivid, didn't matter. Her hunger was a running joke.

The surgeon patiently re-explained her whole case every time he visited. Ashley apparently didn't have much memory when high on meds. He inspected her large scar, explaining that the tumor was in a different location than he expected and they had to revise the initial plan and abandon the laparoscopic procedure, embark on an open one and conduct what was called an extended right hemicolectomy.

That meant they removed the entire right side of her colon, extracted the entire horizontal portion, then reattached the small intestine to the remaining left side. That seemed like a lot of colon to remove for one tumor, but considering she didn't understand medicine, was currently higher than a kite, and wanted out of the hospital, it seemed prudent to go with the current plan.

Except the large, horizontal incision had a mind of its own.

Shortly after the procedure, she meandered down the hospital corridor. As she proceeded, she felt something hit her knee. Gingerly bending to inspect the phenomena, she said, "Somebody dripped cherry popsicle on my leg."

Then another drip hit it. It wasn't cherry popsicle. She opened her robe and revealed her hospital gown glowing with a deep red plume.

"Shit."

Then a red drip hit her foot, soaking into her sock. She gazed behind her and a vivid line of fire engine drips betrayed her path.

*She hobbled to the nurse station, gripping her IV pole. "Ma'am," she
said, "I believe I've sprung a leak."*

*The nurse, clearly overworked and quite busy, responded, "What makes
you think that?"*

*Ashley didn't say a word. Instead she opened her gown. Seeing the
blooming plume, she gasped and said, "Back to your room."*

Ashley said, "I don't feel sick. Can I finish my walk?"

The nurse glared at her. "No. Get back to the room."

*"Do you want me to clean up my trail?" She gestured towards the spots
of blood on the floor. "I honestly didn't know I was leaking."*

*"Maintenance will take care of that," said the nurse, "just get back to
your room."*

*Ashley hobbled towards that accursed room. She longed for the cozy
quilts on her own bed. She wondered how the temp was handling her job.
Her tumor hadn't been staged yet and she wondered what the final numbers
would predict. Most of all, she wondered when she would eat. Although
hunger had dissolved her innards (near as she could tell), the narcotics eased
her worry about the situation.*

But this new development seemed rather disconcerting.

———

Dr. Troy Tonn manuvered his vehicle towards Ike Moe's house. Ike
graciously allowed beautiful Sadie to stay until Tonn was sure the
CSI people wouldn't return to Crossroads.

He grasped his mocha, peeled the thick sticker from the coffee
cup lid, and stuck it to his dash. He smiled, admiring the large
collection of colorful stickers adhering to the dashboard, criss
crossing the instrument cowl.

Ike was a fine person. A long time friend, Tonn recalled how
they immediately hit it off the first time they met. "Twin brothers
from separate mothers," Moe always said. He figured it must have
been in Germany... or was it France... when they really started
working together. They blew up a bridge in Munich. They

poisoned a well in Nice. They took out three operatives in Paris. Near as he could tell, He and Ike had saved at least a hundred people from untimely deaths since they were assigned as partners. Sadly, the body count left in their wake was far higher. But everyone should expect casualties in this line of work. Wrong place, wrong time. So be it.

Since they hit Minnesota, things were much quieter. After the RNF blow up, they thought they would complete their lives in anonymity. Sadly, this didn't seem to be the case.

Ike and Troy never talked about the old days. Instead they fished together. They hopped bars on Friday nights. Moe truly was the brother he never had.

So, when Tonn realized he couldn't euthanize Sadie, he knew the exact person he should call to help perform one of the most amazing stunts in his quiet veterinary career: dupe the CSI team and rescue on damn fine canine. It thrilled him to think that he and Ike would be able to embark on one last escapade.

Moe was more than happy to help, much to Tonn's surprise. Lately Moe was slow to engage in any activity that would involve law breaking... he continually fretted he'd blow his cover.

Not today. He gladly accepted the dog, seemingly thrilled to pull one over on the CSI thugs invading his space. It was fun to see the old Ike in action again.

Tonn slowed down his vehicle and rolled to a stop in front of Ike's house. His fingers ached, waiting to stroke Sadie's firm back. As he exited the Ram, a faint sound... like grass rustling... snagged his attention. He hadn't heard that sound for years... and generally speaking he was the one making it. He thought he caught a shadow out of the corner of his eye. Alarm rose in his throat. He turned.

He didn't have a moment to process what unfolded. Instead, his jaw dropped as if a mute scream exited his lips. A sharp snap cracked the silence. Then everything turned black.

Dr. Troy Tonn fell to the ground like a sack of potatoes, blood oozing from a hole in his forehead. A dark figure lugged his body into the back of the pickup. It dug in Tonn's pocket for keys. Once obtained, the shadow-person hopped into the cab, fired the ignition, and bounced down the street.

Dr. Tonn ceased to exist on a frigid evening as owls hooted, dogs howled, and the many animals he tended in his clinic slept.

———

Ashley laid next to Ned, head resting in the nook of his arm, savoring his scent. She didn't recall feeling this good since... well, since. Her hand resting on his chest, the faint lub dub of his heart vibrated through her fingertips. She didn't dare move. At the moment she felt zero pain. Ned didn't seem to mind that his arm was likely going numb. He lay with his eyes closed, a small smile playing on his lips.

She closed her eyes, hoping sleep would blanket her thoughts.

It didn't.

As much as she hated it, practicality formed in her mind.

"I wonder how long it's been since this carpet has been cleaned," said a voice in her head. She knew who it was. Cancer was back spreading its black notions. "You'll probably get another infection. Just look at this dust. Utter filth. That's where you're laying." She tried to ignore it. "If he sees you when he's not aroused, he'll know he's made a big mistake." She tightened her lips. "Look at you. You didn't even keep your wounds covered. Open wounds. You're an idiot."

Her hand flew to her incision. This time Cancer was right. She recalled ripping off the bandage and cringed. If she got another infection, she wouldn't forgive herself.

"Now that he's got what he wants, he'll go away. He's probably dreamed of fucking a freak... that's what you are. A freak." She breathed deep, pushing the thoughts out of her mind. "If you had any idea how many fetishes there are..."

She shook her head. "No," she breathed, "he's not like that."

"Yeah, well you'll get another infection anyway. Fucking in filth. Smart move."

She ignored Cancer and slowly, in an attempt to not awaken Ned and keep her abdominal pain at bay, maneuvered herself to a sitting position. She scanned the room looking for her clothes. To her right laid a pile of what looked like pants. She thought she could decipher her bra hanging from a piece of the bed over on the other side of the room. She couldn't see any shirts... perhaps they were behind her. She tried to twist to look, but her belly screamed in protest. Beside her rested what was once a bandage.

"Damn," she whispered. "I don't have any extras."

Ned opened his eyes. "What's up?" He grinned.

She knew she should cover at least part of her nakedness, but didn't know where to begin. Sure, she could cover her breasts, but right now they looked better than the rest of her. If she covered her abdomen, she'd probably soil her incision.

Ned sat up. He scrutinized her a few moments. She felt her cheeks redden. Finally, he spoke. "Do you have any idea how beautiful you look right now?"

Her eyebrows flew upward. "Seriously?"

"Yeah," he said, grinning. "I've never seen anyone look so perfect."

Ashley laughed. "You must have dated Quasimodo before you met me."

Ned scowled. "Honestly. Why do you bat back every single complement? I get that cancer is hard. But I wish you could see what I see. You're perfect."

Ashley softened. "I'm sorry. I guess I'm a little insecure."

"Little?" Ned said.

"Lots?"

"Closer." Ned's eyes sparkled. Then they traveled to her belly. "You lost a bandage."

"I noticed."

"We should probably cover it, eh?" He said, "Carpet isn't exactly clean."

"Yeah," she said. Then she added, "This is some pretty erotic pillow talk, don't you think?"

He laughed. "It's reality. There's nothing sexier than reality."

"Well," she said, "be prepared for some incredible sexiness coming from this area of the room."

"Oh, you know it," he countered, laughing.

Chapter Fourteen

EYE WITNESS

Dr. Troy Tonn's pickup would arrive at the chop shop within three hours of his death. It would be completely dismantled in an hour and a half. Luckily for the mechanic, the dashboard, aka, the cowl, was intact, in perfect condition. He'd earn a pretty penny for the ensemble considering the airbags were never deployed.

Sadly, Tonn's fate was far more grisly. Shortly after his murder, his pickup rolled into a grove of trees outside an abandoned farmhouse. The murderer stepped out of the vehicle and breathed deep. The assignment was far easier than he anticipated. But he wasn't finished. He removed his clothing and donned a Tyvek suit, all the while surveying his surroundings, ever vigilant of potential witnesses.

He liked this remote farmhouse. It brought back good memories. Abandoned for decades, it was a perfect place to execute the many grisly tasks required of him. Plus, it was a quiet place to work in peace, without interruption. Prepared for the night's task, he hopped onto the truck bed and dragged Tonn's body onto the ground. It landed with a thud.

Then, he sauntered towards a small shed on the site and pried open the door. Inside a brand new chainsaw glistened.

"Come to me, gorgeous," he purred. "You'll come in handy tonight."

The murderer trotted to Tonn and systematically sawed through each arm near the shoulder. Despite the frigid temps, his forehead moistened with the effort. He paused, noting steam rising from each severed limb.

Without pondering the absurdity of the situation, he revved the saw, slicing off the legs through denim, flesh, and bone. Blood sprayed, staining the snow a deep red. He worked fast, hoping to keep noise to a minimum. No matter, though. He figured the nearest neighbor lived miles away.

After he finished with the limbs, he sliced open Tonn's belly and scooped out his entrails. He slipped them into a bag. Then, he carved the torso in four neat pieces. He wrapped plastic around Troy's head and placed it in a box. "I'll need you later," he whispered. He set it aside.

Then, he bagged individual body sections and placed a large stone inside each sack. Lastly, he wrapped the dripping chain saw in plastic.

After he tossed everything onto the back end of the truck, he removed his white suit and bagged it.

Then Dr. Tonn embarked on his final voyage. As the murderer passed any body of water, whether it was a slough, wetland, pond, river, lake, or stream, he'd pause his truck, step out of the vehicle and chuck one of his bags as far as he could throw. Each package hit the nearly frozen water with a splash.

The murderer worked quick and without remorse. He could have been tossing wood for all he cared. He was a consummate professional: leave no evidence, blend in, better yet, remain invisible.

As the last piece tumbled towards its destination, the murderer said, "God speed. May angels guide you to your final resting place." Then he entered the truck. The box containing Tonn's head sat on the passenger seat. "I have a little project for you." He added, "But first, we must dispose of this truck."

———

Ashley still hadn't eaten. It was three days after her surgery and she expected she'd soon waste away to nothing. Instead the scale steadily climbed. She glared at the IV pole next to her bed. "What do they have in that thing? Lard?"

The nurse laughed. "It's just water weight. You'll be fine."

"When can I eat?"

"When your colon wakes up."

Ashley sighed. Just then, a balding man entered the room. "Hello," he said, "I'm Dr. Lloyd. I'll be your oncologist."

"Why would I need an oncologist," Ashley said, "the surgeon feels he removed the whole tumor."

"Well," said Dr. Lloyd, "Cancer's a tricky bastard. All the while that mass was in you, it was flaking off cells. Those cells entered the blood vessels feeding your tumor. Those cells could, presumably, take root anywhere in your body... most likely your lungs or liver. If those cells take root, you can develop another tumor. Those tumors are what we call metastases, or mets." He waited for Ashley's face to show some sign of comprehension. She still looked puzzled, pondering his words. He continued, "What we do is monitor your tumor markers... special numbers that will now appear on all your blood tests. You'll receive regular exams, blood tests, and yearly CT scans. After five years, if you're still clear, we'll consider you in remission with 'no evidence of disease.'"

Now Ashley's ears perked. "I have to see you for five years?"

"No," said the oncologist, "you'll likely see us for the rest of your life. You'll just have quarterly, then twice yearly visits, then after five years, you'll go in annually... for a while. It all depends on your numbers."

"My numbers?"

"Tumor markers. If they remain steady... nice and low... you'll be in good shape. If they go up, we'll have to revise your treatment plan."

Ashley pondered a moment. "Will I need chemo?"

The oncologist dug through her chart. "Well, you're stage 2A. T3NoMo. That means while your tumor was large... size of a golf ball... it didn't exit your colon. Also, all your lymph nodes came back clear. No metastases either." He pondered a moment. *You're in a very grey area. If we do chemo, you can raise your five year odds of remission by around three percentage points. If you don't do chemo, your odds are still very good plus you'll be able to save your chemo for when you really need it."*

"Really need it?"

"Yes. Chemotherapy treatments don't work forever. We need to cycle them. One will work, then stop. We like to save the chemo for when you really need it. Plus the side effects and possible permanent nerve damage makes that small gain... questionable." He paused, then continued, "You can think about it. Discuss this with your family doctor." He smiled and extended his hand. "You're certainly lucky, Ms Stone. They caught your cancer early. You're the poster child for preventative screening."

Ashley hardly felt lucky, but she extended her hand nonetheless. "I still can't believe I had cancer," she murmured.

"Everyone feels that way," he answered. Then he said, "Do you have any questions before I leave?"

She shook her head. "Nah. You pretty much covered everything."

"Did your surgeon explain everything to your satisfaction?"

Ashley nodded. "I suppose."

The doctor paused a moment. "You know," he said, "I've done this for a long time. You seem unsure. Are you doing OK? Do you need me to order some psychiatric help for you... someone to talk to?"

"No," Ashley said, a bit too quickly, "No. It's just that this happened so fast. One day I'm doing great, the next I'm here. I'm hungry. I'm cranky. I don't think my colon will ever wake up. And what will it be like when it finally does?"

Dr. Lloyd sat back down. "You'll be fine." He dug through her chart. "Extended right hemi. You'll have to be careful with what you eat, but other than that, you'll be fine. Eventually your small intestine will pick up the slack, but this scenario is far preferable to dying of untreated cancer." He continued, "I've worked in this field for a long time. I know you don't feel lucky right now, but you are. Judging from these numbers, you would have been inoperable in two years, dead in five. That's amazing. Your tumor was around 1 millimeter away from perforating your bowel. You were a walking time bomb. Now you're not. I see many good years in your future."

Ashley nodded, wishing her narcotics would lighten her mood. But truth was, her pain was constant and unyielding. She didn't understand what was going on. To make matters worse, she dreaded what would happen when she could finally eat.

Despite the shallowness of the thought, she wondered what would happen to her fuckability factor. It was hard enough to find a kind man to date, but to find one who would date a cancer patient? Her odds of living alone the rest of her life seemed quite unpleasant.

"Are you OK," said Dr. Lloyd.

"I'm fine," she said, forcing a smile from her lips. "You're right. I am lucky. I'm sure I'll eventually feel lucky, too."

He touched her hand. "I'm sure you will."

Dr. Lloyd left her room. Ashley sat in silence pondering their conversation.

Stage 2. It seemed pretty far from stage 4. That had to be good. But she didn't have any symptoms prior to this nightmare. No family history of colon cancer anywhere. How could this have happened?

She closed her eyes and pondered the incredible hollowness in her belly. She wasn't sure if it was because she hadn't eaten in days or if the sensation was due to the amount of colon they removed.

She pondered the utter grossness of her cancer. If she were to be diagnosed with such a dreaded disease, why couldn't she have contracted one of the cool ones like breast cancer. Then she could wear pink and enjoy an entire month of support from every direction including fried chicken sellers offering their wares in pink buckets, coffee drinkers sipping their favorite beverage in pink cups, and even oil rig drill bit makers bathing their equipment in pepto.

Instead she got the cancer that entailed regular colonoscopies, terrible preps, careful diet monitoring, and plenty of Metamucil to manage "bowel issues."

"Jeeze," she mumbled, "my life has become absurd."

Of course all these issues assumed her colon would eventually awaken. If it didn't, she could apparently look forward to ostomy bags and even more rigid diet restrictions.

She decided to wallow in her grief a while. After all, her narcotic was *waning, reality was evidently closing in on her, and she figured she'd never eat again.*

Then the nurse walked in.

"Did your meeting with Dr. Lloyd go well?"

"As well as it could have."

She paused. "Didn't go well?" Ashley shrugged her shoulders. The nurse continued, "It's not as bad as all that. You're one of the lucky ones. You really are. I know you feel terrible right now, but I've seen people die of colon cancer. It's gruesome." She shuddered. "Absolutely gruesome."

"Is that supposed to make me feel better," Ashley asked.

"Yes," she answered. "You really dodged a bullet."

"If you say so," said Ashley. She sank back into her bed and closed her eyes while the nurse pressed the stethoscope against her belly. She pressed repeatedly, moving the apparatus each time.

She finally spoke. "I hear something," she said. "Bet you'll be able to eat shortly."

Ashley's mood brightened. "Seriously?"

"Yup," answered the nurse.

———

McNally patrolled the town on foot when he saw him. Just as he was about to step out of the shadows and onto the street, a movement caught his eye. He froze, turning towards it. Someone was lurking in the shadows. He stepped next to a tree and focused his eyes. He saw it again. The shadowy figure blended into the dark night as well as he did. It was a pro... just like him.

"Nobody can do that unless they're an agent... an active agent," he thought.

He kept his distance, always maintaining the figure at the very edge of his sight. He kept far enough away to keep himself hidden, close enough to observe its movement.

It appeared to linger just outside Ike Moe's house. This intrigued McNally. He grasped his phone and silently dialed. When he heard the click, he whispered, "Ike Moe. Extreme caution." Then he hung up. He expected Jim would show up shortly.

He laid on his belly surveilling the shadowy figure, while it evidently surveilled Moe's house. Except, he didn't seem to be watching the house as much as he watched the street.

McNally felt Jim arrive. He glanced behind him just as Jim's shadow darted between two trees. McNally smiled. Jim served as his right hand man since he was a child. He saved his life on more occasions than he could count. Their friendship ran deeper and longer than any relationship he'd ever had.

Jim slid next to McNally. "What 'cha see?"

"Over there," McNally whispered. "By Moe's house."

Jim focused his vision in the general direction. He squinted and concentrated. Eventually the shadow shifted and Jim nodded. "Yup. Moves like an operative."

"That's what I thought."

"What's he doing there?"

"No idea. It'll be interesting to find out," said McNally.

"Indeed."

Chapter Fifteen

DEATH WINS

Ashley melted into Ned's pickup seat. "I hope you had a good time," he said.

"I did."

Long pause. They proceeded down the bumpy gravel road. Ashley silently blessed the pain killer she popped just before they left Ned's cozy farmhouse.

Ned spoke. "I'm sorry. I feel awkward. We aren't awkward, are we?"

Ashley laughed. "Nope."

"You OK?"

"I'm doing very well." Ashley smiled.

Long pause.

"You sure you don't want to spend the night at my house? I'd love waking up next to you."

Ashley turned to him. "No. I need to go home. I've got some bandaging to do."

"I wasn't too rough..."

"No. You were perfect."

Ned smiled, seemingly relieved. A few more miles passed

before he spoke again. "You know... I have bandages at my place. I'll be happy to help. Like I said, you don't need to do this alone."

Ashley turned to look at him. "Tonight was perfect. I just need to clean up."

"If you want, I'll happily stay at your house. Either works."

Ashley said, "Ned, you're wonderful. But you don't need to see all this. I swear, we'll spend the night together... eventually. Just not tonight." She paused, then continued, "I'm a little overwhelmed. I've got dripping wounds. I just did something I haven't done in a long time." Ned looked deflated so she added, "I'm a good kind of overwhelmed, but I need to think about this. I need to get cleaned up. I need to see where I'm at concerning this whole situation." She studied his face. "I hope you don't mind."

"Of course I don't mind," he interjected. "I just don't want you to forget me."

"I'd never forget you. Tonight was incredible. Plus, we're partners at the paper. I'd have to work pretty hard to forget you."

"You could reject me."

Ashley pondered a moment. "I won't reject you," she whispered, "You're the best person I've met in a long time." She added, "You're perfect."

Ned grinned. "I think you're pretty awesome, too." He continued, "Just don't act like tonight didn't happen."

"I don't think I could do that."

"Me either." Ned glanced at her. "So you'll go out with me again?"

"In a New York minute."

A grin spread across Ned's face.

———

McNally and Jim monitored the shadow person for over an hour.

"What the fuck is he doing?" said Jim.

"Waiting."

"For what?"

"I guess we'll see."

Just then a silver Ram pickup rolled down the street. It came to a stop outside Moe's house. McNally stiffened. Jim held his breath. They watched the driver exit the vehicle. They saw the shadow figure slide into position. The driver turned. A small popping sound pierced the air. The driver fell.

They watched the shadow descend on the driver and toss him onto the pickup bed.

"Woah," said Jim, "He's fast. Definitely a pro."

"No shit."

They saw the shadow jump into the cab and take off.

Acting on instinct, Jim and McNally bolted in the same direction as the vehicle. Luckily their car was parked on the edge of town. McNally hoped it faced the right direction. A U turn could slow them down enough to lose the pickup.

Their pace increased as they raced across lawns, leaped over shrubs, cut corners short, while keeping the vehicle in their line of sight. When the truck turned right, entering the county highway, Jim gasped, "We've got 'em."

Jim and McNally sprinted towards their nondescript vehicle and hopped inside. McNally fired the engine and threw it in gear. No U turns tonight. He left the headlights off as he squinted, trailing the tail lights of Tonn's pickup.

————

Ashley entered her home and collapsed on the couch. She winced. "I shouldn't have done that," she mumbled. She closed her eyes and pondered the night's events. The butterfly in her stomach turned a few back flips as she recalled Ned's touch. She smiled as she relived his embrace. And the love making... it made her toes curl.

"You know it was a mistake." Cancer barged into her thoughts.

"I don't know that."

"Sure. You know. Cancer always wins."

"Perhaps."

"Definitely."

She glanced at the coffee table beside the couch. A letter from the local oncology center rested on top. She picked it up and stared at it a few moments. She turned it in her hands a couple times before she placed it back on the table. "I'll read you tomorrow. Or the next day."

"Delay all you want, I'll wait."

"Shush, you," she replied.

She grasped her abdomen and pulled herself to the standing position. Breathing deep, she hobbled to the kitchen and popped two pain killers into her mouth. Then she proceeded to the bathroom where she removed what was left of her bandages and examined her wounds. "Not as bad as I thought," she mumbled.

She undressed and twisted the knobs in her shower. As she waited for the water to warm, she examined her naked body in the mirror.

"He said I was beautiful," she whispered. She couldn't see what he saw. Her reflection mocked every sensibility she possessed as she stood staring at her reflection. Steam crawled across the base of the mirror.

Bags under her eyes reflected the weariness in her soul. Her abdomen still looked like a war zone with deep, weeping incisions, laparoscopic slits, ebbing rivers of drainage with crusty banks.

She squinted her eyes. The person staring back at her appeared exponentially better.

She scrunched her face while squinting. Now she really looked good; a fuzzy outline of a female form.

She shrugged. "I won't figure him out," she mumbled.

She twisted the cold tap to cool the water's flow. She waited for the right temp, then stepped in, allowing warm water to caress her sore skin, cleansing her of the day's events.

———

"Where do you suppose he's going," whispered Jim.

"No idea." They drove in silence, watching tail lights bob in front of them.

Finally the lights veered onto what turned out to be a long, twisting driveway.

"Lots of abandoned farm houses around here," Jim murmured.

"Suggestions... do we follow him up there, or hoof it?"

"Probably be best to follow on foot."

"What if there's another exit and we lose him?"

"What if there isn't another exit and we're discovered?" said Jim.

"Touché. Park it is."

They drove off the road and stopped their vehicle near a messy grove of trees. McNally made sure to position the car in an advantageous position in case they needed a fast getaway.

Both men exited and padded their way up the driveway, hugging the edges, allowing shadows to cover their presence. McNally's finger rose when they heard a buzzing fill the air. Jim immediately leaped farther away from the roadway. McNally followed, silent as a cat.

They paused and crept forward. The scene that unfolded before them made their jaws drop.

Jim saw it first. Tonn's pickup sat to his right. To his left the shadow figure appeared hard at work systematically dismantling what looked like Tonn's body.

A small pile of dark garbage bags rested behind the vigilant worker.

"Preparing for a body dump, I assume," said McNally.

"Looks like it," whispered Jim.

They watched the saw buzz, then another body part tossed aside. It looked like a big project, especially for one person, but the shadow figure seemed more than competent.

"Do we confront him now or wait?" said Jim.

"Wait. Definitely," said McNally, "we need to see where this leads."

"I suppose," said Jim, "but this guy's beyond anything we ever did."

"Agreed. He's a pro. He's vicious. He's not operating alone."

As the shadow figure finished his business, Jim and McNally made their way back to their sedan. Inside, they waited in silence for the pickup to exit the farm site.

After twenty minutes, they saw lights bounding down the driveway. It passed. McNally waited a few moments before he fired his engine and followed. He didn't turn on his headlights.

———

Ashley sat in her pajamas. She felt marvelous, clean, leaning heavy on the back of her couch, sipping a hard lemonade. Then she heard it. A car door slammed. She heard the crunching of snow as someone approached her door. Then she heard a tapping.

She wasn't sure she should answer, but whoever it was, persisted in their knocking. She stood and proceeded towards the noise. Peeking out the peep hole, she saw Ned's smiling face. She undid the latch.

"Look what the cat dragged in," she said, smiling.

Ned looked sheepish. "Sorry. I know you told me you wanted to be alone. But I found something."

She stepped aside and said, "Come on in."

"Besides," he said, stepping past her, "I'd pretty much take any excuse to come see you... but I assure you, this is kinda big."

"Do tell," said Ashley. She added, "Want a lemonade?"

"You know I do," he said.

She disappeared into the kitchen and returned with a bottle. He smiled as she approached. "You look so good right now."

"I definitely feel cleaner," she answered.

"All bandaged up?"

"Yup."

"How are the wounds? Antibiotics working?"

"Absolutely. It's better. Still hurts. Thanks for asking."

Ned flashed her a million dollar smile. He gazed at her a moment, gorgeous eyes probing her soul, her innermost thoughts. When she looked at him, she almost believed that she could be beautiful. Cancer disappeared. Reality felt sweet, fresh... hopeful. Ned spoke. "Yeah. I can't think about that right now. I'm actually here for a reason." He dug in his pocket and pulled out the mysterious silver key. He held it toward her. "Take it," he said. "You won't believe what I found." She grasped it and examined its exterior. "See that notch," he said pointing at the area he mentioned earlier.

"Yeah..." she said.

"Well, it was bugging me. So, I decided to do a little cleaning on it."

"OK..."

"Well when I was doing that, the damnedest thing happened."

"What would that be?"

"Oh, you're not gonna believe this one," he said. "Here, let me show you..."

———

Jim and McNally watched the shadow figure dispose of each body part, one black bag per drop. Jim carefully marked each disposal on a map. "We'll retrieve them if we need to," said McNally.

"Hope not," said Jim.

"Agreed. But you never know."

After the final drop, they trailed the pickup to its final destination. It weaved through Crossroads, presumably assuring they hadn't been tailed. McNally and Jim easily maintained their slow speed pursuit. When the pickup rolled into the Crossroad's Herald parking lot, Jim furrowed his brows. McNally gasped when he saw who exited the vehicle.

BOOK 3

Chapter Sixteen

BOO HOO

She fingered the ancient brass key, stroking its ragged edge with her soft fingertip.

"It's been so long," she whispered. "I can hardly remember your face." She closed her eyes and tried to envision the visage she so sorely missed. "My first love," she breathed. "Now you're gone.

She rubbed her finger along the well worn edge. "I guess you never forget the first one." She paused, then added, "If you had just told me." She placed the key onto the linoleum table. "If you'd just told me, everything could have been different." She rested her hands on the cool surface. "I could have let you live."

She sighed. Dim music rang in her ears, memories of happier times when unbeknownst to her, the seeds of evil planted themselves in her psyche. Or perhaps it was her psyche's truest desire to navigate the blackest avenues of the human mind.

It didn't matter. Nothing mattered.

For many years she simply followed orders. Today she issued more orders than she received.

"Someday very soon, I'll call all the shots. Fuck anyone who tried to tell me what to do. I'm the best." She snickered. "At least, that's what they tell me."

She closed her eyes as a lone tear made its way down her cheek. "Time hasn't been kind," she mumbled. "I'm not sure I can do this anymore."

Kaufman hurt. But he needed to go. Tonn stung a little more. "He was so pretty."

The next one was going to be torturous. But it had to be done.

She straightened her back. "Do or die." An acid chuckle escaped her lips. "Kill or be killed."

———

Everything within Ike knew something was wrong. He glanced at his watch and clenched his jaw. He knew Troy should have arrived hours ago, but so far, nothing. Plus, he couldn't come up with any explanations for his absence. He called Troy's phone. Nothing. He called Troy's office. Nada.

He glanced at his reflection in the mirror. "So, what's up, buddy?" A ripple of dread trickled down his spine, resting in his belly. "I hope they didn't find you," he whispered.

He briefly closed his eyes, hoping against hope that he'd find a magical solution for this very disturbing situation.

"How, after all this time… could everything go south like this?" He added, "And so quickly?" He slid onto his couch. "One day everything's fine. Right as rain." He sighed. "The next… all hell is breaking loose."

These last few years in Crossroads had been the best of his life. As the quiet community suffered the attritions of an aging population, slowly but surely people like Ike and Troy were able to find a small, oblivious community to call home. And what a nice home it became.

Although he knew it was likely a stupid thing to do, he had become to view Tonn as a brother in every way possible. Their shared common roots bound them tighter than blood. The fact they lived in the middle of nowhere gave them a shared comfort never before afforded. To be able to come, go, shop, fish, hunt,

swim... do anything they wanted without fear of rival organizations... he'd never known such freedom.

While he and Tonn rarely spoke of the old days, memories of
their European missions echoed his his dreams. The scar on his
right hand sometimes buzzed, seemingly remembering the GPS
chip once nestled in his muscle.

"Bad days," he whispered. Then he said, "Good days."

However, today the bad days seemed to revisit his memories as
he pondered the fate of Alex Kaufman. Although he didn't nose
into the situation much, doing so would have made him look too
interested, rumors ricocheted through Crossroads like a bad echo.

"They had to remove the carpeting... totally soaked
with blood."

"They were gathering dog shit for days after. Looking
for bones."

"I heard a CSI agent barfed."

"House still stinks. They can't find a proper cleaning crew."

"Who could have done something like that?"

Ike sighed. He knew perfectly well what kind of person... or
organization... would be capable of such brutal retribution after so
much time had elapsed. He knew because he, himself, had headed
missions like that back in the old days. He recalled the silent
entries, the discrete nab, the exquisite torture, the final release of
life. He knew every technique to diminish DNA evidence and
ways to mar any residual clues. He scratched Sadie's neck.

It had been a long time since the RNF blow up but the training
Ike received felt fresh. And every alarm in his head was currently
screaming a warning cry.

While he didn't know what organization had presumably rose
to power, filling the huge hole left by the RNF demise would be a
coup. Sadly, with every bone in his body, he knew that one of its
prime directives was to hunt down and exterminate any and all
former RNF operatives.

His suspicions originally piqued when word spread about Kaufman's particularly bloody death. "Even a seasoned professional

would have to endure some pretty intense training to pull off something like that." He rubbed his forehead with the back of his hand. "And to leave no evidence... that's really hard core." He pondered the scents of death. The muffled noises of violence. The razor sharp tools of the trade. "And no witnesses. Not even one."

He turned to the large lab filling his living room floor. It groaned and rolled to its side.

The tightness in his belly rose to his throat. "Who could have done that?" he whispered. The dog's tail thumped.

His body stiffened when the next thought entered his mind. "Do they know about me?" His mind darkened. "Definitely. They definitely do."

He jerked his arm and gazed at his watch. "Where are you, Tonn?" He clenched his jaw. "You sure as fuck better not be dead."

Ike sighed. He closed his eyes a moment and pondered his options. A persistent voice in the recesses of his mind begged, "Get out. Get out now."

"I can't," he whispered. "I need to find out what's going on." He added, "Anything that's found me here will find me anywhere." He breathed deep. "Guess I get to face my own Waterloo."

He stepped to his kitchen table and eyed a pile of mail. He grabbed it and snatched open a few envelopes.

———

McNally and Jim watched the shadow figure exit the car and fiddle with the Crossroad's Herald door. It opened.

"What the fuck," whispered McNally.

"Shit just got real," replied Jim.

"No kidding."

———

By the time he got back, the sun was just beginning to kiss the horizon. "It's about time you sashayed through that door," she said. She silently twisted the ring on her finger.

"Listen here," he sighed, "I've had a rough night."

"Boo hoo. Did you get it all done?"

"Yup. Every gory bit of it." He slid into the chair across from her. "And, now I have to get to the office. On time."

"Boo hoo." A small smile played on her lips. "Did he scream?"

"Nope. Didn't even see it coming."

"Damn. I love a good screamer."

"I don't. Not when I'm the one slicing and dicing."

"You are good, you know." A small smile played on her lips.

"I know." His eyes narrowed.

"Don't even think about it," she said, "anything happens to me and you're a dead man.

"You know I wouldn't touch a hair on your head."

"Yeah," she said. "Not one hair."

They sat in silence for a while. He finally spoke. "God. Sometimes I truly hate you."

"Boo hoo. If it weren't for my me, you wouldn't even have a job." She snickered. "Hell, if it weren't for me, you wouldn't even be alive."

"Thanks for reminding me."

"You owe me. You owe me big."

He closed his eyes and leaned back in the chair. "After tonight, I like to think my debt is nearly paid."

"In your dreams. You're mine. I own you. Forever."

"Thanks for reminding me. Again."

"Besides, I got you the best cover you've ever had," she sniffed.

"Presumably."

Her eyes shot towards his. "Boo hoo," she whispered.

"You know I hate it here."

"Boo hoo."

"I wish you'd quit saying that."

"Boo hoo."

———

Dr. Troy Tonn's receptionist was the first person to notice his absence. She called his home. No answer. She called his cell phone. Nothing. Then she called Officer Drake Mallard.

"How long has he been gone?"

"I don't know," she answered, "he didn't show up for work today. That's very unlike him. Plus, the animals don't appear to have been fed in a while."

Mallard pondered a moment. "Well, we generally wait until they're missing 48 hours before we can do much."

"But," said the receptionist, "I know he would have fed the animals. Plus, I can't help but think something is wrong. He's never missed work before. Ever. He's not at home. He won't answer his cell. Can't you do something?"

Mallard sighed. "If this is that out of character for him, I can check into it."

"Thanks," she said, "please find him."

———

Ashley opened her eyes, ready to begin another long day at the office. She turned to her side and paused. She gingerly rolled to the other side.

No pain. Well, at least not a lot of it.

She carefully lifted her shirt. The large scar still grinned at her, but the little draining holes seemed to have dried some. She wiggled. Then she wiggled some more. The third time she shimmied, she felt a few twinges, but they felt manageable.

A grin spread across her face. She rolled to her right and slid out of bed.

She briefly pondered the silver object Ned showed her the previous night. She considered doing an Internet image search, but wasn't sure it would be wise, considering the strangeness of the whole situation.

"I'll check it out at the public library."

"I'll go with you," Ned had replied, "But I think we should do it in Crossfield. Anonymously."

"Good idea."

She rested her head on the pillow. A slow smile spread across her lips as she listened to Ned clink around in the kitchen. "Almost ready to eat?" he called.

"You know it."

She performed her morning duties with nary a grimace. "This is gonna be a good day." She paused. "Nah, it's gonna be a great day."

As she headed out the door, she grabbed a few pain pills. Just in case.

———

Maisy Mills stopped by the bank on her way to work. Her little website project had experienced a particularly profitable few days. "I love you, Ms Muffbottom," she whispered. "If this keeps up, I'll have to find a few more banks so nobody will suspect anything."

She whizzed through the drive through and was a block from the office when she saw it. It never would have caught her eye except she was specially trained to notice the unusual. See the unseen. Act on the ordinary.

The dark sedan blended into the scenery in an overtly normal way. She discreetly slowed down. As she passed it, she examined the driver while keeping her face stock still, gazing straight ahead. She gasped.

———

Ashley and Ned were the last people to arrive at the office.

"You two driving together now," Bart barked as they entered.

"Yup."

"Good for you," said Maisy.

Dick sat sullen, black rings hung beneath his eyelids.

"So," said Bart, "now that you're here, I can get started." The phone rang. "Goddammit." He grasped it with his doughy hand and lifted it to his ear. "What." He listened a few moments, then said, "Great. Thanks." He breathed deep, seemingly gathering his thoughts.

"Well," he said, "we have a problem." His eagle eyes scanned the little group of employees. "Kaufman's dead. Cops have no suspects. Their investigation is going nowhere. CSI folks haven't found anything interesting." His lips tightened. "And just now I hear Dr. Tonn is missing. Folks can't even find his pickup. Either he's skipped town, unlikely... or he's dead."

"Or," said Ashley, "Maybe he just went on a vacation."

"Or his phone broke," said Maisy.

"Skipped work,' Dick drawled.

"Could actually be any number of things," said Ned.

"Good," said Bart. "Investigate it. Write me a great story. Help me scoop that damned Gazette."

He turned to Dick. "I need to talk to you." Dick nodded. "The rest of you," he said, "Get moving. Give me something fantastic."

Chapter Seventeen

MYSTERY DEEPENS

Sex becomes you," said Maisy.

Ashley's cheeks reddened. "Who said anything about sex?"

"Your cheeks. Your hair. Heck, you even move different." She added, "Good God, woman. You're damn near glowing."

"Aerobics," said Ashley. "I've been exercising."

"Yeah. Is that what they're calling it now?" A sly grin spread across her cheeks.

Maisy leaned back into her chair and pondered her morning. The juxtaposition between the awesomely huge checks her website was generating (and all the pleasures copious cash could provide) and the cold reality of Kaufman's gory death nearly took her breath away. Now Tonn was on the list of possible unpleasant topics. Two deaths in one small town in a short period of time? Both former friends and colleagues. This could get bad. She made a mental note to explore her options.

Then she pondered the sedan. "It couldn't have been him," she thought. "What would he be doing here?"

But it looked like him. Perhaps he caught wind of Kaufman.

She felt like her skills had dulled these past few years. "Damn comfort," she thought, "made me soft."

Then she wondered if her web activities had triggered their exposure. "But I was careful. I wore tons of makeup. Softened my face." She focused on her situation. "Plus, I never figured anyone would look that close at my face. But I could have been wrong."

She glanced out the window, hoping to see the sedan again.

Just thinking about the possibility made her skin erupt in goose bumps. "The hottest... and most dangerous... man alive," she murmured.

Memories flooded her mind as she pondered his face, his hands, his embrace. She sighed as she imagined his touch. Her back involuntarily arched as she recalled his body atop hers. Butterflies erupted in her belly when she felt his lips nibble her neck.

"I'm positive it was him. But what could he be doing in Crossroads? Did he see me?" She leaned back in her chair. "He promised to keep an eye on me. He could be an ally. But that was years ago."

But people like him were notorious for making promises. Sadly, they were notorious for breaking them, too. Maisy's face bent into a small grimace.

She felt an uncontrollable urge to find him. Through all this, she wanted a shred of normalcy, an unwritten promise that everything would turn out. A slow smile spread across her face as she pondered hopping in that car and launching into an... interrogation. Then she smiled. "God... damn," she whispered.

"Did you say something," said Ashley.

"Just talking to myself." Then Maisy chuckled.

She lowered her eyes and tried to concentrate on work. She couldn't do it. It had been too long since she saw him. But if he were actually here, why? If he were here for Kaufman, then things were far worse than she hoped. Besides, perhaps she imagined the whole thing. After all, that plain sedan could have belonged to anybody. There were tons of exotic, gorgeous, former lover-looking men perched all over town. She decided to dismiss the supposed sighting. "With all the killing going on, I must have triggered memories."

She sighed.

"It sure would be nice to see him." She grinned. She shivered recalling his tongue on her skin. She almost groaned thinking about his body pressed against hers.

"Good God." A voice interrupted her thoughts. "You planning on staring at your desk all day?"

She turned. Bart scowled. She smiled.

"Sorry."

———

Jim's mouth dropped. "That looked a lot like Maisy,"

"Dunno," replied McNally, "I wasn't watching that close."

Jim studied him a moment. "Ha. You not watching close? That's a first." Then he added, "When's the last time you slept... I mean really slept?"

"Dunno."

"You're losing your edge."

"You think?"

"Yup. In fact, right now you don't appear to have an edge."

McNally sighed. "It's not every day you get to watch what we saw last night."

"Agreed. But you've seen it before. Hell, you've done it."

"It's been a while. Plus, I've changed." He smiled. "I've got Jennifer waiting for me." He pressed his head into the vehicle's head rest. "And it's not every day you get to realize... after all this time.. how easily that could be you."

"Which one? The killer or the kill-ee?"

"Either." McNally shook his head. "I don't understand what's going on. I know the RNF membership list was leaked. I totally get that. But what I don't understand," his eyes narrowed, "is why eliminate potential competition now? It's been a long time. The targeted individuals were in deep cover. They weren't coming out. They posed no threat to anybody." He turned to Jim. "Why?"

"I don't know." Jim closed his eyes against the sunbeams

streaming into the vehicle. "All I know is that we both need rest." He added, "I suggest we head to the motel and get some shut eye." McNally's lips tightened. "You're my best friend," he whispered, "I don't want to see you making any stupid mistakes."

McNally sighed before he said, "You're probably right." Then he added, "I miss the days when we had entire teams to monitor situations like this."

"Those were the days, my friend," said Jim.

"The best of times, the worst of times." McNally threw the sedan in gear and rolled away from the curb.

From within the newspaper office, two sets of eyes watched the vehicle drive past.

———

"What did you think of the meeting this morning?" The intrepid reporter and her fearless photographer bounced down the road in his pickup.

"Weird."

"Everything about this entire situation is weird," said Ashley.

Ned smiled. "Not really. I'll forever feel grateful that Alex Kaufman died. Because of him, I get a crash course in working close with you." He added, "And you're not weird."

"That's gruesome. He didn't die. He was murdered." She smiled. "Plus, I'm as weird as they come."

"It's the truth." Ned flashed a bright smile her way. "And if you're weird, I'm all over ya."

"You're funny." She paused. "Plus, you're morbid. Just saying..." Ashley paused a few moments and said, "You didn't tell Bart about that silver thing."

"Nope."

"Why not?"

Ned pursed his lips. "I'm not really sure." A few more miles passed before he said, "There's something hinky going on."

"Hinky?" Ashley chuckled. "You making up words now?"

"I'm dead serious," Ned said. "Something stinks and I'm not sure what it is."

"You realize, you should probably give that thing to Officer Mallard."

"Not in a million years."

"Why not?"

"Not sure. It's just that something stinks." Ned shrugged.

"Perhaps," Ashley said, "after we find out what it is, we can decide what to do with it."

"Yeah, but when I was fiddling with it, there's this spot on it. When I press it, it vibrates. So weird."

"Agreed." She added, "Plus, you showed me that last night."

"But there's more," he said, "I found a compartment... it looks like a USB thing inside. The whole thing perplexes me."

"Huh."

"I think I should press the button again."

"Nope. Don't. You don't know what that thing's doing. We should leave it alone. Don't take it out of its hiding place until we know what it is."

"What could be the harm?"

"Seriously," said Ashley, "Haven't you watched any spy movies? It could be a homing signal. It could be a bomb trigger. It could be..."

"... a sex toy." Ned interrupted.

Ashley laughed. "Highly doubtful."

"Never know. I'd be willing to give it a whirl."

"Count me out..."

———

Officer Drake Mallard leaned over the report, poring over its contents. Pictures spread across his desk while a magnifying glass glistened in his grasp.

"Find anything, Sherlock?"

He ignored the question, instead focusing on his investigation.

"I thought you were supposed to move on. Weren't you kicked off that case?"

Mallard continued his task, occasionally grabbing a post-it note and affixing it to the photograph. Finally, he grabbed a pile and carried them to his superior's office. He tapped on the door.

"What 'cha want?"

He opened the door. "I have a fast question."

"What?"

"About this." He pointed to a photo.

An annoyed sigh escaped his lips. "I thought you were off this case."

"Yeah," agreed Mallard, "but something's been bugging me."

"Seriously? You're still nosing around?"

"Yes," said Mallard, "but on my own time."

The other officer slightly rolled his eyes. "OK then," he said, "what have you supposedly found that some of the best forensics experts in Minnesota missed?"

"Well," he pointed to the picture, "I patrol Crossroads. I know the people. I'm aware of their vehicle situation."

"Vehicle situation?"

"Small town," said Mallard, "I keep track of the vehicles so I know who's who. When I see 'em on the street, I pretty much know who I'm dealing with."

"OK..."

"Anyway," he said pointing to an exact spot on the photo, "I saw this grey sedan. I don't know who it belongs to."

"Big deal."

"Yeah, but it's in more than one photo." He pulled out more pictures and highlighted the vehicle in each one.

"And this is significant... how?"

"Well," said Mallard, "I don't recognize it. It showed up shortly after the big murder. Now it's hanging out there."

"Your point?"

"My point is that it's worth a look." He paused. Then he repeated, "Definitely worth a look." He added, "I mean, we've got nothing to help solve this case. Big fat zero. Nothing to launch a proper investigation." No response. He clarified. "If this is a lead... or can lead to a lead, don't you think it's worth a tiny peek? I mean seriously. Grey car. Two occupants. Hanging around town after a big murder."

"Got anything else to do?"

"Not right now. Just patrolling."

His superior sat a moment. "Fine. Don't let it interfere with any of your other duties. And do this by the book. Don't go abusing anyone's civil rights."

A wide grin spread across Mallard's face. "Great. I'll get on it."

"Nothing to get on. Just poke around. That's it."

"Definitely."

Chapter Eighteen

ARTIFACT

The text arrived without any warning. Ashley didn't respond.

"Did you hear something," Ned said.

"Yeah," Ashley said, "I thought it was my imagination."

"Someone got a text."

"Seriously? Of course someone got a text."

"Yeah. Wasn't me. Not my tone. Check your phone. Could be Bart."

"I rarely get texts. Couldn't be me."

"Check anyway."

Ashley wrinkled her nose as she dug in her computer case. "This is a lot of work for nothing," she grumbled. She pulled out the device and located the correct app. "I'll be damned," she said, "It was me.

She read the message aloud:

I need to talk to you.

She scrunched her eyebrows. "Huh."

Ned slowed the vehicle and grasped her phone. "Who's it from?"

"No idea."

He turned it over in his hand. "Is this your work phone or

personal one?"

Ashley asked, "We have work phones?"

Ned smiled. "Nope."

"That would answer that, eh?"

Ned breathed deep, words forming in his mind. "Who has your number?" Ned handed the phone back to Ashley.

"I don't think anybody does... except you and my oncologist." She added, "Bart may have it."

His eyebrows rose. "That's weird. Look at the number."

Ashley studied the digits. "Not from you."

"Obviously."

"Not from Bart's number either."

A thick blanket of silence filled the pickup. Ned said, "Oncologist?"

"Dunno."

"Seriously?" Ned glanced at her, eyes filling with worry.

Ashley's heart sank. "Do you suppose it's bad news?"

Ned's heart pounded in his ears, but he maintained a mask of nonchalantment. "Probably not. I don't think oncology offices send out texts."

"That would be weird, wouldn't it."

"Is that the medical center number?"

Ashley dug through her contact list. Relief flooded her mind as she announced, "Nope."

"That's good," said Ned. "How 'bout you text them back?"

"What if it's a spammer? I don't want them to know my number's active."

"Why not?" said Ned. "You could write one of those 'look how I screwed over a spammer' pieces for the Herald. I've read about it on the Internet. Bart would love that. We could join the twentieth century..."

"Nah. Not worth it. I've got plenty on my plate," said Ashley. "If they know my number's active, I could get even more spam."

"I suppose."

Ashley listened to the tires thump over asphalt cracks for a few miles. Then Ned said, "Local number?"

"Looks like it."

"Huh. Probably not a spammer then."

They sat in silence for a few moments before Ashley said, "I think I'll ignore it."

Her phone chirped again. Another message.

I really need to talk to you. It's important.

Ashley stared at the screen. Ned peeked and read. "Weird."

"Agreed."

"How 'bout a reverse phone number search?"

"Not worth the money."

"Newspaper has an account. We get a ton of anonymous tips. They generally come from the same people, but Bart likes to know who called it in."

Ashley's eyebrows rose. "Seriously?"

"Yeah. I've got the login information in my desk."

Ashley sat back in her seat. "Perhaps we'll do that when we get back from checking in with Officer Mallard."

Her phone chirped again.

You better not be ignoring me.

"Yeah," said Ned, "We'll have to definitely check out this one."

———

"I'm leaving early today."

"Hell to the no." Bart Lundquist turned his hefty body towards the door. "You have too much to do. Plus, I feel like you're putting in fewer hours every week. We need you here. I need you."

Maisy smiled. "You know I love the newspaper. You know I'll never quit. But I need the afternoon off."

"Nope. You gotta finish the ads."

"Done."

"You're not that fast. Bring 'em in here. I wanna see what you came up with."

Maisy left the room. She returned, carrying a small stack of space ads.

"This is it," asked Bart.

"Every one of 'em."

A small growl left Bart's throat. "Dick," he barked, "Get in here. Now." He mumbled under his breath, "Lazy ass. He couldn't sell space heaters to eskimos."

Maisy stood silent for a moment before she said, "Dick left for the day." She added, "That whole eskimo thing could be construed as racist."

"Fuck it. Fuck political correctness."

Maisy laughed. "As you wish."

Bart fingered through the papers a few minutes. Then he said, "If Dick's gone and our reporting team is on the road, who's in the outer office?"

She shrugged. "Just me, I guess."

"Then you definitely can't leave."

"Come on. It's dead out there. I've gotta go. I'm sicker than a dog. Period. Cramps. You wouldn't believe..."

Bart interrupted her. "You're not getting outta here. And I'm not falling for that period shit again. You and your lady problems are gonna have to endure."

Maisy laughed. "Yeah, but I really need the afternoon off."

Bart paused. "Where's Dick?"

"Dunno."

"He didn't tell you where he was going? Who he was gonna hit up for ads?"

"Nope and I don't know."

Tense silence stretched across Bart's face. "He sure as hell better be pounding the pavement digging up new accounts."

"Dunno."

"Who does?"

"Dick?"

"Fucker."

Silence descended upon the room. Finally Bart said, "Fine. Go.

I'll be here. But you sure as fuck better buy yourself some pain pills. Next period, you're mine. All afternoon. I got deadlines, you know."

Maisy nodded. "I appreciate this."

"You owe me."

"Always."

She exited the room and grasped her purse. She slipped on her winter gear and dashed out of the office just as the phone rang. She pretended not to hear it.

"David McNally, if you're in this town, you're mine," she whispered as she unlocked her vehicle.

————

He hated these meetings. Clandestine, mysterious, top secret... you'd think he wouldn't have to sit in a freezing car waiting for the phone to ring.

But there he sat.

He poked a few cashews into his mouth. "I should probably lose weight," he thought. "Perhaps I'll start a diet. Tomorrow."

He turned up the heater and turned down the radio. "Fuckers better be on time," he mumbled, "They think they own me, but my time's important."

Then his phone rang. He hated that a large knot instantly formed in his belly the minute the chirp sliced through the silence. He breathed deep. On the second ring, he picked it up and said, "The best broadway show ever is the Book of Mormon."

"The best movie ever is Spaceballs." A pregnant pause ensued while he listened to someone typing on the other side of the line. Finally the person spoke. "Proceed with report."

He breathed deep and said, "Kaufman exterminated. Tonn... exterminated and disseminated."

"Any difficulties?"

"None."

"That's impossible."

"Nope. Everything went according to plan." He tried to sound casual, but something in the tone of the other person tightened the knot in his belly.

"It went perfect, then?"

"Yes." He quickly added, "As perfect as possible."

"Impossible."

A rock of dread joined the knot in his stomach. "I don't know what you mean."

"Is there any evidence to tie us to these exterminations?"

"No."

"I'm assuming any residual evidence has been dealt with?"

"Yes."

"Even the missing Labrador from extermination number one?"

Long pause. "It hasn't been found."

"It wasn't with Tonn?"

"No."

Longer pause. "We were told the animal was with Tonn."

He didn't know what to say, but knew he needed to choke out some kind of reply. He finally said, "I guess your information was incorrect."

"Our information is never incorrect," snapped the other voice. He kept silent as the voice continued, "And the artifact? I'm assuming it's in your possession?"

"Uh... I assumed it wasn't in this vicinity."

"You'd be incorrect. Our best intelligence says it was located at or near Kaufman's place of residence."

"Well, I don't have it. I'm not convinced your intelligence is correct."

Extremely long pause. "We are displeased with your performance. Also, your attitude on this call is being noted."

He jumped into the conversation. "Apologies. Deepest apologies. I amend my report. Immediately." He added, "Your intelligence is correct. I am incorrect. I will complete my mission with my highest quality work."

"You do that." A muffled conversation leaked over the line. He listened intently, but couldn't make out many words. Then the voice said, "You have one more chance to complete this assignment satisfactorily. Your 'best' work thus far has been ranked as dismal. Your work quality must increase substantially or we will no longer require your services."

Now the knot in his belly twisted in circles. He tried to sound confident as he said, "Thank you for your flexibility."

"We do not appreciate sloppy work. We also do not appreciate agents who do not take responsibility for their assignments."

He didn't answer.

"Now... I ask again. Is the artifact in your possession?"

"It is not."

"When will you have it?"

"As soon as I locate it."

"You must locate it. Soon."

"I plan to."

"Did you know we received two signals from it in the last 24 hours?"

"I didn't know that. I am not in possession of a receiver capable of that task. Do you have the origin location of said signal?"

"We're trying to pin point it. It was faint."

"Do you have the capabilities to monitor internet search activities concerning this topic? I do not."

"We do and are."

He said, "I will do what I can to locate it. I will appreciate any assistance you can offer considering I'm flying blind. I don't have access to the equipment needed to complete this task."

"Our engineers will install software on your computer by the end of today." The voice added, "It is your responsibility, and your responsibility alone, to locate that Labrador and eliminate it. Then retrieve the device."

"Understood."

"You must also understand that failure to complete either of these tasks will result in very dire consequences."

"Understood."

"Please proceed with your tasks and understand they should have been completed a number of days ago."

"Understood."

He listened to the phone click, then turned off his own device. He sighed as he verified that his phone had disconnected from the call. Then he pounded the steering wheel of his vehicle. "Fuck, fuck, fuck, fuck, fuck!" he screamed.

———

Ashley and Ned arrived at the office. "Too bad Mallard wasn't at the cop shop," said Ned.

"Yeah, but we'll get his statement soon," said Ashley. "They said he was patrolling Crossroads." She added, "I'm sure we'll run into him somewhere along the line."

"In the mean time," said Ned, "You can find out who's texting you." He opened a black book and paged through it. He glanced at Ashley who was studying his actions with a bemused expression on her face. "Password book," he said grinning, "I have a mind like a sieve."

"You still use one of those," Ash laughed, "I thought computers remembered passwords."

"They do," said Ned, "but if you ever need a new one, sometimes passwords don't transfer. This old school method keeps you connected."

Ashley shrugged, "I suppose you're right."

"Damn straight. Get a password book. Stat." Ned laughed as he handed Ashley the user name for the reverse phone directory account.

She was just typing in the URL when Bart entered the room.

"What did you find out?"

"Mallard wasn't there," said Ned.

"Why not call him? Mileage is killing me."

"It's easier to say 'no' over the phone," said Ashley, "Plus, sometimes I can get leads for other stories while chatting with other cops."

"You're getting info on Tonn, right?"

"So far. From what the secretary said, no report's been filed. He's not technically missing until early next week. We were hoping to talk to Mallard to get some scuttlebutt."

"I suppose..." said Bart, "but scuttlebutt isn't exactly what we should publish. Also, what about..." He never finished his sentence. Instead his face dissolved into an unpleasant grimace. "We'll I'll be fucked with a fork," he mumbled.

Ashley and Ned turned to see what could elicit such a response. Ned chuckled. "Huh," he said, "I'll be damned."

Ashley didn't understand the reactions. All she could see was a tall man slip towards the office. He wore a long, brown coat, shiny shoes, and a black beret. If he didn't look so angry, he'd actually appear somewhat handsome. He opened the door with clear annoyance and tramped into the office.

"I need to speak with Ashley Stone," he bellowed. "Now."

All eyes turned to Ashley. Her eyebrows flew upward. "I'm... er... Ashley." She extended her hand. The man glared at her.

"You ignored me. That's unacceptable." He added, "You are a public servant. You need to reply to your messages." His eyes bore into her. "Do you know who I am?"

Ashley turned to Ned who clearly bit his cheek. However, the smile he tried to suppress leaked through his efforts. "Ashley," he said, clearing his throat, "I'd like you to meet our fine Mayor, Trent Shaw." He breathed deep and said, "Trent, I'm pretty sure you already know Ms Stone."

Shaw wrinkled his nose as he glared at Ashley. "I don't appreciate being ignored."

"I'm sorry," Ashley stammered, "I don't know when I ignored you."

"My texts," he blurted, "You ignored my texts. Three of them."

"I didn't know..." she said.

"Everyone around here knows my number. Everyone answers me. And they do so promptly."

"I recently moved here. I apologize I didn't know who you were."

"It's your responsibility," he turned to Bart, "to make sure your employees know who I am, what I do, and how to respond to my requests."

"Been a little busy, Trent."

"No excuses." Shaw turned back to Ashley. "Allow me to introduce myself," he said. "I am Trent Shaw. My parents founded this town in 1869. There has never, ever been a non-Shaw in the Mayoral chair."

He waited for Ashley to react, but she didn't. He continued, "Me and my family honor the flag, our God, and our community. I take my position of authority very seriously and I need you to take your position in this community seriously as well. To that end, I need you to stop writing about these murders. Now. This minute. No more reporting." As an aside, he added, "I also feel the need to let you know that we will share our evening meal tonight and will be married by this time next year."

Chapter Nineteen

CONVERSATING

Drake Mallard scoured Crossroads from one end to the other... then back again. No grey sedan.

"What the fuck," he murmured. "That fucker was here all last week. Why disappear now?"

He was cruising down the main drag when the call came in: "Mallard. Start a file on Dr. Troy Tonn. His secretary reports him missing."

He rolled his eyes. "I already told the bitch I'd check into it." He spoke aloud. "How long?"

"He didn't show up for work this morning."

"So, it's not an official missing person case."

"Nope. Not yet. A favor."

Mallard smiled realizing he could earn some brownie points for doing something he already planned on doing. "Glad to be of service. I'll poke around and see what I can find."

With renewed enthusiasm, Mallard drove up and down the streets of Crossroads. He paused by Tonn's house. Then he parked by the curb. He got out and strode up the driveway. He peeked in the garage. Empty. He pressed his face near the ground floor windows. Nothing unusual.

He groaned, hating what he'd have to do next. "I despise making nice..."

————

Ashley's eyes shot to Ned. Ned's face was now a mask of suppressed laughter. Trent Shaw continued.

"From the top of the Cascade Mountains, to the mouth of the Mississippi, liberty will roll through the groins of every man, woman, and child like the thunder of freedom will reverberate in the souls of every true American. It is my duty as the divinely appointed Mayor of this fair city of Crossroads to aptly cooperate and control the content of this newspaper to keep those who would shroud the beauty of this tiny metropolis and hinder the advancement of the free enterprise system. It is also my duty to..."

"Hey quack-boy," Bart interrupted, "Get to the point."

Shaw squinted his eyes. "I was doing that."

"Not really," Ned said, "you were rambling." Trent's eyes shot daggers towards Ned. He added, "Just a little rambling, though."

"I was preparing the stage for my big announcement. Now you've ruined my intro."

"Get to the point, Shaw."

"I'll get to my point when I'm good and ready."

Ashley stood slack jawed watching this vignette unfold. Despite her many years working as a reporter, she had never encountered anyone quite like Trent Shaw before. The fact he was the Crossroad's mayor made her a bit uncomfortable. She tried to ignore his marriage announcement, assuming she'd interpreted his sentence incorrectly.

Shaw continued, "As far as the east is from the west, so my love for our fair city grows. And it is in this vein that I must request the delightful staff at this liberal leaning, lame stream media publication, refrain from attacking my administration at every turn. I had high hopes that this new reporter would bring a fair and balanced perspective to the news, but I have come to believe her fear mongering headlines will do nothing to support and uphold the fine qualities within our city that I have worked long and hard to maintain."

Then Shaw stopped and gazed at Ashley. "I know you're a good woman. I have thoroughly checked you out. You have a good resume. I come to personally request that you strive from this day forward to cease tearing down the reputation of Crossroads and instead focus on stories that will show readers the true beauty of our fair city."

"If you're done with your word salad," said Bart, "you can leave. We've got work to do."

"And will the murderous stories continue?" countered Shaw. "Do you realize that with every negative story you run, you effectively murder tourism within our beautiful city?" He turned to Ashley. "I don't think you want to murder Crossroads, do you?"

Ashley breathed deep, realizing all eyes were on her. "Actually, Mr. Shaw..."

"Trent."

"... I cover news. The murders are news. If I don't cover the happenings in town, the newspaper would become a community joke..."

"Joke," said Shaw, "A joke? You're already a joke. A laughable, certifiable joke. Nobody takes what this rag has to say with a modicum of seriousness." He added, "Everyone knows the Gazette has far more journalistic integrity than this puny Herald. I just came here to help you redeem some dignity." His eyes shot to Bart, "But I see I'm too late."

"All right," Bart jumped in, "You said your piece. Now get out."

Shaw turned. "This is a public place of business. I'm the mayor. I have every right to be here."

"Out. Now."

"I hope this won't further slant your coverage of my administration."

"Nope," said Bart, "We write 'em like we see 'em."

"With an evil liberal slant," said Shaw.

"I try to keep my personal politics out of this job and if you want to claim otherwise," Bart stepped forward, eyes boring into Shaw, "that's your right as an American."

Shaw didn't reply. Instead he turned to Ashley. "I'll pick you up at 6:00."

"Uh," said Ashley, "I'm kinda busy tonight."

"Too busy for the most important person in town?"

She nodded. "I guess so."

"Fine. We'll reschedule." He marched towards the door and paused, hand on the knob. "If you want my administration's support, you'll at least tone down your coverage."

"I'll take that under advisement."

"You do that."

Shaw left with a flourish.

"Guess you've got his phone number now," said Ned with a sly smile.

"Guess you're right."

Ned's grin widened. "I had no idea you two were an item. Wish you told me you were getting married next year."

"Yup. Wish I'd told myself that, too."

Ned laughed aloud.

———

McNally's eyes flew open when he heard tapping. He'd slept too soundly. He inhaled a silent breath and focused his attention. Did he imagine the sound? Was it part of a dream? He focused his exhausted mind on the present moment.

It happened again: three quiet taps.

Every muscle in his body tensed. His eyes darted to Jim who laid in the next bed completely unconscious.

He silently slid to his feet and crept to the window. He glanced at Jim, still laid splayed out in the other bed. He gently nudged the heavy curtain aside and peeked outside.

A beautiful blond stood directly in front of the door. She waved at the little crack he created between the window and curtain. He stiffened. Then his eyes narrowed.

"Holy fuck," he whispered. He released the curtain and stepped towards his partner. "Jimbo," he whispered, "we got something going on."

Jim squinted his eyes. "Holy crap," he moaned, "don't you ever sleep."

"Quiet," he whispered, "we've got someone just outside the door." He added, "This one's gonna be weird."

"Seriously?"

"Yup."

He grabbed his pistol and tucked it into the back of his pants. Taking his clue from McNally, Jim grabbed his weapon and slid it under the sheets. "Wait 'till you see this." He crept to the door and peeked through the peep hole. He grinned as he gingerly opened it. His hand grasped the pistol tucked behind him. A tall, slim, blond stepped into the dark room. "As I live and breathe," said McNally.

Jim sat up straight. "Holy shit."

McNally stood stock still, as did Maisy. "What name do you go by these days?"

"Maisy. Maisy Mills."

"Holy shit."

The three of them stood stock still, examining each other. Finally McNally spoke. "How did you find us?"

Jim added, "And how did you know we were here?"

"Seriously," Maisy said, "You set up a stake out right outside my office and you don't expect me to notice?" She grinned at the two men. "Plus the grey sedan. Seriously? You think I wouldn't notice the most ordinary car in the world... right outside my window?" She added, "Plus your so-called disguises could never suppress your gorgeousness."

Jim laughed.

McNally's eyes narrowed. "So, you work at that place?"

"Yup."

"When I saw you enter the building, I wondered if that was you," said Jim.

"I wondered the same thing," said McNally.

"Yeah. But why the surveillance?"

The men didn't answer. "Who you working for these days?" asked Jim.

"Nobody. I gave up that life when the RNF blew up. I've gone legit... mostly legit."

McNally's face tightened a bit. "Care to elaborate?"

"I'm not with any organization, if that's what you mean."

"And?"

"I work for the local newspaper. Graphic design and reception."

"Doesn't sound like you."

"It's not. But it's legit."

"And the non-legit stuff?"

"I have a little Internet business."

"Doing what?"

"Soft porn."

Jim threw his head back and laughed. "Seriously?"

"Look me up. Subscribe. Pay me. Enjoy." A small smile spread across her lips. "I go by Maisy Muffbottom."

McNally shot Jim a look. Jim laughed. "You never fail to surprise."

"But your surprises tend to be deadly," McNally said, "Why you here?"

"I saw you. I work at the Herald. Thought I'd see what you're doing in town. My guess? Those murders. They're professional."

"Nailed it."

"Know anything?"

"Nothing we can share with you."

"Why monitor the newspaper?"

"That's private."

"Ah," she said, "still have the 'trust no one' motto, eh?"

"It's kept us alive so far," said Jim.

"Well, you might benefit from a little inside information."

"We might."

"What 'cha got? I'll show you mine if you show me yours..."

———

Ashley sat alone in the office typing her latest information into a somewhat coherent news story.

"I wish I had more to go on," she thought. "This is the weirdest story. At least in larger cities, new news can bury dead stories. In this small community, I have to squeeze blood out of a dry turnip because there's no new news to replace it."

She sighed, trying to mentally construct another angle to report the Kaufman murder.

Then the door jingled. She looked up and the silhouette of Officer Drake Mallard stood in the doorway. Ashley's eyes darted to her screen. With a sweep of her fingers, she completed her sentence, hit "save" and snapped down Betsy's cover. "Officer Mallard," she said, "It's a pleasure. What can I do for you?"

The cop gazed at her a moment before he said, "I'd like to speak with you."

"Me?"

"Yup."

"Sure," Ashley gestured towards a chair in front of her desk. "Take a seat."

He stepped towards her, paused, looking almost pained, then did as she asked. He sat a moment before he said, "I'm hearing rumors about Troy Tonn. You hear anything?"

"I have," she answered.

"What have you heard?"

A smile spread across her face. "I'll share what I know. But you'll have to share what you know."

"No can do. Investigations are private."

"Even off the record?"

"Do you know the meaning of those words?"

Ashley scowled. "Of course I do."

"I haven't had much luck with sharing private information with the press."

"You've never worked with me before." She studied his face, wondering if it would be worth the effort to charm him. She said, "I'm just hoping to get some kind of direction for my story." She paused. He didn't respond. "It's frustrating. Nobody saw anything. No clues to speak of. It looks like the people who killed Mr. Kaufman will go off scott free. Now, Dr. Tonn is missing."

"That's the looks of it."

She studied Mallard. He didn't look as intimidating close up. She decided to engage a little charm to see where that would lead.

"So," she said, "I met our fair mayor."

A smile spread across Mallard's lips. "Ya don't say."

"Yup."

"And? I assume you got a point to this little story."

Ashley relaxed into her chair. Her abdomen tweaked a complaint. She winced, but tried to disguise it. "No real point," she said, "I just found him interesting."

"Interesting? How so?"

"Jeepers," she said, "You're not a great conversationalist."

"I'm not here for conversating."

Ashley laughed. "However, you're quite skilled at imaginary words." Mallard chuckled, but his eyes appeared somewhat perplexed. Ashley pulled the conversation back on track. "It's just that I found his request rather... discomforting."

"Telling you how to do your job, is he?" Mallard's dark eyes drilled into Ashley's.

She nodded.

Mallard said, "He's stark raving mad, if you ask me."

"He was an interesting one, that's for sure." He raised his hands over his head and stretched. His dark Freddy Mercury physique flexed in a most sensual way. It was at that point Ashley realized Drake Mallard could be a rather handsome man if you looked beyond his macho bravado.

"Ain't nobody but his family been mayor of this town for as long as anyone can remember," said Mallard. "The election's generally fixed in their favor or they outright cheat." Ashley's eyes widened. He continued, "What they want, they get... generally speaking. And from what I hear, they want the paper."

"Seriously?"

Mallard's eyes narrowed. "I got that tidbit of information on good authority. But, Lundquist won't sell." Ashley paled thinking about working for Trent Shaw. Bart may be rough around the edges, but he seemed rather sane in comparison to Shaw. She breathed deep.

"We still chatting off the record?" asked Mallard.

"Sure,' said Ashley. We won't be on any record until I turn on my recorder." Mallard scanned her desk as she spoke. His lazy eyes rose to hers and stopped for a disconcerting amount of time. Finally, he spoke.

"So... I seen your little Smart at the hospital." Ashley's face reddened. "Sources tell me they saw you in the cancer center." He shoved the tip of his pinkie into his ear and twisted it a few times. After he removed it, he examined the tip. "Damn ear wax," he mumbled. Then his eyes rose to hers again.

"I believe that's private information," Ashley said.

Mallard chuckled. "If you want private, don't drive around in a god damned clown car." Ashley felt her ears warm. He added, "Don't worry about it. We're just chattin' off the record." His lips stretched into a faux grin. A rather long, silent pause ensued. Finally, Ashley spoke.

"We got a call from Tonn's secretary. He didn't show up for work."

"I got the same call."

"I feel bad for her."

"Yeah. Whatever."

"I hear she really gets attached to those animals. If something happened to Dr. Tonn, she'd be upset."

"Yup." Mallard appeared to tire of their conversation.

"She's also concerned for Dr. Tonn's new dog. She was hoping to locate it so she could make sure it was cared for."

"A dog? I didn't know he had a dog." Mallard's eyes brightened as he leaned forward.

"Yeah. A golden lab."

Mallard leaned back in his chair. "How long did he have this dog?"

"Not too long. I'm not sure how he wound up adopting it. She was sparse on details. I think she hoped we'll run a 'lost dog' piece on it."

"Interesting." He added, "Well, in the spirit of quid pro quo, I can tell you that a suspicious grey sedan has been spotted in town. It wasn't here before the murder, but it's sure as fuck here now. And with Tonn missing... I sure wouldn't mind speaking to the owners." He stared at Ashley in a very disconcerting way. "You'll let me know if you see it?" Ashley nodded. "This, of course, is off the record until further notice. Correct?"

Ashley nodded again. "Of course. But you gave me a new avenue to explore. I appreciate that."

"I have a bit of info I didn't know, too." Silence descended before he said, "Anything else you care to share?"

Ashley's heart skipped a beat as she thought of the silver key. It would be very easy to mention it now, but she still wasn't sure how far she could trust Officer Mallard. She said, "I can't think of anything off hand."

Mallard dug in his pocket and pulled out a card. "My personal number is on there. Call if you see or hear anything."

"I'll do that." Ashley flashed her sweetest smile. Mallard returned the favor. When he smiled, she was struck again by how disarmingly handsome he looked. Ashley's stomach flipped. The visceral reaction surprised her.

He stepped to the door, placed his hand on the knob, and turned. "Take care of yourself. Cancer's a bitch." He stepped outside and left Ashley red faced and flustered.

After he left, Ashley stood and stretched. Then she winced.

"Time for another pain pill," she mumbled. She hobbled into the bathroom, lifted her shirt, and surveyed the damage.

"Looks better," she thought. The dull pain radiating through her torso told a different story. She dropped two pills in her palm and tossed them in her mouth. She closed her eyes, wishing the relief would kick in faster.

"You're mine," a silent voice whispered in her ear. "Cancer always wins."

"Not this time," she breathed, "I have more to live for than I originally thought."

"Won't be long before the whole town knows."

"Doesn't matter," she mumbled in reply, "most won't care."

"Don't get too happy. I'm waiting for you to let down your guard, then I'll be back with a vengeance."

"Not a problem," she sighed, "Happiness is always an inch away with you around."

Chapter Twenty

DANGEROUS CONVERSATIONS

"So, you call yourself Maisy Muffbottom..."

"Maisy Mills."

"OK. Maisy. I'll just call you Maisy."

"Fine." She plopped into the uncomfortable hotel chair. She laced her fingers behind her head. She arched her back. "Go ahead. Frisk me. I don't have a gun. I have no weapons. No bombs, no triggers." McNally stepped forward and engaged in a quick pat down. "Good grief," Maisy complained.

"We need to be careful," he said, "I'm sure you understand."

Maisy replied, "We used to work together. I just came by to see what you're doing in Crossroads."

"We're in Crossfield."

Maisy narrowed her eyes. "Semantics. Seriously? You're treating me like the enemy? After all we've been through?"

McNally stepped away. His eyes narrowed. "Tell me what you know."

"Only if you promise you'll tell me what *you* know."

"We'll tell you what we can," said Jim. He swept his covers aside and rose from the bed. Stepping onto the dense carpet he stretched his arms over his head. "Ahhhh, nothing like a good sleep to make you feel like a new man," he said. Maisy's eyes widened as she studied his muscular, tight body. Wearing only tightie whities, his fully displayed form flexed with each movement.

"Ho-ly hell," she whispered, "You haven't lost a bit of your appeal."

Jim grinned. "Thanks." He grasped his jeans and slid them over his hard legs.

Maisy could barely speak as she imagined his large hands completely covering various parts of her body. "Got a girlfriend?" she gasped.

He raised his left hand to display a huge, gold band. "Yup. She's a school teacher."

"I never figured you'd settle down," she said. Her eyes nearly consumed him. "She's a lucky woman."

Jim smiled. "Thanks. Janet rocks."

"All right you two…" said McNally, "concentrate."

————

After Mallard left the office, Ashley sat alone pondering the events.

Drake seemed nice. But Ashley knew he needed something… perhaps a new lead. She wondered if she'd tipped her hand too much. At this point, she was glad she didn't spill any info on the mysterious silver key. Something about that thing felt dangerous.

But she didn't want an adversarial relationship with the local police. It paid to cooperate, or at least appear to do so.

"When did this become a contest to scoop the competition who isn't even competition," she mumbled. She stared at her notes. Her fingers tapped on the keyboard.

Everything felt wrong. She sat back and gently stretched her back, hoping the pain would melt away. She closed her eyes. She imagined the events of this murder as a puzzle, each piece fitting somewhere, but she didn't have enough information to construct anything coherent.

She pondered the key, imagining places it could fit. She pondered the crime scene. She thought about Alexander Kaufman and Troy Tonn. "How are you two connected..." she mumbled. Kaufman is dead. Troy is missing. She searched her mind, looking for any common link. Then she remembered Ned's friend. He appeared to have lived here long enough to connect a few of her dots. She grinned. "Perhaps I should talk to Ike Moe."

She tried to remember where he lived. "Ned can help with that," she thought.

Just then a burst of cold air hit her cheek. She opened her eyes in time to see Ned enter the office. Just a glimpse of his face made a broad smile spread across her face.

"Hey beautiful," he said, "I got us something to eat."

"Sounds great," she replied.

He set two bags on his desk and stepped towards her. He removed his mittens and tossed them aside. Something about his eyes made her belly twitter. He dropped his coat to the floor and stepped towards her. At that moment, she felt like the most desirable woman on the planet. Then he bent over and touched her face with his fingertips.

She closed her eyes as electricity buzzed from his skin into her cheek. She felt his warm breath brush her neck just before she felt his lips touch her jawline.

Then he nibbled her ear.

She was just turning her head to touch his lips with her's when he whispered, "How you feeling today?"

She paused. "What?"

"How you feeling today?" he repeated, thoroughly breaking the moment.

"Seriously?"

"Seriously."

Silence.

He pulled away slightly and said, "It's just that you look a little pale." Silence. "You OK?"

She sighed. "Yes. I'm OK."

"You don't hurt today?"

She said, "Of course I hurt. I always hurt. But it'll get better." She added, "Or so they say."

His eyes narrowed. "Did I say something wrong?"

"Of course not. You're perfect."

He chuckled. "I don't feel perfect."

Thick silence rested on them a moment. Then she said, "I wish you didn't know."

"Know what?"

"The big thing. The monster in the room."

He took a step back. His face looked thoughtful. "I'm not sure how to do this conversation."

"Me either."

He stepped to his desk and sat on the chair. "It's just that I care about you. I want to make sure you're OK."

"That's fine."

"But I feel kinda weird. Why wouldn't you want me to know?"

Ashley sighed. "I'm sorry. It's just that I'd rather not have had any of this happen. I wish you didn't know because I don't like being treated like a sick person."

"But you are sick."

"I know. But I just want to... for maybe just a little bit each day... be treated like everyone else."

Ned laughed. "You want to pretend you don't have cancer."

Ashley's eyes darted to him. "Don't say it out loud. I don't have cancer. Surgeon feels they got it all." Her face formed a wall of defensiveness. "Also, I'd appreciate if you wouldn't use the 'c' word in the office."

"I get that... kinda," said Ned, "But you still have to deal with the after effects of that tumor, right?"

"Yeah."

"And one of those after effects is the infection, the healing process, the newly designed innards?" She didn't reply so he continued, "If you recall, my sister is a nurse. I understand more about this than you may think."

"I know."

"I get that you're kind of in a weird middle place. You're a cancer patient, but don't have any tumors. You're not cured or in remission, but you're supposedly free of cancer... for now. It's not a great place, but it could be worse." He touched her knee. "I know you live in a grey area. And I'm fine with that. I just want the freedom to acknowledge all this and still love you."

Ashley's eyes flew to his. "You can't love me. If one stray cell in my bloodstream plants itself in my liver... boom... I'm stage four." She added, "There's no stage five."

Ned looked thoughtful for a moment. "You know, I've never lived my life afraid something could happen. I'm a 'live today' kinda guy. I think it's insanely unfair to not allow love in your life because something could happen somewhere along the line."

Ashley said, "I could counter that it's unfair for you to say you love someone who could wind up dying a pretty gruesome death."

"My point?" Ned said, "We don't know that will happen." His eye twinkled. "And if it gets bad, I'll drop you like a hot potato." He laughed. "I'll throw you out the door." That one made Ashley smile. "I'll chuck you to the curb like yesterday's garbage." Now Ashley laughed out loud.

"That's why I like hanging out with you," said Ashley. A tear streamed down her face. "You make all this seem less dire."

Ned leaned over and kissed her tear. "That's because it's not dire," he whispered, "at least not today. Not right now."

Another tear flowed down her cheek. "You scare the hell out of me."

"That's good," he said, "because sometimes you scare the hell out of me, too." He wrapped his arms around her.

"That's because this is a really scary place to be."

"Agreed."

A few more tears rolled down Ashley's cheek. Ned wiped each away with his thumb. Then he kissed her. He was stroking her hair with his palm when...

"What the fuck's going on now," boomed a voice.

Ashley looked up. Bart stood in the doorway.

"I love this woman," said Ned. Ashley's mouth dropped.

"Well fuck it in a bucket, that was fast," said Bart. "This better not affect your work."

———

Mallard pondered the yellow lab situation.

"Funny how Tonn cremated the mutt before the CSI teams could get to them."

"Funny how Tonn wound up adopting a yellow lab shortly after the murder."

"Funny how Tonn wound up dead."

"Funny how Tonn's lab has disappeared."

"Funny how all these things are happening and there are no clues to be found. Anywhere."

His fingers drummed on his steering wheel.

"Tonn hung out with Ike Moe. Perhaps I should pay him a quick visit."

———

"So, let's suppose that maybe, just maybe we could combine our efforts to find out what's going on here."

"I'm listening," said McNally.

"Come on, David," said Maisy, "we were pretty close at one time. I still count you as a friend. Why all the suspicion?"

"Well," said Jim, "perhaps it's because it appears as though two of our former operatives... both inactive, by the way, have been professionally eliminated."

Maisy's eyes narrowed. "We don't know that Troy's been exterminated."

Jim's face dropped. "We know," he whispered.

"How?"

Jim gazed at McNally who produced a nearly imperceptible nod. "We witnessed it."

Maisy's jaw dropped. Silence filled the room for a few moments. Then she whispered, "When?"

"Couple nights ago."

"Was it professional?"

"Thoroughly."

"Why?"

"That's what we want to know." Jim shrugged.

"You couldn't stop it?"

"Nope."

Maisy placed her head in her hands. "What can you tell me about it?"

Jim glanced at McNally again. He nodded.

"It was fast. Shot in the head."

"Where?"

"Outside Ike Moe's house."

"Ike didn't hear it?"

"Apparently not."

Maisy breathed deep, visibly upset. "Where's the body?"

"Standard dismemberment."

"No body?"

"It's spread all across the county."

"Couldn't even make him a bog mummy." Maisy's shoulders shook. "Damn. Troy deserved better than that."

"Well, parts of him will be mummified..."

"That's disgusting." Maisy rubbed her eye with the palm of her hand. "And disrespectful."

"Apologies," said McNally.

The three sat in silence for quite some time before Maisy sighed. "Where do we go from here?"

More silence. McNally finally spoke. "We're not sure. We followed the assassin to Crossroads."

"Crossroads?"

McNally's eyes narrowed. "He parked right in the Herald's lot."

Maisy's eyes widened. "Seriously?"

"Yup. Had a key, too."

"Holy hell."

"Yup."

"Hence the stake out."

"Yup."

A long few moments passed before Jim spoke. "So, Maisy. You up for one last assignment together?"

————

His phone rang again. It was Trinity's number. He cringed. Two calls in one day. What kind of fuckery was this? He let the phone chirp three times before he picked it up.

"Trinity. On this most holy day, I wish a scourge upon the earth."

"And upon you, too."

Then Trinity chuckled. "I always loved that greeting." He didn't answer. The voice continued. "I hear you got quite a reaming this morning. I guess you should have performed your duties better."

He didn't answer.

The voice continued. "Operatives are on their way. They have software to monitor any internet activity concerning the artifact. They also have an app for your phone that will assist you in acquiring its signal." The voice paused. He didn't respond so it continued. "You must be at the predesignated location at 3:00 on the dot. That's when they'll arrive. Be ready and don't make them wait. They don't wait well."

"I'll be there," he mumbled.

"I also have one more piece of advice."

"What would that be?"

"Don't fuck this up. You'll be an exceedingly unhappy camper if you fuck this up."

"Fully aware."

Officer Drake Mallard stood outside Ike Moe's house. He rang the doorbell. A large dog barked inside. Mallard smiled.

He waited a few moments, then rang the bell again. No answer.

He descended the steps and headed towards a window. The shades were drawn. He stepped back and surveyed the front of the house. All the windows were blocked. He swore under his breath. A voice broke his concentration.

"Hey Mallard, you a peeping tom now?"

Chapter Twenty-One

DOG FOOD

It had been a quiet morning at the Moe residence. Ike couldn't take his eyes off Sadie.

"Who's a good girl," he cooed. Sadie's tail thumped on the floor as he scratched her back. "Who's a good girl…"

He ran his fingers across her golden fur and watched hairy tumbleweeds form around her writhing body. "Dingbat," he said, as he gathered the puffs, wadded them in his hand, and shoved them in his pocket. "We must not let anyone know you live here." He added, "No evidence."

He sat on the floor, allowing the dog to crawl onto his lap. "You're quite the lover girl," he said. Her fat tongue slathered his arm. "Some day, you're gonna save my life. I know it." He pursed his lips as thoughts, various scenarios, passed through his mind. "Things look rough," he said, "but I know this could work." He pushed the dog off his lap and proceeded to the kitchen table. He scanned the various items arranged neatly on its surface. The candle glowed. The paper cut. Indelible ink pen set to go. Can of stinky dog food at the ready. Everything was in its place. His stomach growled.

He poured himself a bowl of cold cereal and worked intently, feeling rather smug that he thought of such a foolproof plan.

"With any luck, you'll be my ticket to safety," he said.

As he sat at the breakfast table, he slowly chewed while the candle burned directly to his right.

"Sorry, little lady," he said, "I couldn't find an unscented one." He picked up the jar. "Pumpkin Spice. Shouldn't be too bad."

He felt candle heat radiate next to his skin while he carefully wrote a few strings of numbers on a small paper in front of him.

Then he heard the door ring. Sadie launched into a barking spree.

Dread hopped from his belly to his throat as he scribbled like a mad man, folded the paper in as small a unit as possible. Then he hastily dipped the entire, small square into the hot wax.

Ike placed the wax square in the palm of his hand as he scampered to the window.

Ike noted Mallard's cop car parked on the street. He stiffened when he heard the bell again. Sadie scurried at his feet, threatening to trip him.

He dashed to the kitchen in search of his coat, boots, and mittens. He also grabbed the leash.

He half expected the door to go crashing inward as he scrambled into his winter gear.

Sadie, observing Ike's movements, focused her attention on him and eagerly awaited her invitation to go outside. She eyed the leash in his hand. Meanwhile, Moe gingerly tip toed to the front door. Peeking through the window he watched Mallard step away and another person approach.

It was Ned Stevens. The new reporter followed him. A slow grin spread across his face.

He clipped the leash onto Sadie and dashed towards the back door. Before he opened it, he grabbed the can of dog food. He and Sadie flew outside.

———

"Hey, you a peeping tom now?"

Mallard turned.

Ned Stevens strode towards Mallard, a grin spreading across his face. Ashley followed.

"What the hell are you doing here?" barked Mallard.

"We're here to see my good friend, Ike."

Mallard's eyes darted to Ashley. "I thought you weren't going to use my information for your own purposes."

"This was my information," Ashley said. "Your information included something about a grey sedan."

"Oh. Yeah." He added, "Well, don't get in the middle of my investigation."

"I'll try not to," laughed Ashley, "as long as you don't get in the middle of my story."

Ned's eyebrows scrunched. "When did you two talk?"

"Tell you later," said Ashley.

Mallard derived smug joy sharing personal information with Ashley. He smiled sweetly at her, then drawled, "How ya feeling, darlin'?" His eyes darted to Ned.

"Just fine," Ashley replied, cheeks reddening. "Thanks for asking."

Ned watched the interaction with amused bewilderment.

She stepped towards Ike's stoop. "Nobody's there," said Mallard, "except what sounds like a large dog." He added, "Could be the mysterious Labrador we discussed."

Ashley rang the doorbell and was greeted with silence. "That's one big dog ya got there, Mallard," said Ned. He laughed. "Yup. Sounds like a real monster."

"It was just there a minute ago," said Mallard.

"Uh-huh. And I believe you."

Mallard elbowed Ashley away from the door. He grabbed the doorknob and gave it a twist. It wasn't locked. He opened the door. "Anybody in here," he called.

No answer.

Mallard gingerly stepped into the house. Ned and Ashley followed.

As Mallard crept from room to room, hand resting on his firearm, Ashley scanned the living area, feeling somewhat sheepish for having invaded Ike's home.

Ned stood at the door, refusing to enter the building. "Find anything," he called.

"Shut the fuck up," Mallard hissed.

Ashley laughed.

"Smells like pumpkin pie in here," said Ned.

"I doubt that Ike's been baking," Ashley observed.

Then something caught her eye. A movement. Outside. She silently signaled to Ned who followed her gaze.

They watched in silence as Ike Moe darted onto the street, a beautiful golden lab beside him. He dragged a children's bicycle behind him. Once he got to the street, he dropped the bike and ran directly to Ned's pickup. He opened the rear gate, heaved the dog and shoved her into the vehicle. Then he tossed in the leash along with a metal object. He silently pushed the gate shut and secured the vinyl tarp covering the bed.

Ned watched the proceedings gape mouthed. Ashley remained silent.

Then Ike hopped into the bicycle and pedaled away like a mad man.

Ashley stepped closer to Ned and glanced over her shoulder. Mallard was now ascending the stairs, hunch backed, eyes focused directly ahead, creeping forward like a ninja.

"What the hell did I just see," whispered Ned.

"No idea," she said, "but I think we should probably leave."

"I think you're right," said Ned.

They exited the house, hopped in the truck, and left town. By the time they got to Ned's farmhouse, the dog was in full howl mode.

———

At 3:00 that afternoon, the Crossroad's Herald offices were completely empty. Ned and Ashley were with Mallard. Maisy was in Crossfield working up a plan of action with McNally and Jim. Dick was hanging out in parts unknown. As for Bart Lundquist... if his wife knew what he was doing, she'd be most displeased.

———

Ashley and Ned stood next to the rear gate of his pickup.

"How we gonna do this?" asked Ned.

"No idea."

Ned scratched his head, then he said, "Wait here." He trotted to the dilapidated barn and disappeared inside. Ashley stood shivering next to the pickup, watching the vinyl tarp pop each time Sadie raised her head. A few moments passed and Ned reappeared carrying some twine. "We can use this as a leash," he said.

"Sounds like a plan."

He formed a lasso and nodded to Ash. "Go ahead. Open it. I'm ready."

Ashley pulled open the gate and Sadie came flying out like a cannon ball. In her excitement, she gallomped from one person to the other, leaving dirty paw prints on every item of clothing. She leaped on Ashley, pushing her to the ground. She tackled Ned who had long since dropped the twine. The dog's thick tongue slathered his face.

"Dear God almighty," panted Ned, "this dog's gonna kill me."

"Or at very least she'll make you up your laundry skills," sighed Ashley.

She pulled herself to her feet and eyed the leather leash. She reached into the truck and retrieved it. "Sadie," she said with an excited tone, "wanna go for a walk?"

The dog burst into a new round of enthusiastic leaps. Ashley tossed the leash to Ned who grasped Sadie's collar with one finger and snapped on the leash with his free hand. "Good God," he moaned, "what was Ike thinking?"

"Dunno."

Ashley peered into the bed of the truck and remarked, "Ike threw something in here. I think I see it. Might be important."

Ned peeked inside. "I see it, too."

He handed Ashley the lead and crawled inside. Sadie still leaped from side to side. Ashley had the distinct impression she may have to have some of her incision restitched after this escapade. Ned finally emerged from the dark recesses of the pickup bed carrying an empty can of dog food. "What the hell..."

They slipped, slid, and maneuvered their way to Ned's front door. "I really should shovel more out here," he groaned.

"Do it in your leisure time."

"Yeah," Ned snorted. "Leisure. What's that?"

Sadly, the front entrance was completely blocked with a fresh drift. After a minor snow shovel job, Ned cleared the porch enough to get the door opened. They stepped inside. It was at that point that Ashley realized it was colder inside the building than outside.

"I'll start a fire," said Ned, "Then I should probably rev up the furnace."

"Sounds like a plan."

"Hope the damn thing works."

"Me, too."

While Ned tended to his duties, Ashley examined the dog.

Sadie looked healthy. Her enthusiastic attitude hadn't diminished since she entered the house.

"What's your story, girl," Ashley whispered.

The empty can of dog food rested beside her. She lifted it. Written on the label were the words, "Look inside! It'll come out eventually."

Ashley knit her brow. She listened to Ned fiddle with the wood stove. She watched steam exit her nostrils. She pondered the strange words on the dog food can.

"I wish people would just say what's on their mind." She turned the can over in her hand, "I hate all this cryptic stuff."

———

The gray sedan came to a stop outside the Crossroad's Herald office. Two people sat inside the vehicle.

"It's 2:55. Place is empty."

"As it should be."

"Think he'll make the appointment?"

"Sure as fuck better. Dude's on his last legs."

"Well, you have to admit, he's flying blind."

"He's incompetent."

"I probably wouldn't do much better under similar circumstances." Long pause. "Neither would you."

Another pause. "You getting soft?"

"Nope. Just realistic."

A cigarette burned in the ash tray. Its plume fingering the dashboard. "Realistic?"

"Yup. We're both getting older. We've got a ton of enthusiastic youngsters biting our heels. The thing I've noticed about this new organization is the lack of fidelity. No honor. One mistake and boom... you're toast."

"Don't think about it too much."

"Hard not to." Silence. "It's 2:58. Should we go in?"

"Not yet. Follow the orders."

"Think we'll find it?"

"How am I supposed to know?"

"And if we don't? Do we wind up like Tonn?"

"Fuck no. We treat our own better than the enemy."

Silence.

"But how do we decide who our enemy is?"

"Stop thinking. It's almost time."

At 3:00 sharp, two figures exited the grey sedan. One of them pulled a key from a pocket. They crossed the street and headed straight to the Crossroad's Herald. There, they inserted the key and entered the building.

They paused, both heads turning towards the road. At that

moment, a lanky man sped past on a small bicycle. The front tire appeared to be low on air. Steam exited his thin lips as he pumped his way through snow drifts.

The two figures paused and pondered the sight. "Weird," said the first figure.

"No shit. If I hadn't seen it with my own eyes, I wouldn't have believed it."

"Agreed." An uncomfortable silence ensued. Then he said, "I suppose we better get back to it. Hope we find something."

"If we don't... I don't know what Trinity will do."

Chapter Twenty-Two

ESPIONAGE

Ned rolled the tin can around in his hand. "Look inside! It'll come out eventually," he read.

"What do you suppose that means," asked Ashley.

"Dunno," mused Ned.

The two sat on his dusty couch. Sadie rested at their feet, curled in a large ball of exhausted yellow fur. Between the wood stove and furnace, the house was now a toasty cocoon in the middle of a freezing wind tunnel. Windows vibrated and squeaked as winter squeezed through the weather stripping.

Ashley leaned against Ned and closed her eyes.

"You feeling OK?"

"Yeah. I kinda hurt, though."

"Damn dog."

"Not really. I understand. She had a rough day, too," said Ashley. They sat in silence. Then Ned spoke.

"I'm wondering something weird."

"What would that be?"

"Well, remember how Ike's house smelled like pumpkin pie?"

"Yeah. Smelled yummy."

"Yeah but… Ike didn't know how to cook."

"Weird."

"Yeah. He definitely couldn't bake."

"Probably not."

"But why would his house smell so good?"

"Dunno."

"Well, what smells like that?"

Ashley's eyebrows knit together. "Well… it could be a cleanser of some sort."

"Seriously? Ike clean? Did you see that place?"

Ashley laughed. "I suppose you're right."

They sat in silence for a few more minutes. Ashley finally spoke. "You know… the smell wasn't quite right, not like any pumpkin pie I've ever baked. The smell was… chemical. Kinda waxy."

Ned's eyes brightened. "Waxy? Like a candle?"

"Definitely could have been."

"But why would Ike burn candles?"

"Why does anyone burn a candle?" said Ashley, "because they smell nice? Because his house was stinky?"

"He wouldn't notice anything like that," said Ned.

Silence descended again. Ned picked up the dog food can and read the label again: "Look inside! It'll come out eventually."

"Dude has a warped sense of humor." He tipped the can upward and examined what was left of the contents. Stinky pate lined the edges. He dipped his finger inside and scraped the edges. His eyes narrowed as he did it again. He scraped harder. Finally he whispered, "I'll be damned."

"What?"

"Touch that," he said.

"Ewwww. You sure?" she said, "I hate pretty much everything about dog food. The smell… texture… everything."

"Just do it."

Ashley gingerly touched the side of the can. Her finger met a smooth surface. "Huh. This part. It's hard," she said, "solid. Very different from what I'm used to."

Ned chipped away some of the residue and held it to the light. "Do you think this could be wax?"

Ashley examined it. "Could be."

"Do you think this could possibly be wax from a pumpkin spice candle?"

Ashley said, "Possibly." She added, "But what could that mean?"

Ned looked thoughtful. "You know... I have an idea. Might be crazy... but it sounds like something Ike would do."

————

The whole process was humiliating. First they checked his phone. Then they plugged it into a laptop. Then they scanned it.

"You spend far too much time on gossip websites."

"That's my business. Not yours."

"You've downloaded some pretty lame porn, too."

"Whatever..."

The geek rolled his eyes. "It becomes my business when you fail to complete your assignments." He added, "Do you have any idea what I could be doing today? Instead, I get to come out to the middle of nowhere and net-nanny a device. So lame."

He tapped at his keyboard some more. "I'm blocking every un-useful site from this device. All you need are the ones that will provide you the information you need to complete your mission."

"Fine." He felt resentment bubble in his belly.

The geek tapped some more. He said, "Now... every time the artifact is activated, it will broadcast a weak homing signal. The software I'm installing will release a tone when it senses it."

"Something subtle, I hope."

"It will sound like a text... give or take."

"Will it pinpoint where the signal originated?"

"If it's strong enough. Otherwise it will alert you so you're aware it's in the vicinity."

"Vicinity?"

"Yes."

"Define 'vicinity.'"

"Within a few mile radius."

He breathed deep. "Seriously? How's that going to help me find it?"

"That's not my problem. You're the operative." Then he mumbled, "You're the fuck-up."

He bristled, but chose to ignore the slur. "And another thing. This artifact. I don't know what I'm looking for. What is it? How big is it? What color? Got any clues? Anything I can hang my hat on?"

The geek stared at him. "That information is classified."

"Do you know what it is?"

"I cannot answer that question." He added, "However, that may be something to ask your superiors."

"I have. They won't tell me."

"Then... good luck." The geek snapped his laptop shut. "I also placed an alert on your phone. You'll get a ding when anyone does an image search for the artifact."

"So, what you're telling me is that my phone apparently knows what I'm looking for, but I don't."

"That would be correct."

"Is there any way I can reverse that image search so I can see what I'm looking for?"

"Not without half the organization crawling up your dick."

He felt rage bubble in his throat. "This is impossible, you know."

The geek said, "Look. I know this mission is tough. I guess that's why they want you to do it. From what I hear... and this is off the record..." the geek looked to his right, then his left, "the artifact is small. Fits in your hand. But it's really important to get this thing to Trinity. That's why they won't tell you what it is. Trinity wants it and Trinity doesn't want anyone to know what it is and what it does." He continued, "Everyone's looking for this thing.

Whatever organization gets it, it'll be unstoppable." He added, "Hope that helps. And I didn't tell you anything. Nothing at all. You nark on me, and I can make your life a living hell."

He pondered the geek's words. "Thanks, man." The geek was packing up his gear when he said, "About the whole organization crawling up my dick. If I'm hearing you correctly, other operatives are looking for this thing?"

"Yup. But you're the main one. The rest are monitoring your movements."

"Monitoring me?"

"Yup. Installed the software myself. I'm amazed at the number of fail safes involved in this assignment."

"Damn. If I fail, I'm screwed."

"Yup," said the geek, "screwed in every way possible. Operatives from here to California are poised and ready to take your place." The geek stood at the door.

"One more thing. Why call it an artifact?"

"Cause they don't want anybody to know what it is."

"Weird. So it's not necessarily something old."

"Correct."

With that, the geek exited.

He sat down and pondered his options. He couldn't think of any.

"This is a one way street." He knew what happened to operatives who failed their assignments. "Guess you chose the wrong side this time." He pressed his hand against his face. "Fuck."

———

"I know who can probably help us," said Maisy, "Ned Stevens has been on this story since it broke. And our new reporter, Ashley Stone is pretty sharp. I wouldn't be surprised if they're sitting on some information that they haven't released yet."

McNally glanced at Jim. "You think it's wise to expose ourselves like that?"

Jim's brows knit together as he pondered a moment. "Likely wouldn't hurt to see what they've got."

"We could use some kind of cover."

Maisy interrupted. "I wouldn't advise that. Ned's an on-the-ball guy. He'd smell a scam a million miles away. Best bet is to be as truthful as you can."

"But he could be a plant... someone who works for whoever is ordering all these assassinations."

"Doubtful," said Maisy, "He's a local."

"So was Kaufman."

"Not really," said Maisy. "Kaufman never really assimilated into the community."

"You have a point," said Jim. He turned to McNally. "Do we dare trust them?"

McNally said, "If Maisy trusts him, I guess we'll have to. We've got to figure out a way to get to the bottom of all this."

Maisy laughed. "Just this morning you didn't trust me. Now you do? What changed?"

"Nothing," said McNally, "except now I evidently need you to get some information."

"You romantic devil."

———

"So, what 'cha thinking?"

A slow smile spread across Ned's face. "This might be weird. But Ike was definitely an odd duck."

"Just say it."

"Well," said Ned, "Don't judge me."

"Never."

"Well, here's what I'm figuring..."

———

When Bart returned to the office, something felt askew. He

opened the door to his office and everything looked the same, but everything felt different. The outside door squeaked open. He peeked into the main area and watched Dick enter. He also paused, eyes scanning the room. Bart heard him mumble, "What the fuck?"

"What 'cha up to," yelled Bart.

Dick turned. "Just finished a meeting."

"With a potential advertiser?"

"Yup. Sure."

Bart sighed. "You know sales are down, right?"

"So's circulation."

"Circulation is my department," said Bart. "Besides, numbers are up, thanks to this recent murder."

"I hear we've got two possible killings."

"Correct."

Dick's eyebrows rose. "Any details?"

"None I want to share with you."

Dick wrinkled his nose and proceeded to the chair directly across Bart's desk. "Listen. I know I'm probably not the best salesman you've ever had."

"You're the worst."

"But you know I care for this paper." Bart's eyes bore into Dick. He continued. "Your sister has a lot of financial and emotional investment in this business. I just want to help."

"Then sell ads."

"I do."

"Not lately. Sales are dismal. Profits way down. Almost all the ads currently running are long timers and ones I've personally sold." Bart pursed his lips. He added, "What the hell do you do around here anyway?"

"I'm married to your sister. Happily married. Quit bitching."

With that, Dick stomped out of the room.

"Fucker."

Chapter Twenty-Three

POO

Ned scrolled the webpage on his phone. "It says here we can expect some action in seven to ten hours."

"I can't believe you're doing this."

"All in the name of good reporting," laughed Ned.

"It's likely the grossest thing I've ever thought of," said Ashley.

"Well, the only way to know if my hunch is right is to... well... try it."

"Yeah, but," said Ashley, "your logic in this situation is... weak."

"It's all we've got."

"Explain it to me again."

Ned leaned back in his chair and laced his fingers behind his head. "Well, Mallard's after the dog because... thanks to someone," his eyes narrowed while staring at Ashley, "he knows it could have belonged to Tonn."

"Sorry..."

Ned laughed. He continued, "Well, everyone with a horse in this race is apparently focused on this mutt right now."

"Don't call her a mutt. She's beautiful. Probably a purebred."

"Whatever. Anyway, for some reason Ike had Tonn's dog.

Tonn's dog probably ate Kaufman. Now Tonn's gone missing...
under suspicious circumstances." His eyes narrowed. "Ike tossed
this mutt..."

"Dog."

"OK. Dog... into my truck along with an empty can of
dog food."

"Yup. I was there."

"The writing says what?"

Ashley picked up the can and read: "Look inside! It'll come out
eventually."

Ned laughed. "Knowing Ike, that means the dog is about to
expel something interesting. Ike would love knowing we're sitting
around focusing on a canine anus."

"Expel. Anus. You make the whole process sound respectable."

"Yeah. The dog's gonna shit. And knowing Ike, it's gonna be a
doozie."

Ashley sighed. "Great. When does all this excitement start?"

"Like I said. The website says seven to ten hours."

"I can't wait."

———

Maisy dialed her phone. It rang twice before the recipient
answered. "Hey," she said, "what 'cha doing?"

Long pause.

"Sounds interesting. What 'cha doing at 4:30?"

Long pause.

"Well, I was wondering if you wanted to meet at O'Neils.
Coffee... drinks... doesn't matter."

Pause.

Maisy laughed. "Nah. I'm not up to anything. I just need to
chat with you and Ash."

Pause.

"Sounds like a plan then?"

Pause

"Great. Talk soon."

———

Ned set down his phone. "Strange. That was Maisy. She wants to talk to us."

"Both of us?"

"Yeah."

"That's weird."

"Yeah. Know what's weirder? She wants to meet at O'Neils."

"Not the office?"

"Nope."

"When?"

"4:30."

"So soon?" Ashley said, "We gonna do it?"

"Why not?" said Ned. "The dog won't shit for quite a while. Besides, it's a perfectly weird ending to an incredibly weird day."

"Touche."

———

Ned and Ashley stopped by her house before heading to O'Neils.

As they stepped inside, Ashley ran to her bedroom to change clothes. Ned lingered in the living room. He noted the pile of mail laying on the table next to the front door. He picked it up and stared at the letter resting on the top of the heap.

"Dr. Laurie Pence. Crossfield Oncology Center." He sighed.

He set the pile of mail back on the table. Seeing the word "oncologist" made him pause. The whole situation felt far too real. He gathered his thoughts, reining in his emotions, hoping to somehow label the feelings tumbling through his head. The violent mixture of helplessness and anger pooled in his mind.

"Cancer," he thought. "It really happened." It was too easy to pretend the violent act never took place. It was easy to simply move forward without a thought about the reality of the situation.

A wave of impotence rushed over him as the realization dawned that this was a situation he couldn't control. The thought struck terror into his marrow.

And the entire row of negative dominoes got triggered by one white envelope.

Rather than deal with the multiple scenarios tumbling in his mind, he headed to Ashley's bedroom. "How 'ya doing' in there?" he called.

"Fine," Ashley answered. "I'll be out in a sec."

Rather than wait, he turned the knob and gently slid open the door. He watched as Ashley sat on the side of the bed, arm resting over her incision; eyes closed, shoulders hunched. Ned stepped closer, concern spreading across his face. "You OK?"

She breathed deep. "I will be. Just give me a sec."

He sat next to her. She cringed. "Need a pain pill?" he said.

"I'll get one in a minute. I just need to sit for a bit."

He placed his arm on her shoulder and she rested her head against him. "We don't have to go anywhere," he said.

"I know. But, I want to." She added, "It could be something about the story."

They sat a few moments in a warm, comfortable silence.

Ned said, "I noticed your new oncologist sent a letter."

"Saw it."

"Care to open it and see what she has to say?"

"Not particularly."

Another long pause enveloped them.

Ned said, "You know you've stolen my black heart."

Ashley laughed. "I feel pretty bad for you then."

He kissed her hairline. "I feel pretty fine about it."

Ashley didn't respond.

"Do you want to open it together."

"Not really. I'd rather be happy a while longer."

Ned laughed. "I think we can be happy either way."

Ashley didn't answer.

———

Maisy arrived first. The hostess led her to a private room.

Ashley and Ned arrived at precisely 4:30. They joined Maisy.

Ned strode into the large dining room, dozens of fully dressed tables peppered the floor. A single table appeared occupied. "Day just got weirder," he said.

Ashley nodded her head.

Ned proceeded directly to Maisy. "So. What 'cha got cooking?"

"I need to talk to you about something."

"What would that be," said Ashley.

"Let's get beverages first." She added, "Something alcoholic."

"Must be bad," said Ned. He placed his arm around Ashley's shoulder.

"No," said Maisy, "Not bad. Just... awkward."

"Then let's get right to it, eh?"

Maisy glanced at her watch. "We can start at 4:45. That's when they come."

"They?"

"Yeah. The people I need you to meet."

"Dear god," said Ned, "What have you gotten us into?"

Maisy laughed. "Nothing. I just rounded up a couple people who can help you with your big story."

Ashley's eyes lit up. "Seriously?"

"Yeah."

"Where did you come by these mystery people?" asked Ned.

"I have my connections," said Maisy.

"In that case," said Ned, "I'll await the big news." He sat at the table. Ashley joined him.

"If I'd have known this was about work, I would have brought my gear," said Ashley.

"Probably not a good idea," said Maisy sitting down, "most of this will likely be off the record."

"I hope I can take notes..."

"We'll have to see."

"Then I have dubious expectations about how this can help with my research," said Ashley.

"Oh," said Maisy, "It'll likely help."

They waited in silence, clock ticking echoing across the room. Finally a rustling outside the door interrupted the incessant sound. The door opened and two men entered. The first was likely the scariest man Ashley had ever laid eyes on. With piercing eyes and intense expression, he seemed to violate her soul. She discreetly pushed her chair closer to Ned. The other man was likely gorgeous, but Ashley couldn't take her eyes off scary-man. She did note, however, that man number two had the largest hands she'd ever seen. Her eyes flew to Maisy whose genuine smile did little to diminish her apprehension.

Maisy spoke first. "Ashley... Ned. I want you to meet David and Jim."

All four nodded. The two men sat across from Ashley and Ned. Maisy pulled up a chair and sat at the end of the table. The seating arrangement felt crowded.

The one called David spoke first. "I hear you may have some information about the Kaufman murder."

Ashley's eyes narrowed. "I heard you had information to share with us."

All eyes flew to Maisy. "Hey," she said, "I just said you guys could likely help each other."

The man named Jim breathed deep. "Maisy said you two were good at gathering information. We just thought we'd see what you've got."

Ned laughed. "Seriously?"

Jim's eyes narrowed. "Seriously."

Ned said, "Maisy. You disappoint me."

"This is just weird," said Ashley, "I think I should go."

"Wait a minute," said David, "There's more to this story than meets the eye."

"No shit Sherlock," said Ned.

Jim rubbed his eyes. Ned turned to Maisy. "Seriously? All this cloak and dagger? All for a big nixie meeting?"

Maisy said, "I really think you guys can help figure this out."

Ned sighed. "I don't see it working." He stood.

"Wait a minute," said Ashley, "Let's just breathe."

"Agreed," said Maisy. "I mean, you're all here. What could it hurt to at least share a little information?"

"You seriously think we can trust these two?" said Ned.

"With your life," answered Maisy.

Ned's eyebrows rose. His eyes slid to David. David nodded to Jim. Then Jim said, "Listen. We expose ourselves big time by revealing any of this to you. Please excuse our reluctance to share what could likely be very dangerous information."

"Sounds like some pretty serious shit," said Ned, descending to his chair, "but do go on."

Jim nodded. "What I'm about to share is off the record. We're coming to you because Maisy says you're legit. You should also be aware that if this information gets out, we're dead men."

Ashley's eyes widened.

Ned spoke. "I'll keep quiet." He turned to Ashley.

She nodded. "Off the record."

Jim turned to David who nodded. "Thing is," Jim said, "Alex Kaufman was one of us. He worked with us... quite a while ago."

"He worked with me, too," whispered Maisy.

Ned's head swung towards Maisy. "Seriously?"

She nodded.

"What did you guys do," asked Ashley.

"Well," said David, "... depending on who you spoke with, we were either freedom fighters or..."

"Terrorists," said Jim.

Ned leaned back in his chair. He chuckled. "I'm just looking for the cameras. You're filming this for some 'gotcha' show, right?"

"I wish we were," said Maisy. "This is scary stuff. Someone's killing our operatives and we don't know who's next."

"Wait a minute," said Ashley, "You said 'operatives.' Not 'operative.' You mean to tell me there's more than one?"

Maisy nodded glumly.

Ashley said, "You're not saying..."

"Dr. Tonn," said Maisy.

"He's one of these terrorists?"

"He was," said Maisy. "He was fairly low level, but yes... he worked with us."

"Holy crap," said Ned, "speaking in past tense? That's weird." He added, "How many of you guys live in Crossroads?"

David paused before he said, "A few. Quite a few."

Ashley breathed deep. "Since when did Crossroads become a hub for retired terrorists?"

"Ha," said Ned, "a terroristic retirement community. That's a good one."

"Not exactly," said David, sobering the room, "we need to backtrack a bit." He paused, breathing deep, then continued. "A couple years ago... remember hearing about an organization called the RNF? The Republic National Forces?"

"Nope," said Ned.

"I recall something with those initials. Wasn't that somehow tied in with someone from Minnesota... a terrorist organization... an abduction... I never heard how all that ended."

"Well," said David, "it apparently ended here."

"How so?"

"What happened was that the main RNF membership list... and I mean the entire list... was leaked. Media got it. Authorities got it. But worst of all, our competing freedom fighters..."

"Terrorists," Ned interrupted.

David McNally's eyes narrowed in Ned's direction, "Freedom fighters. Our rival freedom fighter organizations now had the opportunity to either recruit or pick off everyone not associated with their goals."

"You still haven't answered my question. How did so many wind up here?" said Ashley.

"We need to back up a bit," said Jim. McNally nodded.

"Thing is," he said, "many of us were recruited as children. With economic unrest, children were a liability." Jim nodded in agreement. "It was pretty easy to deposit children in the care of RNF members because parents believed they were doing their children a service." Jim nodded again.

"What they didn't know was that the children... and in my case, an adolescent... were not only taught how to fight, kill, and maim, but we were taught an ideology. Our keepers were viewed as kind, just, and correct. The ideology ingrained over such a long period became truth."

"I've heard stories like this before," said Ned.

"Well, now you've met three who have lived it," said Maisy.

"I truly thought the crimes I committed for the RNF were for the good of all," said Jim.

"What changed your mind," asked Ashley.

"I met Jennifer," whispered McNally.

"He couldn't kill her," said Jim.

Ashley's eyes widened.

"I knew the order to kill her wasn't fair. It wasn't just. It wasn't right. Hence, I began to question my group... the only family I'd ever known."

"So, he got out," said Jim.

"Before the blowup?" said Ned. "I'm probably wrong, but I have a hunch that RNF-type organizations don't let people retire just like that."

"That's an understatement," said Jim.

"It's a long story," said McNally, "I don't have time to go over the details, but suffice it to say that after far too long, I realized I couldn't devote my life to the RNF anymore."

"So you came to Minnesota?"

"We did."

"And others followed you?"

"Apparently," said Jim.

"Near as we can tell," said McNally, "One of our cohorts... a man who joined the organization later in life, originated from this area. He returned home. Many followed because they enjoyed his stories of ice, snow, and... well... the remote nature of this area."

"It seemed like a safe, quiet place," said Jim.

"Until our former operatives started going down," said Maisy.

"Which brings us to today," said McNally, "We've shared more than we should have. You could have all three of us arrested for all the crimes we've committed. But here we sit. Asking for your help."

Ned scanned the faces of the people sitting around him. "What, exactly, do you need from us?"

"Information," said Jim.

"For the first time in a very long time, we need a team. This is unfolding to be something rather large."

"If these people aren't active in your particular trade, do you have any idea why your... er... operatives are getting eliminated," said Ned.

"Kind of. I'm making some fairly large leaps in knowledge here, but according to what's left of my feeble network, it appears the people behind this might be looking for something," said McNally.

Jim said, "Agreed. It's unlikely they'd randomly show up in Crossroads and start whacking people. They're looking for something. We just aren't sure what."

"Hmmm..." said Ned, "I can't imagine what anyone would want here."

"Me either," said Maisy, "but that house was trashed. Tonn's missing, no pickup."

"Ike Moe just ran out of town."

"What?" said McNally.

"He was one of ours, too," said Maisy.

"Seriously," said Ned, "I'll be damned..."

"So weird," said Ashley. She paused, then said, "We saw him run off on a bike."

McNally's brows knitted together. "When? Where?"

Ashley said, "Ned and I went over to his house to ask some questions."

"Mallard was there, too," said Ned.

"He wasn't home. But then we saw him take off on a bike."

McNally said, "Did he leave anything behind?"

Ned and Ashley exchanged glances.

Chapter Twenty-Four

LIBRARIAN WARRIORS

"The wife's gonna kill me," thought Bart as he gently fingered the glazed donut resting on his desk. He smiled. "But what she doesn't know, won't hurt me." He laughed as he raised the greasy bread to his lips. He rolled his eyes as the sweet goo dissolved in his mouth.

"Yup," he mumbled, "perfection on a plate."

———

"We probably shouldn't have told them about Sadie," said Ashley.

"I know," said Ned, "but by revealing that little factoid, we didn't have to tell them about the silver thing. Plus," he added, "I didn't tell them we actually had the dog. They're probably driving all over the county looking for her." He added, "Having them calling every animal shelter this side of Crossfield should give us enough time to do a bit of research on that weird key. Plus, I won't mind having those creepy dudes out of my hair for a while."

"Agreed" said Ashley, "Those men scared me."

"Me, too."

Ashley smiled. "I suppose you could have charmed them with your rock star looks and witty personality."

"Ha ha," said Ned, "my wiles generally work better on women than men."

They drove in silence, both pondering the events they'd just witnessed, the surreal week swirling in their minds. Murders, clandestine meetings, terrorists, freedom fighters. Oy.

Finally, Ashley spoke. "What time are you meeting Mr. McNally?"

"Chop shop will be active around 8:oo tonight."

"I still can't believe you set up that meeting." She added, "However, that was really a brilliant move," said Ashley.

"I thought so." Ned smiled.

"It was yet another decoy to turn any and all attention away from that thing you found. Plus, you got them occupied for a while. That was brilliant."

"Well," said Ned, "hopefully we'll know what it is after we're done at the library."

"Hopefully."

Then he added, "Besides, I've been gunning to get to that chop shop ever since I found out Troy's pickup was missing. I'm not sure I'd be comfortable going there unless I was with someone pretty rough. Those two hooligans we just met fit the bill."

"I'll ignore the hooligan comment," said Ashley. "What makes you think you'll find something there?"

"Well," said Ned, "If something happened to Troy, chances are his pickup could wind up at a chop shop. That's the only chop shop I know of in the five county area. If something's amok with Tonn, it could be there." He added, "Actually I hope it's not. I hope he's OK... off fishing somewhere. But if he's not, it would be nice to know what's going on."

"Yeah," said Ashley, "I agree. I hope the news is better than I suspect."

A few more miles disappeared under their truck tires before Ned spoke. "Think we can actually trust Maisy and her new crew?"

"I don't know," said Ashley. " You know Maisy better than me. What are your thoughts?"

"I thought I knew her. But this one surprised me. A lot." He sighed. "I mean seriously. She's a former terrorist? She's got terrorist friends? I don't know who to trust anymore."

"Me either."

Then Ned's eyes glinted. "I trust you."

"Always." Ashley laughed. "You crack me up, Superstar."

———

McNally closed his eyes. "Head hurts," he groaned.

Jim grunted. "I know. I was hoping for better luck."

"I have no idea what you two are whining about." Maisy slapped the back of McNally's head. "Grow up. Deal with it. Be the professional you used to be."

"I didn't figure I'd be doing shit like this." He tapped the screen on his phone. "I had no idea there were so many yellow labs in shelters throughout this county."

"Yeah," Jim agreed, "There's a lot of 'em. As for professionalism, you have to acknowledge we're a little rusty."

"Tough shit. Do you want to figure this out or not?" Maisy squinted into her computer screen.

McNally sighed. "I know." He paused a moment then said, "But those two newbies. I don't know."

"What don't you know," asked Maisy.

"I'm not sure I can trust them."

"You don't need to, numb-nuts," Maisy said, "You just need to run with what little information they dole out."

"They didn't give us much." He added, "And looking for a stray yellow lab is like looking for a needle in a haystack.

"But you've found a way with less."

"I know."

Silence descended around them. Jim finally spoke. "That Ned had a good lead. It took a bit of inside information to know about that chop shop."

"I know," said McNally leaning forward, "But did you watch the female? She appeared calm and all, but she was sprung tighter than a violin string. She was definitely sitting on some information. We need to find out what it is."

"What did you expect," said Maisy, "I kinda sprung you guys on 'em."

"I know. But I kinda figured those two country bumpkins would be easier to crack."

"Nope," said Maisy, "never underestimate a bumpkin. They may look a mite simple at times, but it's a ruse. There's a lot going on in their noggins. They're cagy. And smart." She added, "Believe me, I know what I'm talking about."

Jim's eyes narrowed, "You sound like you speak from experience."

"Yup," said Maisy, "You got that right."

"You'll have to share stories."

"Someday."

————

Ashley and Ned entered the Crossfield Public Library. "I don't have a card," whispered Ashley

"Don't need one for what we're going to do," said Ned.

They entered the large building and scanned the interior. Ned nodded to a bank of computers to his right. "There," he whispered, "let's go there."

Ashley nodded in reply. They headed to the machines and settled next to the most remote one. Ashley whispered, "I'm not sure why we can't just do a reverse image search on our phone." She added, "Or how 'bout doing this in the privacy of our own home?"

"I'm just being cautious," said Ned. "You never know who is monitoring."

"You've read too many spy novels."

His eye sparkled. "You know it." He spoke low, almost whispering. "Also, I happen to know the IT guys for this library system. They keep the computers top notch. They set the machines to delete caches upon exiting. They're all about security and patron privacy. And the librarians..." He chuckled. "The librarians are anti-patriot act warriors." He said, "They're fearless when it comes to butting heads with authorities when it comes to their patrons. Anyone wants our info, they'll have to go through those tough bitches." He nodded towards the petite women organizing papers at the main desk. He added, "They're pretty amazing."

Ashley's eyebrows rose. "I guess I believe you."

"Damn straight," said Ned, "Never mess with a librarian."

Ashley laughed.

Ned fired up the browser.

"Search terms..." he whispered.

"Silver key?"

"Silver key... large head... microchip inside..."

"Smooth blade," she added, "rounded tip, irregular milling."

Ned shot Ashley a side eye. "When did you become an expert on key lingo?"

Ashley chuckled. "I've done a little research since we found this thing."

"Not online, I hope."

"Nope. Just a book."

"You had a key book laying around?"

"You got me. I may have browsed one at the hardware store..."

Ned nodded, pursing his lips. "I'm impressed."

He typed the keywords into Google and hit "return." Both of them narrowed the space between their noses and the screen.

Ashley silently read the results while Ned perused the images.

"See anything?" said Ned.

"Not yet."

Ned slowly scrolled, eyebrows knitting together.

Finally Ashley chirped. "Here. Click this one."

He did so.

The screen filled with images... a few similar to to their key, most unlikely matches. Ned clicked an image that somewhat resembled what they were looking for.

"Holy shit," he breathed. "This is really weird."

———

His phone chirped. Damn. He was in the middle of something. It chirped again.

"Excuse me," he said. He pulled the phone from his pocket and stared at the screen. "Holy shit," he whispered. He turned to the person across from him. "Apologies, but I have to go. It's an emergency."

The person rolled their eyes and smiled sweet. "No problem."

He ran to his car and scrambled inside. He gazed at his phone and poked at the screen with his finger. He waited a few moments and a quiet beeping sound emerged. He tapped the screen and the sound increased in volume.

He tapped it a few more times and a group of numbers popped up: 192.168.4.3.

"What the fuck does that supposed to mean," he mumbled.

He punched a few more numbers.

"The sky is grey today."

"Not in Nicaragua."

A self satisfied snort emerged from the other end of the line. "I just love those things."

"Good for you," he said. "I got a hit. 192.168.4.3"

"Excellent. Give me a moment."

He listened to someone tapping on a keyboard. He heard mumbling. He heard more tapping. Silence hung on the line for a few moments. He waited patiently. Finally the other end of the phone perked up.

"That address comes from one of the computers at the Crossfield Public Library," the voice said, "I'd suggest you arrive there as soon as possible. This could all wrap up today. That would please Trinity."

He sighed. Another day of work lost. Fuck. "I'll get moving," he said.

———

Ned printed the Internet page with the photo of what could have been his key's relative. Not a perfect match. But close.

He grabbed the papers as they rolled out of the printer. He dug in his pocket and pulled out a few coins.

Ashley exited all programs on the computer. Ned double checked that they were thoroughly logged out.

As they exited he placed the coins on the main desk and with a quick, "Thanks," they exited the library. When they entered his pickup a block from the library entrance, Ashley expected him to drive away. He didn't. Instead he sat, reading what he had printed.

"We going to leave?"

"In a minute. Check this out." He handed her a page. With eyebrows scrunched, she did as he asked. Soon she was engrossed in the text.

"Who knew reading about keys would be so interesting," she mused.

"Indeed."

They sat in silence around ten minutes before Ashley heard Ned say, "Well, well, well. I'll be damned."

Ashley's eyes swerved towards him. "What?"

"Check it out," he nodded forward.

Ashley gasped.

———

He ran into the library in a near panic. He never dreamed it would take so long to get there. "Damn traffic."

He launched inside and ran headlong towards the computers.

All were occupied. He nonchalantly strolled parallel to the machines, sneaking a peek at each screen. He didn't see anything that could remotely look like some sort of artifact.

He made his way back to the counter. "Excuse me," he said, "but did you have anybody use any of your computers today?"

The librarian cocked her head and stared at him. She nodded towards the group of students. "They're all in use now," she said.

"Yes. But earlier. Has anyone use these computers today."

"Uh, yeah."

"Could you give me a list of today's computer users?"

"No."

"Why not?"

"Privacy issues. Plus, we don't keep track. People come, people use them, they leave."

He sighed. "Can you give me a list of internet searches performed so far today?"

"Nope."

"Even if I had a court order?"

"Do you have one?"

"No."

She laughed. "No. I can't help you. Besides, the computers purge all activity once the person leaves. I couldn't give you information even if I wanted to."

He pursed his lips. "Fine. I'll figure something out. Thanks for nothing."

———

"You don't suppose..." said Ashley.

"Jeez, I hope not."

"That sure would complicate things."

"No kidding."

Ned leaned back in his seat, resting his head against the soft fabric. They watched him exit the library, glance at his phone, then run to his vehicle.

"Well," Ashley said, "things just got exponentially weirder."

———

That evening, Ned and McNally entered the chop shop. It was a noisy, greasy garage, the sound of pounding metal and squealing bolts ricocheted off metal walls. When they entered the office, an oil streaked man strode over to them.

"What can I do you for?" he drawled.

"Looking for parts," said McNally.

"For what?"

"We're restoring a Dodge Ram. Silver."

"What 'cha need?"

"What 'cha got?"

"A lot."

"Like?"

The man nodded to his left. "If ya need a cowl, this just came in. Airbags still intact. Perfect shape, 'cept for all the stickers. I can get 'em off with Goo Gone. Won't even know they were there."

Ned's breath caught in his throat. It was Troy's. Definitely. All the stickers from his decaf mocha collection glowed bright under the harsh lights. "Shit," he breathed.

McNally examined what was once Troy Tonn's dash. "That might work. I'll double check the interior's color," he said.

"We'll think on it," added Ned.

With that, they left the building.

"That was Tonn's," said Ned.

"I figured," said McNally, "you weren't exactly subtle in there."

"Guess I'm not a terrorist schooled in the art of deception."

"Freedom fighter."

———

Ashley arrived home that evening more exhausted than she

expected. Her abdominal wound ached with a dull thud every time she moved. She limped to the bathroom and gingerly shut the door. As she stood before the mirror, she carefully lifted her shirt to view the damage.

Somewhat relieved, her wound didn't look as bad as it felt. She wondered how things were going for Ned at the chop shop. She wasn't sure if she could trust McNally and Jim. They seemed nice enough, however they most certainly possessed an unmistakable terrorist vibe.

She lowered her shirt and leaned on the vanity. She pondered her options. She could become an annoying girlfriend and call to see how things were going. She could keep quiet and enjoy an evening of solitude. Or, she could conduct a small investigation of her own.

Ned said he was concerned about outsiders monitoring Internet activity surrounding any image searches of that mysterious silver key. She wondered how anyone could possibly monitor her Internet activity if she were to use her personal cell phone. She figured if she were to conduct a quick search, shut down her phone, and glean useful information, what harm could come of that?

She didn't have much time to ponder her plan because a sudden rapping on her door interrupted her thoughts. She tiptoed into the door and peeped through the hole.

She gasped when she saw who was standing outside.

———

Ned and McNally made their way towards the farmhouse in silence. The road thumped under their tires creating a surprisingly steady rhythm. The events of the evening ricocheted through Ned's mind.

His life and become such an absurd whirlwind of crazy since that danged murder. He almost longed for the days when Crossroads was a quiet, lazy village. He hoped he could someday go back to the good old days when the greatest controversy concerned whether or not the most recent chocolate chip cookie recipe belonged to one family or another.

But everything was different now. Today, at this moment a former terrorist sat in his vehicle. And to add insult to injury, this frightening terrorist was probably the most trustworthy individual he'd met in a long time.

Except for Ashley.

Ned wasn't sure what was going on, but all he knew for certain was that woman had managed to steal his heart. Whether this was a good thing or bad thing, he wasn't sure.

"I guess the heart wants what the heart wants," he mumbled.

"What 'cha thinking over there?" said McNally.

"Nothing."

"We saw some pretty upsetting stuff tonight. You sure you can process it all?"

"Nope."

The two men sat in silence for a few more miles. Then, McNally said, "Look. I know things are nuts. I know your life is upside down. But we're really trying to make this right." Ned didn't respond. A few more miles thumped under the truck before he spoke again. "I'm playing a pretty vague hunch here. I know I shouldn't trust you and you definitely shouldn't trust me, but you're all I have. Jim and I spent the entire afternoon looking for that damn lab." He paused for a response the didn't get one. He continued, "Ike and I were friends. We were colleagues. We made promises to help each other no matter what. We were like brothers and I need anything you can tell me that will help me help him. I need to find that Labrador."

Ned continued to drive in silence as a few more miles evaporated. McNally spoke again.

"I can't help but notice we're not heading towards Crossroads."

Ned replied, "Nope."

"Care to tell me where we're going?"

"My farmhouse."

McNally stroked his chest, assuring himself his firearm was in place. Ned didn't seem to notice. A few more miles passed under the truck. Ned said, "I've got something at the house that you should probably see."

McNally didn't reply.

Chapter Twenty-Five

DOG DUNG

Ashley pressed her back against the front door and breathed deep. She had no idea how to react, she had no idea what to say. She hated that, for the first time in quite a while, she was alone.

She stood a few moments in silence. Then the loud rapping resumed.

"I know you're in there," said a voice, "open up, I'm freezing."

Ashley paused a moment, then turned and peeked through the peephole.

"Just open the damn door," the voice said. "Honestly, I saw you. You're in there. Just open up."

Ashley's heart was beating in her ears. Her hands shook. She didn't know how entangled she wanted to get in this mess.

The knocking resumed in earnest. The voice said, "Listen, you gotta let me in. Trent Shaw's on my tail. I should be halfway to California by now."

Ashley turned around, undid the latch, and twisted the knob. The door exploded open and Ike Moe burst into the room.

"Fuck," he said, " you have no idea what my day has been like." Ashley stood with her mouth hanging open while Ike slammed the door closed. "I can't believe Shaw saw me. Damn idiot has been following me all night. Never thought I'd lose him." He scampered to the picture window and closed the drapes. Then, he proceeded to peek at the street via the curtain edges.

Ashley found her voice. "Ike Moe," she said, "what the hell's going on?"

Ike's eyes twinkled. "I miss Sadie."

Ashes jaw dropped. "You came back for the dog?"

"She's more than a dog," Ike said, "she's my responsibility. Troy told me to take care of her. It's the least I can do considering what likely happen to him." He added, "I have fucked up most of my life. I'm not going to mess up this final promise to my best friend." He scanned the room. "So," he said, "where is she?"

————

McNally exited the truck and stepped into the inky darkness. He glanced at Ned and double checked the position of his handgun.

Ned said, "Follow me."

McNally hesitated, not sure what Ned had in mind. He watched him make his way towards the farmhouse before he reluctantly followed suit. When Ned plunged the key into the lock the explosion of barking inside the house make McNally smile. "Is that what I think it is," he said.

"Possibly."

The door swung open and a golden lab burst outside. "Catch her, catch her!" yelled Ned. McNally lunged forward and looped his finger through the collar. The dog twisted and yanked out of his grasp. "Don't let her poop, don't let her poop," shouted Ned.

McNally leaped in front of the dog, but she dodged him. Ned scampered towards the animal and she slammed into his chest, knocking him to the ground. The animal's wide tongue slathered his face.

McNally leaped towards Ned, shoved his finger under Sadie's collar, and held tight. He hauled the dog towards the house.

Ned scampered to his feet, brushed snow off his pants, and

followed. "Damn dog," he mumbled as he slipped and slid towards the door.

The trio stepped inside and locked the door behind them. McNally gasped when he viewed copious piles of fecal matter peppered throughout the living room. "Damn," he said, "that's one messy dog."

"Excellent," Ned breathed, "this just may work."

———

Within a few moments Ike and Ashley were heading towards the farmhouse in her little Smart. Ashley had no idea what to do with Ike so she figured the short trek to Ned's place was likely appropriate.

They sat in awkward silence for a mile or two before Ashley spoke. "So," she said, "I suppose this means Dr. Tonn is dead."

"Yup," whispered Ike.

"How did you get Sadie?"

"Long story."

"How do you know Dr. Tonn is dead?"

"Long story."

"What are your plans after you get the dog?"

"Long story."

Ashley didn't respond, instead keeping her eye on the road and concentrating on getting to the farmhouse before becoming too frustrated with Ike. However, had she been a little more obser-vant, she would likely have noticed the pair of dim headlights in her rearview.

———

"Holy shit."

"Agreed," said Ned, smiling.

McNally watched in disgust as Ned snatched a pencil off the

desk and proceeded to hop from pile to pile carefully poking each turd into smaller pieces.

"What the hell are you doing," he said.

"Not sure," said Ned, "just playing a hunch."

Ned poked some more, carefully jabbing each group of tightly bound fecal matter. "Feel free to help," he said.

"I'll just watch," said McNally.

Ned poked some more before he said, "I'll be damned."

"What 'cha got there?"

"Not sure."

McNally stepped forward, carefully avoiding stepping on additional piles, and stood next to Ned. "What's up?"

Ned poked at the turd. "This," he breathed, "This right here."

McNally lean over and gazed at the substantial pile. "What on earth did that animal eat?"

Ned grabbed a tissue and pulled it out of the mass. He wiped away a substantial amount of debris before he lifted it to his nose.

"What the fuck..." said McNally.

"Pumpkin spice," declared Ned, "I knew it."

"That's it," said McNally, "You're officially, certifiably insane."

Ned held the object towards McNally and repeated, "Give it a whiff."

"Not on your life."

Ned laughed. "Seriously," he said, "This is something big."

"Do tell."

"Well," said Ned, poking at the object, "When Ike left Sadie in my truck he happened to leave behind a short message on the label of a dog food can."

"Seriously?"

"Yup."

"What did it say?"

"Look inside! It'll come out eventually."

"That's weird." McNally scratched his head, tousling his hair.

"Yup. Sounds like Ike, though."

"I suppose," said McNally, "he always had a weird sense of decorum."

Ned ignored the comment and continued, "So, I played a hunch figuring he made the dog eat something I should see."

"Again... could be plausible."

"Especially true now that I found this."

"Possibly. But the mutt could have just eaten something stupid. Labs do that," said McNally. "But what's up with the pumpkin spice?"

"His house smelled like that. I know he doesn't bake. Had to be a candle."

"Candle?"

"Yup."

"You figured he sealed something in wax?"

"Possibly."

"Dunno. Ike's great in a pinch, but he's not exactly ranked high in the smarts department..." McNally stepped forward and examine the object. It looked like carefully folded paper dipped in brown wax. "You don't suppose," he said, "we'll have to pick that thing apart..."

"I'm sure you've done worse... terrorist and all."

"Freedom fighter. And no. I can't say I've ever dug through dog shit before." He added, "Keep calling me a terrorist, and I'll have to refer to you as 'superstar.'"

"Fine with me," said Ned, "I am a superstar." McNally rolled his eyes. Ned set the brown wad on a nearby coffee table. He poked it with a pencil for a few moments before he finally picked it up with his fingers. He carefully scratched off some wax with his fingernail and pulled the paper open. McNally peered over his shoulder mumbling quiet encouragement.

When Ned concluded his task, he spread the paper flat on the table and read its message.

"What the fuck," he said.

———

The grey sedan rolled to a stop. He leaned forward, narrowing his eyes, squinting at the farmhouse. He knew he should probably check in with his superiors, but he figured if he could nail this assignment, he could get in good with the organization.

He watched intently as the new female reporter exited the Smart with Ike Moe. He watched them proceed to the front door the farmhouse. The door opened. They stepped inside.

He exited his vehicle and crept towards the building.

He paused when he spotted another vehicle bounce up the driveway.

———

Ashley and Moe entered the farmhouse. She gasped when she noted the copious fecal matter covering the floor. Each pile appeared to have been most unfortunately disturbed. She glanced towards Ned.

"You didn't..." she said.

Ned and McNally stood silently, eyes fixed on Ike. "What the hell," said McNally.

"You're back," said Ned.

Ike smiled. "You bet. I couldn't leave poor Sadie behind."

"You expect me to believe that," said McNally.

"Of course," he said, "I love dogs."

"More like," said McNally, "you realized you gave away your only copy of something important and you figured you come back to get it."

Ike's face reddened. "You found it, eh?"

"We most certainly did."

"But you don't know what it means, do you?"

"Nope. Do you?"

"Nope."

"Kaufman? Did he know?"

"Dunno," said Ike shrugging.

McNally breathed deep. "You realize, without a way to decipher these numbers, this information is useless."

"Not exactly useless," said Ike, "More like part of a puzzle." He stepped to the table and examined the paper. "Not too bad, if I say so myself." He added, "I think I was pretty clever, hiding something so important inside a dog."

"Agreed," said McNally, "if this string of numbers are, indeed, important."

Ashley and Ned stood, watching the proceedings, mouths open. Finally Ned spoke. "So this paper, it's just a list of numbers. And nobody knows what they represent?"

"Nope. Not a clue."

Ned turned to Ike. "You have no idea either?"

"If I told you I'd have to kill you," said Ike, smiling.

"Ha ha," said Ned.

"He probably knows. He's just not spilling yet," said McNally.

"Seriously?" said Ned, "Wasn't the RNF some sort of terrorist organization? I thought you were on the same team. Why aren't you sharing information?"

"Freedom fighter," said McNally glancing towards Ike. "We were freedom fighters."

"Yeah," said Ike. "The RNF was definitely the good guys."

McNally laughed. "That's a good way to put it. Good guys. I like it."

Ike shrugged. "But yeah. A lot of what we did was covert. They liked to use blind mules. I'm one of 'em, I guess 'cause I have no idea what those numbers mean."

"Thing is," said McNally, "whatever they represent, the RNF big wigs wanted to protect it. So, they spread the love, gave various operatives various objects... information... to keep whatever they were protecting safe."

"Rumor has it, if you try to retrieve the protected information without all the correct pieces, the damn thing will explode... literally or figuratively," added Ike. "Either way, you won't get what you were looking for."

"Do you guys have all you need to retrieve this crazy important object," asked Ned. Ashley's eyes shot towards him.

"Nope."

"Do you know where to find it all?"

"Nope."

"Any clues on where it could be?"

"Rumor is that Kaufmann was the keeper of one piece of the puzzle."

"I heard he stole it," said Ike.

"That's why he was murdered?" asked Ashley.

"Yup. Probably."

"The people who murdered him," said Ashley, "did they get what they were looking for?"

"At first I thought they did. Now I'm not sure," said McNally.

"Weird," said Ned.

"Indeed."

Thoughts ricocheted through Ashley's mind. She pondered revealing the location of the key but thought better of it when she saw Ned's face. She glanced at the copious piles of dung surrounding her and realized how absurd her life had become. The men continued to discuss their options while she pondered her's.

She bit her lip and gazed out of the window, towards the moon. That's when she saw it.

"Guys," she said, "I think you better look over here."

A pair of headlights bobbed up the driveway. A tall figure exited the vehicle and strode towards the house.

"Holy shit," McNally breathed, "that can't be..."

"It looks like it is," said Ike. "Shit. I gotta hide." He added, "But where?"

————

He watched the proceedings with great interest as he crept closer to the farmhouse, hoping he would be able to listen to any ensuing conversation. So far, no luck. He crept closer. And closer. And closer...

Finally, he sat below the picture window, back pressed tight against the wall. He could make out a few words, but not many. However, he was able decipher the words, "object" and "paper" more than once. The hairs on the back of his neck stood on end. Dread choked his throat as he noticed a pair of headlights bounce up the driveway. He scampered around the corner of the house hoping the driver wouldn't catch him in his headlights.

————

Anger bubbled in his belly. Never in his entire life had he been treated so shabbily. He slammed the car door with utter disgust.

"I will never allow anyone to treat me like that," he grumbled.

He marched towards the house with a flamboyance reserved only for the rich and famous.

————

McNally, Ned, Ashley, and Ike peered outside as the familiar car rolled to a stop. Ashley's mouth dropped as she watched the driver exit the vehicle and sashay up the well worn path to the front door.

Nobody moved when the person outside pounded on the door and yell, "Open up. I know you're in there!"

McNally's gaze shot to Ned. Ike rolled his eyes. Ashley breathed deep. The pounding resumed. "In the name of all that is right and just, I demand you open the door."

Finally McNally stepped forward. He paused a moment, then twisted the knob.

Trent Shaw stood before them in all his mayoral glory. "I demand to know," he said, "what Ike Moe is doing in town. I was under the impression that he was currently on the lam." Ike's eyebrows rose significantly. Shaw continued. "It is my duty, as the mayor of Crossroads, to be aware of any and all illegal activities in and around my fair city. It is also my constitutional duty to enforce the law. I am fully aware that the Crossfield police department is currently searching for Mr. Moe to question him about the disappearance of Dr. Tonn." He gazed around the room triumphantly. "It is to that end that I must now conduct a citizens arrest." He added, "I also demand to know why this room is filled with dog shit."

"You've got to be kidding me," mumbled McNally.

Ike remained silent.

Shaw continued. "This place is filthy. What's up with all the dung?" He scanned the room, nose wrinkled, clearly disgusted.

"Long story," said Ned.

"Well you'll tell that long story to the police when they arrive. In the meantime feel free to have a seat and we'll wait for justice to be served."

"Not on my watch," said a new voice, "I'll take that paper."

All eyes flew towards the open door. A large figure filled the jam, a shiny pistol glinted in the light. Ned's mouth dropped. McNally's hands rose.

"Well, I'll be damned," breathed Ike.

"Dick," said Ashley, "what are you doing here?"

He chuckled. "I'll take that paper off your hands. I'll also take anything else of interest."

"Sorry," said Ike. "no such luck." He grabbed the shit sheet, wadded it, and shoved it in his mouth. With three large gulps, the paper disappeared down his gullet.

"Oh my Lord," whispered Ashley, "that was possibly the grossest thing I've ever seen."

"Dude," said Ned, "I don't recall your washing that thing."

"Now," said McNally, "that was unfortunate."

Trent yelled, "I want to know what's going on I want to know now."

Dick took one look at Trent and promptly shot him in the leg, the bullet grazing his thigh. Trent's ensuing scream pierced the evening air. McNally seized the moment to leap forward and tackle Dick. Ike joined him. Ned grasped Ashley's hand and held tight.

Chapter Twenty-Six

NED

"Oh dear God," Ned breathed, "Ike ate the shit sheet."

"That's all you have to say after everything that happened," whispered Ashley.

"Well, it's not everyday that you get to watch your friend presumably poison himself with E. Coli."

"I'd just be glad if you quit calling it a shit sheet."

"Is poop paper better," said Ned.

"Not really."

"Shut the fuck up, you two." McNally shot them a look that could possibly wilt the freshest flower.

The scene had become absurd. Trent Shaw yelled while limping throughout the living room grinding fecal matter into the old carpet. Ike and Dick rolled throughout the matter, long ago having lost track of why they began the wrestling match in the first place. McNally stood, holding the pistol, waiting for the insanity to ebb.

It was at that moment that another figure darkened the door of the tiny farmhouse.

"Jimbo," yelled McNally, "welcome to the asylum."

Jim's mouth dropped, eyes widened, and hands dropped. "What the hell's going on?" he said.

"Just another day in paradise."

After ten minutes, Ike and Dick tired of their wrestling match. Both sat leaning against the couch, brushing dog crap off their clothing. Neither experienced much success. Ashley watched in horror as they smeared fecal matter deeper into their clothing.

McNally viewed the scene with disgust before he turned his gaze at Dick. "So," he said, "who do you work for?"

Dick didn't answer.

"Suppose we need to make it worth his while," said Jim.

"Dunno," said McNally, "It probably depends on the costs of failing this assignment."

Dick cringed as the men studied him. Finally McNally turned to Ashley. "That paper. The one dipped in wax. The one Ike ate. We've got to get it. Suppose you can you help Ike upchuck it?"

Ashley's stomach churned. Ike piped in, "Dude. I'm a professional. I can upchuck on my own, thank you very much."

"Well hop to it," said, McNalley, "get out of your belly before you smudge the ink." He added, "Do it in the kitchen sink. I don't want that thing floating in toilet water."

Ike hopped to his feet and trotted to the kitchen. Ashley listened to him gag.

"I truly didn't believe my life could become weirder. But here we are," she mumbled. Nausea washed over her.

Ned grasped her hand. "You gonna be OK?"

"I have no idea."

Ned and Ashley watched the surreal events with detached horror. Dick sat on the floor looking sullen, McNally and Jim hovered over him barking questions, Ike stood with his head hanging over the sink while attempting to regurgitate paper, Trent Shaw limped around the room shouting obscenities. Ned silently held Ashley's hand, feeling like her only anchor to sanity.

Finally, Ike entered the room triumphantly waving the waxy paper. "I got it," he yelled, wiping his lips with the back of his hand.

"Good for you," said McNally, "now hand it over."

"Hey," Ike complained, "I worked hard for this."

"Fine. Just give it to me. You can't handle it."

Ike reluctantly placed the paper in McNally's outstretched palm. "Double cross me and you're dead."

"Yeah. I know."

Ned's eyes focused on Dick. "What the fuck, Dick?" he said, "I thought you were a friend."

"I'm more of a friend to you than these assholes."

"I'm not so sure..."

"I guess you'll find out when they end me, won't you?" Dick's eyes burrowed into Ned's face defiantly.

"Why do you figure they'll end you," said Jim.

"What else are they gonna do to me?" said Dick, "We all know what happens to failed freedom fighters."

"I can think of a few things," squeaked Shaw.

"Forget the small talk," said McNally, "who you workin' for?"

"When you find out, you'll be sorry."

"I'm already sorry," chirped Ike.

Just then, a single pop pierced the air. Dick slumped, eyes glazed. A red splotch bloomed on his forehead. Ashley felt Ned pull her to the floor. The sounds of Trent Shaw's shrieks filled the air.

"Holy shit," Ned breathed, "what the fuck just happened?"

"Dunno," said Ashley, "but I think I just broke my incision."

———

"I hear Haiti is warm this time of year."

"Not if you're in Antarctica."

Long pause. "I hear it did not go well."

"It didn't."

"Our operative?"

"Dead."

"Did he leak any information?"

"Not to my knowledge."

"Your cover?"

"Intact."

"Excellent."

"What's our next move?"

"Call this number tomorrow. 5:00. I'll update then."

"Thank-you Trinity.

———

Ned and Ashley stepped into her home. Neither spoke, both too overwhelmed to communicate. Ashley marched straight to the kitchen and grabbed a bottle of pain killers. Ned stood by the door pondering the evening's events. He watched Ashley down her pills and lean against the counter. He breathed deep.

Stepping towards her, he paused, eyes drawn to the small table by the door. The letter still sat there, the one from her oncologist. He picked it up and carried it into the kitchen. He wrapped his arms around Ashley's shoulders.

"You know I'm completely in love with you."

She burrowed deeper into his chest. "After all the weird things that happened... heck, after everything that's happened since I moved here, there's one thing I'm sure of: I'm glad I met you."

His fingers traced her spine, drawing a line between her shoulder blades, brushing her neck. He held her firm, yet gentle, and traced kisses along her cheekbone. When their lips touched, she knew she could be his forever.

They stood together, the gentle warmth of their love enveloping their physical bodies. She could've stood like that forever, but it was him who broke the embrace.

"How's the incision."

"It's fine," she said, "just a little raw from twisting around." She added, "I'll be fine."

He hugged her and buried his nose in her hair. They stood in silence, enjoying the embrace a little longer. Then Ned spoke. "You haven't opened this." He showed her the letter.

"Nope."

"Why not?"

"I don't want to know. Healing's hard enough. I don't want to know any lab results right now."

Ned looked thoughtful a few moments. Then he said, "But I want to know. Do you mind?" He stepped away and held the envelope in front of him.

A long moment of silence weighed heavy on them. She finally said. "I suppose."

He broke the seal, pulled out the enclosed letter. He lifted it and read. His eyes looked thoughtful. Finally, he spoke aloud.

"It says 'No Evidence of Disease. NED." His eyes sparkled. Relief washed over Ashley's face. "I like that," he said, "We're both Ned."

"For now," she added.

"For now," he said, smiling.

He tossed the letter aside and swept her in his arms. He kissed her soundly. They relished the moment, silently savoring the pure joy of incredible news.

Unfortunately, they didn't fully comprehend their role in the reorganization of a worldwide terrorist network or how the resulting conflict would would leave a plethora of dead bodies in its wake — some of them close friends.

Nor did they realize they were on the brink of a treacherous betrayal by someone they counted as a friend.

However, today they were oblivious to the gathering storm clouds that would test their fledging love to its utter limits. Because at this moment, in this one embrace, they relished a brief, tranquil moment in the eye of the hurricane.

***** The End of Book 1 of this Trilogy*****

Author Note: If you enjoyed Reclaimed Haven: Murder on First, find out how Ashley and Ned fare in Reclaimed Haven: Murder on Second. Hint: Things get messy. You can get all the juicy details here:

http://bethannerickson.com/beths-books/reclaimed-haven-trilogy/

Chapter Twenty-Seven

NOTES FROM MINNESOTA

Notes from Minnesota

Oy. Cancer's the gift that keeps on giving.

Just as I was about to release this book, a crazy thing happened.

I was sailing through my fourth cancerversary, thinking all was going well. Then, as was the case when I first received my diagnosis, I failed my final test... the CT scan.

All I had to do was get a clean scan and I could go on my merry way. That didn't happen.

The radiologist found a mass, a "complex lesion," on my left ovary. Gynecologists in the Twin Cities (three hours away) were alerted to my situation. I was set to head to their clinic to be evaluated for a complete hysterectomy, biopsies, and recommendations for chemo.

It was pretty ugly.

But first, I had one additional blood test: a tumor marker for ovarian cancer to verify everyone's suspicions.

I rushed to the clinic to get blood drawn on a cool Friday afternoon. With tears in my eyes, terror flowing through my veins, I knew the likelihood of three radiologists and one oncologist being incorrect were slim to none.

I donated the blood and endured one of the longest weekends of my life.

Before 8:00AM on Monday morning, the phone rang. It was my family doc.

"I thought I'd call before things get crazy," he said.

I'm not sure I recall the entire conversation except that my tumor marker crossed his desk and he immediately called to tell me the number was... totally normal. No ovarian cancer.

The Twin Cities plans got canceled. I got to visit a local gynecologist to check out the mass. Life didn't feel as overwhelming anymore.

I just returned from that appointment. Turns out he was a UCLA trained physician who practiced in the Twin Cities the lion's share of his career. "You would have visited someone like me, had your tumor marker been elevated," he said.

He reviewed my scans. He pushed on my belly. Turns out, my "mass" was nothing to worry about.

That was terrific news.

The whole experience made Ashley's situation even nearer and dearer to my heart. Like Ned, my dear husband stood by my side through the whole ordeal.

True love isn't always dramatic. Sometimes it's simply a solid presence during uncertain times.

So today, I'm happy to release the first third of this story. I hope you enjoy reading it as much as I enjoyed telling Ashley's tale.

Head to BAEricksonBooks.com and become a VIP reader. Check out the other books in this series. Then ponder areas of your life you need to reclaim...

I look forward to meeting you,

Beth :)

P.S. Nab Book 2 in this trilogy: Reclaimed Haven: Murder on Second to find out how this crazy story unfolds. Trust me, it's a doozie...

http://bethannerickson.com/beths-books/reclaimed-haven-trilogy/

ABOUT THE AUTHOR

Beth Ann Erickson is the founder of Filbert Publishing and editor of the long-running zine for freelance writers, Writing Etc. She's worked as a freelance writer since '95, launched Writing Etc. in 01, and wrote 10 titles during that time. She's the author of multiple novels and storytelling is her first love. Diagnosed with cancer in '13, Beth put the brakes on all other writing pursuits and decided to pursue projects near and dear to her heart. You just finished reading one such project. :) So far, Beth remains cancer free. Keep an eye on how she's doing, nab her latest project, read journal entries, become a VIP reader, and more by surfing here: http://BAEricksonBooks.com .

BOOKS BY B.A. ERICKSON

Please visit your favorite ebook retailer to discover other books by Beth Ann Erickson. Better yet? Nab swag. Get in on contests and special deals. I've got freebies and news, too. Just become a VIP reader here: http://BAEricksonBooks.com

Current titles (as of this book's publication) include:

Stand Alone Novels in the Reclaimed Series:

Reclaimed Trust: Screams Fall Silent in the Desert

Reclaimed Love: Evil Lurks in Friendly Places

Reclaimed Hope: Her Truth is a Lie. His Lie Holds the Truth

A Reclaimed Trilogy:

Reclaimed Haven: Murder on First

Reclaimed Haven: Murder on Second

Reclaimed Haven: Murder on Third

Shorter works:

Novella: Reclaimed Wonderland (Free when you become a VIP reader!)

Reclaimed Life Series: (Currently Under Construction) :)

The Recruit

The Crossroads Flood

The Poisoned Letter

The Mysterious Key

Cop Shop Mayhem

The Hot Summer

The Unfortunate Scoop

Get the complete updated list at http://BAEricksonBooks.com

Connect with Beth Ann:

Friend me on Facebook: https://www.facebook.com/bethannerickson

Rather be Facebook Fan?: https://www.facebook.com/pages/Beth-Ann-Erickson/143474998699

Follow me on Twitter: https://twitter.com/bethannerickson

Subscribe to my Blog: http://BethAnnErickson.com

Become a VIP Reader: http://bethannerickson.com/free-books-2/

Visit my Website Bio Page: http://bethannerickson.com/about/

<<<<>>>>